D0903111

By the same author

CHIMERA
FOLLOWER
VALLEY OF LIGHTS
OKTOBER
DOWN RIVER

-STEPHEN-
GALLAGHER

Rain

Steve Gallagher

3/2/90.

NEW ENGLISH LIBRARY

British Library Cataloguing in Publication Data

Gallagher, Steve
  Rain.
  I. Title
  823'.914[F]

  ISBN 0-450-52460-4

Published by New English Library,
a hardcover imprint of Hodder and Stoughton,
a division of Hodder and Stoughton Ltd,
Mill Road, Dunton Green, Sevenoaks, Kent TN13 2YA.
Editorial Office: 47 Bedford Square, London WC1B 3DP.

Photoset by Rowland Phototypesetting Ltd,
Bury St Edmunds, Suffolk.

Printed in Great Britain by
Mackays of Chatham plc, Chatham, Kent.

PART ONE

Death and the Maiden (I)

ONE

The first time that he saw her was across the parking lot of a motorway service area. It was about a quarter to midnight, and it had been raining. He could see that she was tired and cold and that she'd probably been on her feet for some time. She didn't look much more than sixteen, although he knew that she was older. She shifted from one foot to the other, waiting with her awkward bundle of papers under her arm like some census-taker worn down by a few too many rebuffs. He saw her walk up and down under the forecourt's dripping canopy, watching her for about fifteen minutes as she killed time and waited for new arrivals; and then, after she'd covered the same piece of ground more often than he could count, he saw her turn and go back inside.

He got out of his car, and followed.

At the glass doors, he hesitated; now she'd stopped a lone driver at the foot of the overpass stairway, and although the sound didn't reach him at this distance he was able to supply his own dialogue track as she fumbled out her well-worn photograph and made her familiar pitch.

'Excuse me. I wonder if you can help me . . .'

She'd been opening with the same line every time, trying not to catch them too much off-guard but still making them wary of some imminent request for money, or a lift, or worse. They'd look at her suspiciously, and the suspicion wouldn't entirely clear until they'd heard her through and were able to back away, shrugging and shaking their heads. After which she'd repack her papers, stuff the bundle under her arm again, and carry on.

He knew how to observe without being seen. On the outside there were plenty of shadows but inside, and at this hour, there was no crowd to hide him, and so he waited before pushing through the glass doors to follow. She'd gone ahead into the cafeteria, a long gallery of blond wood and oatmeal-coloured tile at the far side of the concourse; from here to there was mostly dead space at night-time, the Game Zone and the magazine shop darkened behind roll-down chain metal shutters. His footsteps echoed in emptiness as he crossed the vinyl floor.

Once inside the cafeteria, its windows a long gallery of darkness overlooking the motorway, he made sure that he kept his distance from her. There were two or three dozen people already inside, most of them late-night, tired-looking, and slow. The haulage drivers were grouped together, spinning out their supper breaks; the rest were bleary tourists in twos and threes, huddled over trays of Danish and tall paper cups of Coke. He was the only one who sat alone.

From a corner table, he watched. When she moved, he would move after.

Two hours of this. It might even have been more.

There was a pattern to what she was doing. For a while she'd stand out front as she had before, walking the length of the building and looking over the cabs of the lorries pulled nose-in toward it, and then as her energies and her attention flagged she'd go inside and sit for a while, and instead of cabs she'd scan faces, and edge nearer to lorry drivers' conversations as if in the hope of picking up something useful. Some of them knew her, some of them seemed to know her well. Sometimes she'd sit with a group of them although never, in any sense, did she seem to get close to anyone.

He studied her. From every angle, at every distance apart from close-to. A mousy little kid with a self-administered peroxide job that had almost grown out, weary and driven and dressed in cast-offs like some refugee from an earthquake zone. He saw her tackling strangers, he saw her with her guard down at a corner table when she thought she was unobserved. There, she had the look of a child; some distance travelled, some illusions still intact. But then there would be a new influx of late-running haulage drivers, ambling in bantering and sometimes tousling each other's hair, and she'd rise to the occasion with a face that read *business as usual*.

It grew late. Then it grew later. By now most of the tourists had moved out and even the professionals were beginning to disperse, some back to the road and others to sleep in their cabs. He knew that she'd noticed him a while ago; nothing special, just one new face in a night when there were plenty of new faces mixed in amongst the regulars, but it placed a limit on how long he could continue to stick around without making her suspicious.

So then he went outside, and waited to see what she'd do next.

He stood under the awning, as she'd stood some time before. Even at this hour, there was activity; freight and haulage vehicles had moved in and taken over the daytime car parking area, and their sounds were a backdrop to the night. The engines of static lorries beating time, the occasional hiss and release of air brakes, chains rattling and shackles crashing as furtive uncouplings took place in the distant darkness. Way out beyond the trees there were even more of them, all crowded in together like sleeping cattle; and as he looked, his eyes were caught by the movement of a police Range Rover taking a slow cruise along one of the aisles.

Another world, he thought. Another life, lived by another people. She moved among them, and they seemed to treat her like a mascot.

He wondered if she knew how dangerous this might turn out to be.

A big United Transport wagon, its cab backlit like a dark-faced jack o'lantern, was moving into one of the few empty spaces alongside the main building. Its lights were a smeared trail on wet asphalt; the rain was so faint that it was barely perceptible apart from where it showed up directly under the floodlights, but it was a presence that couldn't be ignored. Many of the nearby drivers had their engines running and their heaters on, their windshields steamy and streaked on the inside.

He decided to go over and wait in the car.

Sitting with his window half-open and the radio playing low, his attention was caught by the police Rover again. It was now beyond the diesel island, its lights snapping on after a prowl along the perimeter road without them, and he half-smiled in the darkness. When the night was long and at its lowest, perhaps it could take a little more than patience to get the boys through.

Night games, he thought, just night games, and as the Rover passed behind his car he glanced in his mirror. He could just about make out the white blurs of the faces of its occupants, and the distinct yellow slash of the reflective bands that they wore over their uniforms.

And then, as they moved on, he returned his attention to the night game that was his own.

She came out only a couple of minutes later. Same spot, essentially the same routine. Jesus, did she never grow tired of it? He switched off the radio and leaned well back, but she wasn't even looking his way. She was sorting through her papers, looking at them, checking, compiling, rearranging as if for the thousandth time. He felt his heart go out to her as it might to some noble thing reduced to the indignities of a zoo where it could only repeat the same futile pattern of behaviour again and again.

Someone came out through the glass doors behind her, catching her by surprise.

5

TWO

'Excuse me,' she began, but the man was ready.

'No, sorry,' he said.

He was youngish, with a towel over his shoulder and a soapbag in his hand, his hair in dark spikes from a coldwater splash and a vigorous rub; he wore what had to be one of his oldest sweaters, out at the elbows, and he carried under his arm a two-litre Pepsi bottle that he'd filled at one of the washroom basins. He'd seen her through the glass, had probably decided that at the very least she had to be tapping people for spare change, and had taken the furthest of the doors with the intention of putting himself beyond her range as quickly as possible. He didn't even pause, or meet her eyes.

'You don't even know what I was going to ask you!' she called after him as he hurried out and onto the tarmac.

Perhaps it was the indignation in her voice. Or perhaps it was some streak of common decency, that faulty defence mechanism that forces people to sit through a sales pitch for something they know they don't want, and which sometimes even persuades them to buy. But he stopped, and he turned.

'I'm sorry,' he said, flinching a little under the faint, needling touch of the rain. 'But I can't give lifts. It's a company rule.'

'I'm not looking for a lift.'

'Then it's money.'

'No.'

'What, then?'

'I just want you to look at a picture of somebody.'

The driver looked at her warily, as if to say, And you mean that's *all*? But she'd already extracted the photograph from her bundle and was holding it up to show him.

He peered at it. They were about a dozen yards apart, and he'd have needed the eyes of a spy satellite to make it out with any clarity. With an air that he was somehow going to be sorry for this, he came back under the awning and out of the rain.

She didn't let him take the photograph but held it up before him, and he made a show of looking. An ordinary snapshot, postcard sized, lousy exposure.

6

'Very nice,' he said without any particular feeling. 'Who is she?'

'My sister.'

He took another look, with some interest this time; becoming involved in spite of himself, his wariness already dimmed a little by curiosity, and after glancing at the picture and then again at the face of the girl who was holding it, he said, 'I reckon she is, at that.'

'Did you ever see her before?'

'No, but I wouldn't turn down the chance.'

'She's dead,' the girl said flatly, and returned the photograph to join her other papers. The young haulage driver stood rumpled and nonplussed as the girl went on, 'She died about a year ago. She was hitching up from London. I'm looking for the driver who dropped her off. All I know is that his lorry had some kind of a cross on the front.'

'What, a Jesus-type cross?'

'No, a . . .' She didn't have the exact word, but she raised her forefingers and made an X in the air between them.

The young man said, 'I don't get it. This is what, last year?'

'Yes.'

'And you're still looking?'

She seemed to be avoiding his eyes, running through her papers again as if in search of something else. 'Yes.'

'What about the police?'

'The police aren't interested now.' She pulled out a well-worn, handwritten list. 'Absolutely the last question. Do you ever get around any of these places? They're all lorry parks and service areas.'

This time, she let him take the paper. He ran his eye down the list and said, 'Some of them.'

'Can you keep your eyes open for anything that could be a cross on the front of a cab? It might be painted or a trademark, I just don't know.'

Some kind of cab design in the form of a St Andrew's Cross? Such a feature might not be quite as common as a set of wheels and a tailpipe, but it wasn't exactly a rarity either, especially not here on one of the main southbound routes coming down out of Scotland and the north. Shivering a little as the night's cool touch began to seep into him, the driver said, 'Well, it's a bit vague . . .'

'I know. Somebody saw her being picked up, but that's the only thing about it they can remember. She was dropped off less than an hour from home, and that's when someone ran her down.'

'In a truck?'

'It could have been a truck or a car, nobody's sure. The police

7

reckon it was hit and run, that's why they're not so interested now. They said it was probably joyriders.'

'They could be right.'

'I'd still like to know.'

He handed back the list and said, 'Suppose I see something. How do I get in touch?'

'Here,' she said, taking the paper, 'or any of these other places. I'm always around.'

'Every night?'

'Just about.'

He shifted the Pepsi bottle from where he'd tucked it under his arm. It was the clear plastic kind, no weight at all when it was empty and as awkward as anything to carry when full. The girl was reassembling her bundle again; each of them was about as well organised as the other. At the photograph of her sister, she stopped and looked at it as if some once-hidden detail had now been identified for her.

'You really think there's a resemblance?' she said.

'Absolutely. What's your name?'

'Lucy Ashdown. My sister was called Chrissie.'

He shifted the bottle again. 'Listen,' he said, 'I was going to doss down in the cab for a couple of hours. But if you like, I could take you around a few places that you haven't covered.'

She looked up from the picture.

'No, thanks,' she said.

Maybe he'd sounded too eager, changing his tune too quickly. Or maybe it was simply that she could read him better than he thought; their eyes met and hers were firm and steady while in his could be seen the realisation that, near-child or not, this kid was pretty well bullshit-proof.

He shrugged, and gave her a smile.

Her expression didn't change.

So then he turned and walked away, back through the rain toward the shelter of his cab.

THREE

She watched him go.

Lucy Ashdown, just a couple of months shy of her eighteenth birthday. She knew that she looked younger, that was why some of them tried it on. Probably assumed that a kid out so late had to be a lost cause already, so what the hell? Most of the men that she spoke to reacted to her in some way or another, but she'd quickly learned to distinguish the would-be protectors from the would-be seducers, and to get some idea of all the shadings in between. It hadn't been easy knowledge to acquire, and a couple of times she'd come close to paying heavily for it. Each time, it had been exactly like this – somebody who'd think himself ordinary, nothing in his background to say otherwise, reading in just a little more than her questions could justify. What might follow, if she was stupid enough to let it, could be the first step toward a doorway that would open for him onto an awesome and exhilarating darkness with the realisation that the question *Why not?* didn't necessarily have any answer. To such men she was just an open wallet on the ground, with no name attached and no-one to observe; and whilst this wasn't true of everyone, she could see its potential in more than a few.

Lucy had learned to spot this some time back near the beginning . . but for her sister Christine, the lesson seemed to have come too late and at the end.

She looked at her watch. It tended to run slow and the date display never worked at all, so it was only a rough guide at its best. Almost two a.m., and a diminishing likelihood of action between now and the first of the breakfast arrivals around five. There would be a steady drip of possibilities, night-freight drivers on their midway breaks, but no more than that.

What the hell. A quick check over the acreage of parked vehicles, and then she could go back inside to keep warm for a while. There was a new night manager – new to her, anyway – so she might have to try to stay out of sight a little more than usual, but once he understood the score with regard to his main clientele she'd probably be okay. She didn't try to fool herself that she had any influence, but out of the through-flow of regulars she certainly had some friends.

After stowing her papers in a carrier bag which she then tucked under her arm, she set out for a circuit of the parking lot.

The rain could be seen more than it could be felt, a continuous spattering of light-rings on the surfaces of puddles. She didn't mind it, much; not when it didn't soak her or drive her off the job, as she tended to think of it. The rain reminded her of something that Chrissie had once said to her. They'd never talked much, never even been particularly close in the way that sisters sometimes could be; in a perverse kind of way, Lucy felt closer to Chrissie now than she ever had when she'd been alive. Alive, Chrissie had mostly seemed to ignore her. Now, with the last traces of her fading from notice elsewhere in the world, it was almost as if she belonged to Lucy alone.

'Hello, kid,' she said out loud, because now she'd reached the spot where it had happened.

There was a sloping grass bank over on this far side of the perimeter road, topped by a line of bushes that screened the main service area from a business motel on a spur. The motel had an all-car clientele, vehicles lined up outside their doors like a row of sleeping puppies, somehow giving the impression of being both a safe haven and a soft option. The police had traced most of the guests who'd been registered on the night of Chrissie's death, and not one of them had seen or heard a thing. Chrissie had been discovered in the bushes, thrown more than twenty feet by the impact of her collision with some unknown vehicle. Her hand luggage had been found on the roof of a removal van. She was a mess. She hadn't died straight away, but she was dead by the time that she'd been found.

Looking down at the spot, Lucy felt almost nothing. It was no more than a stretch of oil and rain-streaked boundary road, right out on the edge of the lighted zone. No ghost walked here. The only lingering charge from the event wasn't material, but emotional. And Lucy carried that with her wherever she might be.

If anything, she reckoned as she turned to recross the perimeter road, she'd grown to like it around here.

Let's face it, she thought, the place had become almost like home. She'd discovered a great and unsuspected sense of mystery in this world, this transient network in which she'd been searching for most of a year; it was almost a separate and self-contained reality where no-one else lived but was just passing through. Where the great powered beasts were the dim intelligences and the rumpled, out-of-shape men that they carried merely their passengers. As she stepped down from the bank and onto the tarmac, she could see a number of

10

them that had grown familiar to her; Road Trains, sixteen-wheelers, five-axle artics, ferry freightliners, semi-trailers, Strato tractors, tankers, tippers.

These weren't just individual vehicles to her. Each had a place somewhere in her network; she could match faces to many, and routes to a few. The process of discovery had been an eye-opener for her. She'd come to realise that she'd spent almost seventeen years of her life without any real purpose to it, and without any real sense of a place where she belonged; whereas now, thanks to her obsession, she seemed to have both.

As she took a zigzag path to return through the maze of vehicles, only one caught her attention as a total novelty and this was a motorised horse transporter, interior lights on and its side-door open to allow the animals some air; she could glimpse their heads nodding and the moving flanks of live horseflesh as they turned in their stalls. She went around to the front of the blacked-out cab but there was no hint of an X-shaped design of any kind, just a bumper sticker that read *God Made the Scots a Wee Bit Better*. She thought about taking a note of the number, reckoned that it was probably on a once-only run, on the way to a race event maybe, and decided against.

Wearily, and with the dampness finally getting in to make itself felt around the shoulder seams in her coat, she headed back for the bright lights of the main building.

There was a spot down by the Game Zone where she knew she could settle for a while, out of everybody's way and with enough floor space to check through her documentation. She had more than just a photograph and some lists in her bundle. She had maps of the motorway network, notes on drivers seen and leads suggested, names of drivers who might have mentioned seeing an accident around the time and whom she'd yet to track down. She had all the cuttings from the time of Chrissie's death, and the brief coverage of her funeral from the local newspaper.

She had a photograph of their father. He knew something about what she did at nights, and didn't approve. She hadn't told him everything. And she'd never told him that she carried his picture, either.

She sat cross-legged in the alcove off the main concourse, her papers spread before her and her coat drying out by a warm-air vent at floor level. It had been a slow night and there was little to add, but there was always something to recognise. Sometimes this gave her satisfaction, sometimes not. Sometimes, when she looked at the vast and disconnected amount of information and thought about the haphazard manner of its gathering, she felt a surge of something dangerously close to despair. In the arcade on the other side of the shutter, the Thunderblade game machine ticked ominously through the night with a pulsing sound that was unsettlingly close to a heartbeat.

Someone tapped her, none too politely, on the shoulder.

'Miss . . .' he said firmly, as she looked up.

It was the night manager, the new man. He wore a caramel-coloured uniform jacket that only a blind man would have sported out of choice. As he stood over her, he said, 'I want you to pick up your stuff and leave. Right now, please.'

Oh, damn, she thought.

'I'm not causing any trouble,' she said.

'If you want to move through and buy something, fine. But you can't just hang around the premises all night.'

'I can't buy anything. I haven't got any money.' Which was true. Until her next Giro came through, she'd be surviving on goodwill and pennies and maybe a little light shoplifting when she really got close to rock bottom.

'Then there's nothing here for you. Come on. Out.'

What was needed here was some sharp reply, something that would dumbfound him and destroy his authority and send him away humiliated. But damn it, as usual, the words just seemed to escape her. Wasn't that always the way? And so instead, flushed with reluctant embarrassment, she regrouped all her papers and took her coat from the vent and clambered to her feet.

She winced a little as she put her coat back on. There had barely been time for it to dry out at all. She wondered if it was worth trying to explain about Chrissie, but decided from the look of him that there probably wasn't. He looked the kind who could probably suck up honey and shit a pickle. She gave him a quick, tentative smile as she fastened her toggles, and it was deflected like spit from a propeller.

'I'm not trying to be hard,' he said, and was clearly unconcerned whether she believed him or not. 'But if any of the customers complains, it'll be me who has to answer.'

He held out his arm, palm upward, to guide her toward the doors. Where she went beyond that, he didn't seem to care. Lucy moved as directed, knowing that she had little choice; she survived as she did almost entirely on the goodwill of others and when the goodwill ran out, as it seemed to have here, then much of her buoyancy was lost. Barred from the main building, there would only be one place for her to go; down to the motorway sliproad, to stand on the hard shoulder and wait out the night until a sympathetic ride decided to pull over and pick her up . . . and she hoped to God that it *would* be a sympathetic ride, and nobody like the nutter who'd stopped for her a couple of months back and then, after about ten minutes of apparent normality, begun a long and rambling confession while calling her by some other woman's name.

But then, through the plate glass, she witnessed the impending arrival of the cavalry.

The cavalry took the form of three Aberdeen fleet drivers. One looked like a mountain, another looked like a mouse, the third looked like a regular human being but hardly ever spoke and when he did, his accent was so dense that Lucy had difficulty following it. They wore blue uniforms in a way that always made her think of some attic dressing-up chest, and drove spotless refrigerated trailers carrying beef and bacon for the big supermarket chains south of the border. They'd come down in convoy, take a breakfast break at this or some similarly unsociable hour, and then split three ways toward their various distribution centres.

The glass door bounced back before the mountain and the mountain said, '*Lucy! How're you doing, girl?*'

And with a glance at the manager, Lucy said, 'It looks like I'm leaving.'

The mountain understood her meaning immediately. His name was Wilfrid and he called himself Ted, although everyone knew him as Jock. He put a gentle hand on her shoulder and didn't even appear to register the manager's presence, just steered her around and away from his influence to leave him somewhat dazed and stranded in the concourse behind them.

'Not when we just got here, you don't,' Jock told her, loudly and for the manager's benefit. 'We're going to buy you some tea and a bap.'

And, amidst the safety of friends, she was borne back into the lighted haven of the cafeteria.

Well, she hadn't been able to come up with any saving put-down. But this would do quite nicely.

They'd changed the counter display since she'd last been in here, resetting to be ready for breakfast. There was bowl after bowl with those farting little packets of cereal that she'd loved as a child and detested ever since, there were pastries, there were undercooked rolls. Over on the hot food counter there were the usual stews and pies and sausages getting dried out under the heat 'n' light units. Jock sized her up and wanted to buy her the works, but she lied and told him that she'd already eaten. They sat her in amongst them like Goldilocks amidst the bears and, for the first time in what had been a long, long night, she allowed herself to unwind a little.

Someone brought her tea. Someone else, a bacon roll. The roll

13

was too soft and the bacon had the texture of a pair of braces, but she put it away like a locust.

These men counted as friends. She'd see them twice, sometimes three times a month. They knew her and they knew her story, and they kept her informed; and if any of them had ever been tempted to suggest that her self-imposed mission was likely to prove both futile and dangerous, he'd at least managed to keep it to himself.

Until tonight.

They swapped tales, traded a few rumours. There was an owner-operator who'd called her a Road Slut about three weeks back, and the word was that two of the boys had finally caught up with him. His wagon had been spotted alongside the small public toilet by Stonehaven harbour, and they'd ambled in and stood either side of the urinal stall and introduced themselves as the Friends of Lucy Ashdown, Lothian Branch. Then they'd explained what they were considering doing to him and why, and then one of them had said, quite genially, 'But finish your pee, first,' after which he'd tried to keep on going for so long that he could have written his autobiography with it in a field of fresh snow.

She told them of the progress she'd made since last she saw them which was, essentially, none.

And Jock, with all of the gentleness of which big men can be capable, said, 'And say you find the man. What do you propose to do?'

'Talk to him,' she said. 'Ask him what she said. And what he saw.'

'And this is going to bring your Chrissie back, is it?'

She looked at him, a little blankly. 'What do you mean?'

'Dead's dead, love. When it comes to the end of it, all your Perils of Pauline stuff is going to get you nowhere except hurt.'

'I can look after myself.'

'I'm not sure you can. Nobody can, not all the time. You've been lucky so far, that's all. *I* wouldn't like to see myself in some of the situations that you risk getting into.'

The Mouse tried to lighten the tone by saying, 'Not much danger of that, is there, Jock?' But Jock ignored him, as if he hadn't even spoken; as if he and Lucy were the only two people in the place, and that it was suddenly essential that he made himself understood.

'I'm serious,' he said. 'What does your poor old dad think? I bet he doesn't sleep at nights. One wee girl dead, and the other one out there asking for more of the same. The lads can't always be on hand, you know.'

'I know,' Lucy said.

'But you still won't give up.'

She shook her head.

'Eindhoven,' the third man said, his first word in the entire conversation, and the rest of them turned to look at him as they might at a potted plant which had suddenly asked if there was any chance of getting a drink.

'What about Eindhoven?' Jock said.

So the third man told them what he'd heard.

It wasn't easy to follow, although only Lucy seemed to be having trouble; but it seemed that he'd been told of a driver who was rumoured to have applied for a route switch suddenly about a year before. Whether it was because he'd had some scare, or for whatever reason, the man couldn't say for sure although this was the impression that he had. All he could supply was the name Billy, and that of a big electrical firm that had a regular Eindhoven run. Lucy wrote it all down, yet another item of intelligence to add to the others, and then squared it all away with the rest of her papers.

Jock pulled a TachTrak from his breast pocket, a calculator-sized device on which he could keep a log of his hours on and off the road; anything approaching a violation, and it would buzz to warn him well before the tachograph in the cab could record an infringement. Right now it was showing the time, and a mealbreak symbol; Jock said, 'Well, wagons roll,' and the others dug out devices of their own and the Mouse said, 'Oh, shit,' because he'd forgotten to reset his.

The three of them started to rise.

Lucy stayed where she was.

Jock said, 'You look after yourself, girl. There's people worry about you.'

'Thanks,' she said, and managed a smile. She heard stuff she didn't want to hear all of the time, but from someone like Jock it could cut a little deeper. She knew that he meant well. She knew almost nothing else about him, what his house was like or who his children were, but she knew that. Somehow, his concern made it even harder to take.

Staring down at her empty cup after they'd gone, she was aware of somebody moving in alongside her table; and she remembered the new manager, and realised then that she should have gone along with one of them and at least picked up a safe ride to another of the night-venues on her list, because now they were gone and she was right back in a position she'd occupied when they'd arrived.

She looked up. It wasn't the manager.

'May I see the photograph?' he said.

FOUR

He studied her in that first, frozen, rabbit-in-the-headlights moment, and wondered if she'd recognised him from sometime earlier in the evening; but then he decided that her reaction was one of simple, defensive surprise. Either that, or she had great potential in next year's Oscars.

She recovered quickly. Her bundle was on the table before her and she rummaged through it until she found the photograph, and then she held it out for him. Now she was watching, waiting to see if he reacted to the image.

'Did you ever see her before?'

Instead of just looking, he took the picture from her hand. Held it up where the light was a little better. She'd parted with it reluctantly, but wasn't making any big thing about it. From somewhere behind him came a clattering sound of dishes being cleared at another table.

He said, 'May I sit down?'

She was still watching him, and now she half-smiled with more than a faint trace of cynicism. Her face was young, but those eyes . . . no, don't be fooled, he told himself, because those eyes were something else.

'Don't tell me,' she said. 'You couldn't help overhearing.'

'I was listening. I'd like to know more.'

She watched him for a moment longer; trying to read his thoughts, take a guess at his motives. Then she shrugged, making no objection – at least, nothing for the moment, but it was clear as he slid in along the bench on the opposite side of her table that it was tolerance, not trust, that he was getting here.

Well, what did he expect? At least it was a start.

Over the photograph, he said, 'You seem pretty determined.'

'You mean it shows?'

He shook his head. 'A hit and run. It's a year old, there's no evidence, and the only witness can't be found. You realise that you're probably wasting your time?'

'If I find him, it won't be wasted.'

'And if you don't?'

16

'I still think a person should have a purpose in life.'

She seemed serious, and he didn't smile. He let the photograph drop onto the table and reached across for the list that lay next in order on top of her bundle, the handwritten rota of service areas, transport yards, truck stops, roadhouses, lorry parks. Some of them were just road or motorway junction numbers, with the word *unofficial* bracketed alongside.

Looking it over, he said, 'How often do you get around these other places?'

'As often as I can,' she said, gathering the photograph in again. 'It depends on when I can get the rides.'

He nodded, aware that someone was approaching their table. Someone in a jacket that would have been an embarrassment at a fancy dress ball, and he didn't have to look up to know any more. He'd witnessed the scene out in the concourse by the Game Zone; he hadn't planned to interfere, but he'd probably have waited for her out on the tarmac if the rescue party hadn't come along in time.

He sensed it as Lucy flinched a little at the night manager's arrival, and was aware of the man putting his hands on the table and leaning over the two of them. He didn't look up. That uniform didn't improve at a lesser distance.

Still without taking his eyes from the list, he said quietly, 'Go away.'

Nothing happened for a moment.

So then he let his gaze travel upward to where the night manager waited, mouth hanging slightly open like a player piano with its roll suddenly gone adrift and its triphammers grabbing away at nothing. He locked onto the man's eyes, saw weakness there, and knew that he'd done about as much as was going to be necessary.

And only a few moments later, the night manager was gone.

He looked at Lucy. Now he smiled, faintly.

And when she smiled back, it was with less of the wariness that she'd shown him at first.

He said, 'I'm doing nothing right now. Why don't we drive around some of these places, and you can tell me more?'

'Why?'

'Because I'm interested.'

'I haven't any money. So I can't pay you for petrol.'

'That doesn't matter.'

Her eyes narrowed, just a little. 'I'm not offering anything else, either.'

'I don't want anything from you. If you don't even want to talk, that's okay.'

She was studying his face again, trying to make some kind of an

17

assessment. He could see that she was less than one hundred per cent sure of him.

But at least she was tempted.

He had to admit it. She really knew some places.

After a while he wanted to suggest that with a little more organisation she could put the list into some kind of order and cover them all in half of the time, but he said nothing. She was working to some scale of priorities, but they were entirely her own and impossible to fathom. First a big commercial yard with its vehicles in neat floodlit ranks on the far side of a high wire fence, and then twenty miles down the motorway to a spot where no more than half a dozen lorries could be found hibernating in the darkness beneath a concrete overpass; and then, with no great logic, back to check on the waste ground behind a travellers' hotel that stood less than five miles from their first stopover. It was now close to four a.m., an hour of night that belonged almost exclusively to travelling shiftworkers and beat-up minicabs, so at most of the places they had no-one to speak to and no reason to do much more than slow down and cruise on by. Sometimes she'd wind down her window and ask him to back up so that she could lean out and take a second look at something, but then moments later she'd be dropping back into her seat in disgust. Every now and again they'd graze the edge of town, but mostly they kept out in the nearby countryside.

They cruised by just about every style and type of road haulage vehicle he could imagine along with a fair number of cars, vans, and old ambulances with home paint jobs. In between stopovers she'd fiddle around with his car radio, looking for music but usually finding talk shows. The phone-in callers seemed mostly to be shift workers and off-duty minicab drivers. He noted maybe half a dozen sleeping trucks which carried some kind of X-form decoration – lights, pennants, or whatever – but none of these seemed to hold any special interest for her.

'I know most of these,' she'd say.

'What, personally?'

'Most of them.'

After that first hour he told her that it was time to take a break. He could sense the return of her apprehension as he found a quiet spot and pulled in, but he said nothing. He didn't want her to be scared, but it wouldn't hurt for her to be a little edgy.

Nervous people tended to give more away.

They were on land behind one of her fringe-of-town stops, a

Victorian commercial hotel that backed onto railway sidings. Between the hotel and the tracks there was a broad cobbled parking
area broken only by the recessed plates of a disused weighbridge,
but the hotel's business was slow and the yard stood mostly empty.
Sodium lights out over the tracks gave the area something of the
feeling of an all-night basketball court. He'd pulled in by the old
weighmaster's office, the face of its big scale just visible in the
shadows beyond its kicked-in windows. Across the way, the hotel
showed no lights at all.

He didn't switch off the engine, but let it idle.

'You really get around, don't you?' he said.

He wasn't being entirely serious, but she took it as straight
comment. 'That's the beauty of an area like this,' she said. 'You get
a lot of main routes all converging and passing through. You can
meet a lot of drivers.'

'How far does that get you, though?'

'You never know. It's not just a network, it's like another world.
Things happen in it that people outside never get to hear about. It's
got its own gossip and its own personalities.'

'Does that include you?'

He couldn't see her too well, but he could sense her reaction. She
was offended. Whether because he'd hit the bullseye or missed the
target completely, it was impossible to say.

'That's not why I do this,' she said.

'I know,' he said. 'Don't be so touchy.'

She looked down.

'Sorry,' she said.

It seemed unlikely that he'd get anything more from her right
now, so they moved on.

Half an hour later they were on a long country lane that ran out
from a motorway junction and carried on at least ten miles into
nowhere; it was a nothing road with nothing but fields around it,
but along one side there was a grass verge wide enough for a vehicle
to get completely over the kerbing and off the carriageway. For long
stretches the verge had become rutted with tyre tracks, the grass
turned to mud, the hedgerow speckled with blown paper waste.
About two miles out, a couple of dozen lorries stood in a silent
convoy as the car rolled by them.

'These aren't legal,' Lucy said as she scanned each one in turn.
'Most of them are parked here to save on their overnight allowance.
Some of them would get shot if their bosses found out they weren't
in a lockup yard. Can we go back?'

'Back home?'

'Back to the last one.'

He did as he'd been asked. This had happened so often now that he was hardly paying attention; he was looking up at the sky for any hint of the dawn, and seeing only stars. As the car reversed, she was winding her window as far down as it would go.

'Stop level with the cab,' she said, and he did.

He was wondering which was more deserving of respect, her dedication or her energy, when he realised that she'd clambered up to kneel on the seat beside him and was hanging right out of the window. Directly above her was the cab door of a red Bedford truck, its side-mirrors out on stalks like a bug's eyes, and before he could speak she'd raised both of her fists and begun to hammer a drumroll on the panelling that was sudden and surprising and shockingly loud.

She paused for one second.

'POLICE!' she shouted. 'VICE SQUAD! THIS IS A RAID!'

And then she started hammering again.

He made a fast takeoff spraying grit, his left hand clutching at the back of her coat to prevent her from pitching headfirst out of the window. She was dumped back into her seat like a sack. The last sounds that he'd heard before the revving of his own engine had been a muffled female shriek and a lower, louder roar that had something of the quality of an angry bear about it. A brief flash of naked flesh above them, and then they were gone. He didn't care to stick around to see any more; in his mind he was picturing a figure like that of Bluto from the Popeye cartoons, only bigger and meaner, and the figure was down out of the cab and peeling back the top of his car without the benefit of a can opener.

'He'll not catch us,' Lucy said confidently. 'He was all boxed-in.'

He looked at her in disbelief. She was grinning happily in the reflected light of the dash.

'Just an old score,' she explained.

He shook his head, momentarily lost for words, and then he looked at her again. Her eyes shone, her face a deep-sea angel's lined in green.

And damn it, he couldn't help it, he started to grin as well.

FIVE

He was beginning to like her.

And that could prove to be a mistake.

They'd covered a fair number of the places on her list, only a couple of locations left; she seemed relaxed, low in the seat with her knees up against the dashboard and a newly-opened bag of caramels in her lap. The radio was playing *Blue Bayou* and she was posting the used wrappers out of a half-inch gap at the top of the window, to be ripped away by the night and the wind.

The night would soon be coming to an end. The clear blue-black of the sky was taking on a certain opacity. He wanted to yawn, but he fought against it.

She'd told him that he could jack it in any time, drop her off somewhere, not to worry, she was used to this and he wasn't, but he'd told her that he'd stick to it as long as she did. By now he'd given up wondering how she managed to keep going, or why she felt so driven; but what he did find hard to understand was her apparent lack of curiosity toward him. She hadn't asked his name, or anything about him, or even his reasons for what he was doing. He'd all the necessary answers ready, and no call to use them. Maybe she considered herself such a good judge of character that no answers were needed.

Not that it really made much difference. None of them would have been true, anyway.

As they were checking out an empty lay-by on the edge of some woodland, she pointed out a spot where she'd often seen a family of foxes come trooping out of the trees to rummage around in a big wire litter-cage in search of picnic rubbish.

'Always at the same time,' she said. 'You wonder how they know.'

And then she offered him a caramel, and they sat in the car and watched the rubbish cage for a while, and nothing whatsoever happened.

And then he began to do some wondering of his own, since she'd protested that she'd no more than nine pence to her name and had been at least as stony-broke as this for the past two days; specifically, he wondered about the provenance of the confectionery.

21

'From by the cashpoint back at the services,' she explained when he'd asked her. 'When the management wasn't looking. Serves him right, for being such a bastard.'

He stared at her. She beamed.

They drove on into the dawn.

They came in over autumn moorland, the distant hills in layers of grey over a pale mirror of standing water. She checked her watch, and reckoned that it was around five-thirty; he looked at his own, and said that it was closer to six. They were on an old pack route, a minor-looking road that went up by forestry land and reservoir and which would be used mostly for local haulage to the northern-most parts of the county. It was a region of dye works, and paper works, and grim little villages; field walls were of low stone, their gates broken and patched with barbed wire, and on the roadside verges were deep and untrodden stands of nettles. This was an area for passing through, not for stopping; harsh-looking country, braced for the worst.

'Just along here,' she said. 'Watch for the sign.'

It would have been easy to miss, a board with a handwritten legend that read TEAS, COFFEES, SNACKS, *OPEN*, and below that an arrow. It had been wired to a gatepost and had almost become overgrown, and it stood at the entrance to a narrow lane. He followed the sign, and found himself on a forest track with dense conifer woodlands blocking out the light to either side. The track was rutted, and seemed to be leading nowhere.

But there was life ahead.

They came into a clearing, a widened stretch of the track where a number of vehicles had already pulled over. Some way ahead the track wound onward and out to rejoin the main road, but right here the focus of attention was on a snack wagon that was puffing out steam into the early-morning chill.

He joined the line of vehicles. She was opening the door and getting out almost before he'd come to a stop. He stayed in the car, and watched as she crossed the open space to where the wagon stood.

It was an old, square-sided caravan conversion with a lift-up flap braced to make an awning above the counter, and a two-man dining room at its end reached by a step that was actually a wooden fork-lift pallet. It was pretty run-down, and looked as if a good kick would probably make it spring apart at the seams. A portable generator was beating away somewhere around the back, powering a couple of lines of sixty-watt bulbs that had been strung, fairground-like, to adjacent pines. The entire setup seemed vaguely illegal, but more or less permanent.

Three men were waiting for service, one of them wearing a NORWEB uniformed overall and all of them shuffling on the spot to keep out the cold. She waded in and got their attention straight away, and moments later he saw the photograph being produced. He saw heads shaking. The conversation continued.

He yawned.

Surely she couldn't crash on for much longer. The supply of truck drivers had to dry up sometime, and salesmen in company cars reading newspapers and dodging the office would be all that remained. He'd been tired for a while. Now he was hungry, as well. He was beginning to wonder if the night had been wasted. His timing had been good and he'd gained about as much of her confidence as it was reasonable to hope for, but she still hadn't exactly opened up. He knew everything about what she was doing, except why.

And without the answer to that, he still had nothing.

A long, empty flatbed went by, wheels bouncing in the ruts and the overhanging branches scraping at its cab. As the tailgate cleared his line of sight, he saw that she was heading back toward him. She seemed thoughtful.

'Anything useful?' he said as she got back into the car.

'I don't know,' she said, and seemed about to add something; but then, with no more certainty, she simply repeated, 'I don't know.' She got a biro from inside her coat – the pen had a half-inch of loose chain at its end and looked suspiciously like standard Post Office counter issue – and started to make some notes.

'But you heard something new.'

'Just something that could tie in with something else.'

He watched as she wrote. He didn't make any big thing of it, but he was able to read down most of the page on her knee. She was concentrating hard, and didn't seem to be aware. She had reams of the stuff, her writing tiny and cramped and filling the paper without margins. A couple of times she paused, and checked back to some earlier entry.

When she'd finished, she sat back and said, 'Okay, I'm ready.'

'Anything useful?'

'Could be something, could be nothing. Perhaps you brought me luck.'

'A pleasure,' he said. 'Now let me get us some breakfast. I'm running on empty.'

'Fine, but not here,' she said quickly. 'Charlie's all right, but his food's bloody awful. Even the badgers won't steal from his bins.'

'It's six o'clock in the morning. Where else did you have in mind?'
'Trust me,' she said.

In town, the streets were quiet and the backstreets were dead. Cats
scavenged amongst the trashbags and boxes that had been stacked
before the shops, but even the tramps in the doorways had barely
begun to stir beneath their newspapers. In the shadows of an alley
near to the docks one neon sign flickered, like a hangover of the
night. It read

KOWLOON RESTAURANT
Open 24 hrs

and he looked up at it, doubtfully.

He said, 'Who eats in a Chinese restaurant at this kind of hour?'

'Us, and a load of night-club drunks who can barely find their
food when it's put in front of them. Come on, this is on me.'

And before he could ask how she planned to pay, she was through
the door and heading down the stairs.

It was all very basic.

The lights were pretty dim. But at least they were brighter than
the tablecloths and the tablecloths were a shade brighter than the
wallpaper, which in turn was marginally brighter than the carpet,
which was too dark to be seen in the general gloom. All that he
knew as they crossed to their table was that it stuck to the soles of
his shoes with every step, as if something had once crawled in and
died upon the floor. They both took seats, and a waiter took their
order.

Hot tea, hot soup . . . he supposed it could be worse. He rubbed
his eyes. *I feel like shit*, he thought, but then he glanced across at
Lucy. If anything, she seemed brighter than at the beginning of the
evening; as if the night's routine had recharged her rather than run
her down.

Better make an effort. 'Where are you living?' he said after their
order had arrived.

She made a face. 'I'm in a squat. I had to move into town, to get
closer to everything.'

'That the only reason?'

'That, plus my dad didn't like to see me staying out all night.'

'And this way's better?'

She looked down into her bowl, and at the stains in the cloth around it. 'I ring him whenever I can. But I couldn't stay at home, he was on at me all the time to give it up.'

'He's got a point.'

She raised her head and gave him a suspicious look. 'Did he set you up to come looking for me? Run me around for a while and then try to talk me out of it?'

'Is that what you really think?'

She shrugged, letting it pass. 'I know what it's doing to him. That only makes it harder. But I know what I'm about. I'm over eighteen.'

Well, almost, he thought.

There was silence for a while, broken only by the sounds of their china and a gentle snoring from somewhere over in the corner. Then she suddenly said, 'I don't live the way I do because I like it. If you saw the place I have to sleep, you'd know.'

'Why, then?'

'It's like breathing. You can try to stop, but you can't do without it for long. It's not even as if we were close . . . she was ten years older than me. And she made friends easily, and she was *really* good looking . . . you've seen the picture.'

He'd seen the picture. It hadn't even begun to do her justice.

'Me, I was hardly ever in school because of my asthma. And I bleached my hair, but it only made me look like a Woolworths girl. But God, I looked up to her. She was everything I wanted to be. And when she went to London I thought, *one day* . . . And then she came running for home, and we never knew why, and someone just . . .' She waved her hand briefly, a small gesture to indicate the passing of a life. And she shook her head, as if words would never be enough to explain how she felt.

'Don't get upset,' he said quietly.

'I *am* upset. All the time. Only mostly, you don't get to see it on the outside.'

She reached over and took a folded paper napkin from the glassful at the centre of the table, shook it out, and then loudly blew her nose on it. The sleeper at the corner table awoke briefly at the sound, before slumping back over his rice bowl. Their waiter passed from one doorway to another, coasting vaguely through the shadows under the guidance of some automatic pilot.

She seemed to be feeling better, now. She glanced around, and then she glanced at him, and gave a little smile as if to show it.

'Keep eating,' she suggested.

'I've had enough.'

'Pretend, then.'

'Why?'

'He'll come and hover if he thinks we've finished.'

She was keeping her voice low, almost conspiratorial, and he couldn't understand why. He said, 'I'm not with you.'

Now she was beginning to hitch her chair back from the table, but surreptitiously, as if she didn't want anyone to realise.

'All right, then,' she said, 'just get ready. I'll give the signal.'

She was making no sense at all to him, or at least, she wasn't until she started to rise, and then it all clicked into place. Suddenly she was out of her chair and heading for the door, and clearly expected him to drop everything and follow. Given a good burst of speed, she'd be in the street and running before the staff could get the message; he felt completely wrong-footed, leaping up almost before he'd realised what he was doing and upsetting the table so that it rose up into the air and came down again with a crash as plates, cups and glasses danced and rolled. There was a yell from the direction of the kitchens, but the door was already swinging shut after Lucy and he could see the heels of her trainers disappearing up the stairs; he was only halfway out and around the table with a *what the fuck* expression on his face, and then suddenly there were at least three pairs of hands grabbing hold of him and he was moving at what seemed like an unreasonable speed toward the wall.

It was like being carried by the tide, and dashed down just as hard. All of the breath went out of him. The wallpaper was a kind of flocked velvet, he noticed, although he'd never have known it from a distance. They turned him around and slammed him again, hard. He tried to speak, but nothing came out. Over on the far side of the restaurant, someone was emerging from the kitchens and he saw the shiny-metal flash of stainless steel.

It was a cleaver. Had to be.

He tried to speak again, but nothing came out.

Two of them held him, the grey-suited one searched him. They were all shouting, but not in any language that he understood.

Again, he tried to speak. The chef with the cleaver came shouldering into the crowd.

They found his notebook, and let it fall to the floor. The same with his keys. But then they found his wallet and flipped it open looking for cash, plastic, anything they could shake out to make him pay.

Over what they found, they grew quiet.

And those who were holding him, let him go.

He straightened himself out. His dignity and the power of speech returned, both of them somewhat ragged and incomplete.

'Police business,' he said hoarsely, retrieving his warrant card from their hands. 'Now tell me what we owe.'

Six

She was waiting for him beyond the end of the alley, about a couple of hundred yards further down the road. He didn't even know that she was there until she hopped out from behind a builders' skip and joined him, matching him step for step.

'Did you pay them?' she said.

'What do you think?' he answered darkly.

'Chicken. That was supposed to be my treat.'

'Well, I've been treated enough for one night. I'm tired and I'm sore and I don't care if I never see another lorry or a layby or a radiator with a teddybear on it for as long as I live. Which won't be very long, if I stick around in your company. You'd better be able to get home from here, because this is as far as it goes.'

'Have I annoyed you?' she said.

He stopped. Tried to compress his feelings down into something like an answer. A simple 'yes' might have done it.

But he said, 'Annoyed me?' He turned to face her. 'All right. You want to know what *really* annoys me? The sight of a kid who's still trying to impress a dead sister who never loved her back. It's futile and it's stupid and it's downright dangerous. There's no sane or solid reason for you to be pissing your life away like this. It's a waste, and it's tragic, and *that's* what gets me mad.'

She didn't answer. And he realised that he'd probably gone too far.

'Look,' he began. 'I'm sorry . . .'

But she was calm, and she was serious.

She said, 'Give me just another half-hour.'

He didn't know what had come over him. He hated to lose his self-control, and that was pretty much what he'd done. No harm, as it happened, but that wasn't the point. You lose control, you show things about yourself that you don't want seen, you risk becoming vulnerable.

You risk doing something that you might regret.

The suburbs were stirring into life. These were big, old houses with gardens of some size; some of them well-kept, some of them less so. But the area spoke of past money even if the fabric had begun to fray a little over recent years, and even the most run-down of its properties would still be entitled to the elusive cachet of the 'desirable address'. A wide avenue, tree-lined. They left the car around a corner and walked the rest of the way.

'We'll go around by the back,' she told him. 'I'd rather we weren't seen.'

A narrow fenced passageway between two of the houses led them to a bolted gate. The bolt was on the inside, but she tinkered around for a couple of moments and then slipped it with ease. The gate stuck as it opened, its hinges dropped and unoiled. They moved through into the garden.

This was one of the shabbier houses; nothing that a little paint and some attention couldn't cure, but over the last few years it didn't seem to have had much of either. The garden was rambling and overgrown, long grass standing under the rusted frame of a child's swing. Beyond the swing was an outbuilding, part garage and part garden shed; with a glance toward the house, Lucy was making for this.

The key was under a broken flowerpot. Once they were inside, she took a piece of blanket which she hooked across the window in lieu of a curtain and then switched on the light. This came from an unshaded bulb in the rafters, which it shared with a lot of dust and a few hundred cobwebs. Down below, there was no order to anything. Tools, broken furniture, old toys, old shoes. Spare pieces of carpet, cardboard boxes, camping equipment, more cardboard boxes.

'Here's where we put all of Chrissie's stuff,' Lucy said, tugging a small dusty suitcase out from under a stack of old newspapers. She carried it over to the workbench, its surface a mass of old sawcuts, and set it down. 'This is the bag that she had with her on the night that she died.'

He moved around behind her, to watch as she unzipped it.

'All of her clothes and makeup, everything. We never threw anything away. All this stuff's what she had when she first set out. Nothing to say what she'd been doing, or anything. It wasn't a happy time for her, when she left. I'll always remember what she told me. She said, whenever it rains, think of me, because I'll probably be out there in it somewhere.'

She pulled out some of the clothing and other pieces to show him; the half-read paperback book, the leather purse with its small amount of cash still untouched, a few receipts, some postage stamps.

28

Whatever life she'd had in London, it was almost as if Chrissie had deliberately shed it before making the run for home that she would never complete. Lucy laid out the items on the workbench; no relic was ever handled with more care. He touched nothing, but moved in closer as Lucy went back to the junkpile and lifted a couple of big old mirrors aside to get to something else.

He didn't know what he could say to her. That the dead moved on, into darkness or maybe to something better, and that what she was doing here was nothing more than giving way to self-deception? Lucy was a bright kid, but she was wasting her life on the impossible. He'd seen death, often close-to. It defied romance, it defied imagination.

The box was heavy, and she apologised as she bumped him aside to get it up onto the bench.

More clothes. Christine's schoolbooks.

Lucy rummaged around, and came up with a roll of stiff paper held together with an elastic band. The band snapped, perished, when she tried to take it off. 'It's her old school photograph,' she explained.

It was one of those yard-wide, inches-high affairs taken with a special camera, row after row of monochrome faces all smiling, squinting, scowling; one fragile strip of frozen history, its players now long-dispersed into marriage, jobs, prison, divorce, all poised to scatter from that one spring morning when they'd lined up on the school hall steps. Lucy gave him an end to hold, and unrolled the photograph to its full length. She held the other, and scanned around in the middle for a moment before pointing.

'There she is,' she said. 'It was taken when she was fifteen.'

He looked more closely. She stood in the next to last row. Those to either side of her were looking straight at the camera, but her attention seemed to have been diverted for a moment. Christine Ashdown, her life already more than half-over.

'And that one's you,' Lucy said.

He was nodding politely, and then he realised what she was saying. He looked, and she was right. His fifteen-year-old self, a walking embarrassment and, even in school uniform, a fashion disaster zone.

Then he looked at Lucy.

'Since when did you know?' he said.

She took the photograph from him, and studied her sister's long-ago image. 'I suppose I could look like her, just a little,' she said.

And then she started to re-roll it. 'I knew almost from the beginning," she went on when I saw you watching me. At first I was worried, then I thought you looked familiar. And then when you started dodging around and playing games and hiding, I worked it

29

out. You're Joe Lucas, the one who surprised everybody and joined the police when you left school.'

'You knew that all along?'

'Of course. You don't think I'd have ridden around all night with some stranger I'd just met, do you?'

Dodging around. Playing games. Hiding.

He said, bleakly, 'Anything else you know about me?'

'A few things.' The rolled photograph went back into the box, minus its rotted band. 'Chrissie talked about you sometimes. She said you could make her laugh.'

'Really?'

'I reckon she actually thought a lot of you. Back then, anyway. But it didn't come to anything, because you never asked her out.'

Something had begun to hurt in him; something old, something almost forgotten.

'No,' he said, quietly. 'No, I never did.'

She turned around and leaned against the bench. The unshaded light was hard and unkind, but her face was young enough to take it. She really was something, he couldn't help thinking.

She said, 'So what's this all about, Joe?'

'You were right,' he admitted. 'Your father asked me to get involved. He asked if I could find out exactly what you were doing, what kind of danger you were putting yourself in, and then help him to find some way to talk you out of it.'

'You're still with the police?'

'I'm still with the police.'

'But this is nothing to do with the way that Chrissie died. It's all about me, and getting me back under control, isn't it?'

'That's not being fair to him. Think what he's going through. Accidents happen, people get hurt, but . . .'

'Life goes on, right?'

'I know it can sound hard. But that's exactly what it does.'

She turned abruptly, jerking open her sister's valise again and reaching inside. Whatever she was looking for, it took her a moment to find it.

'You asked me for one sane and solid reason,' she said. 'Well, how about this?'

There was a blur, a distinctive click, and suddenly he was facing one of the most lethal-looking switchblades that he'd ever seen.

'She didn't have *this* when she left home,' Lucy said. 'She told us that she had a job in an office.' With the blade, she gestured toward the half-finished job of unpacking on the workbench alongside her. 'There's nothing here to say what she did or where she lived, or anything. It's like she didn't want to bring any part of it back with her. That doesn't seem to bother anybody else, but it really bothers me. It's all wrong. And I don't think she died by accident.'

Before he could say anything, she seemed to hear something that he didn't; some sound from outside, and so she quickly switched off the light and reached for the old piece of blanket that covered the window. She raised it no more than an inch at the corner, and peered out. He didn't know how she could expect to see much through the thick layer of dust and cobwebs on the inside of the glass, but after a few seconds she seemed to be satisfied and let the makeshift curtain fall again.

He said, 'Do one thing for me, will you? Just listen to yourself, and see how you sound. One dangerous toy doesn't make for a whole conspiracy. You're making something out of absolutely nothing.'

The light stayed off. In the shady, musty twilight of the shed's interior, she carefully closed up the spring-driven blade from her sister's luggage.

She said, drily, 'Well, thanks for the advice, Joe.'

He could see that it would be pointless to keep on hammering at her. His cover was blown, he'd learned what he could and said what he had to, and all that remained was to bow out so that he could crawl home and catch up on some sleep. He had calls to make, letters to answer, problems of his own to consider.

He said, 'What are you going to do now?'

She laid down the folded weapon. 'I'll stay here a while longer. Then I might go over to the house. I haven't seen my dad in weeks.'

'Good idea,' he said.

He hesitated a moment longer.

And then he left her there, with the dust and the mirrors and the memories.

She waited until Joe had gone before she spoke again.

'She did love me back,' she said softly. 'I know she did.'

SEVEN

'I think I blew it,' he told her father.

Jack Ashdown didn't look good. He was in his fifties, but carried it like a man at least ten years older. He'd begun to dress and half-completed the job before apparently losing heart, at which point he'd thrown on a rust-coloured bathrobe and called himself ready. They sat by the kitchen table, which still had the half-cleared remains of some other day's breakfast on it. The house itself wasn't exactly a pit – he seemed to have made some effort to keep it tidy – but it was obvious that his mind had been somewhere else. He'd offered Joe some tea, coffee if he preferred it; but after a glance at the crockery-filled bug farm that was the kitchen sink, Joe had declined.

He told the night's story, skipping only the incident in the restaurant. There was plenty of colour without it, and he reckoned that Ashdown was probably already getting as much anxiety as he could take.

'I can see your problem,' Joe said as his account reached its end. 'She's quite a handful.'

'Don't I know it,' Ashdown said dispiritedly, shaking his head and tracing patterns in something on the table. There didn't seem to be anything in the story that had surprised him too much; he had the look of a man who'd lived with his certainties for too long for confirmation to make any kind of a difference.

'I've never seen anybody so obsessed with a single idea,' Joe said. 'You've heard the theory she's come up with?'

'The murder business. I don't know what to think anymore.'

'Have you thought of psychiatric help?'

'I've got tablets from the doctor, but they only give me the shakes.'

'I meant for her.'

Ashdown gave a slight shrug. 'I've made appointments, but she never turns up. She's as good as an adult. I don't see how you could force her.'

'There are steps that can be taken,' Joe said.

'I know,' Ashdown said. He pushed back his chair, stood, and wandered over to the window. He ran a hand through his thinning hair which looked as if he'd cut it himself, and none too recently.

He said, 'I tried talking to her, so she moved out. So then I stopped giving her money, but somehow she's managing. I lost one of them, Joe. Now it looks like I'm losing the other.'

Joe got to his feet. 'I'll find out about the procedures,' he said. 'Nothing you have to act on, just something to be thinking about.'

Ashdown nodded, absently. 'Where did you leave her?'

'She's in your shed, still going through Chrissie's stuff.'

That got a reaction. Ashdown turned and looked at Joe, his eyes widening. 'She's *here*?'

'Yeah. Sorry I couldn't do more.'

Now Ashdown was looking down at his ragbag assortment of night and day clothing, as if suddenly realising that it wouldn't do. His own daughter, Joe thought, and he doesn't want to make a bad impression. 'Thanks for that,' Ashdown was saying. 'Thanks for that, anyway.'

Joe shrugged and they shook hands, Ashdown glancing anxiously out of the kitchen window in the direction of the shed. Then they parted company.

He'd almost reached the end of the street when he heard Ashdown calling his name.

He stopped, but didn't turn straight away.

He could walk on. Pretend he hadn't heard. He'd done so much in the past eight or nine hours, surely no-one could ever blame him if he did.

But then, wearily, he turned around.

Ashdown was a distant figure at the end of his own driveway. He was waving his arms and pointing back toward the house, but Joe couldn't make out what he was saying. He seemed pretty agitated.

Joe went back.

The two of them went into the shed. It was empty – or at least, it was empty of Lucy Ashdown. One of the big mirrors had been propped up on the workbench and wiped more or less clean. On the bench and the floor before it lay a mass of cut hair, most of it bleached, and the rusting old scissors that had made the job possible. Lucy's clothes were in a heap to one side – everything, right down to the underwear. Christine's clothing and case were nowhere to be seen.

'I don't understand it,' Jack Ashdown said. 'What does she think she's doing?'

Inwardly, Joe sighed.

I could look like her, just a little.

'I may have some idea,' he said.

33

EIGHT

She'd had a definite feeling about the night. Things had seemed to be running her way, even before Joe Lucas had come along and provided a free set of wheels; and then thanks to him she'd covered more of her network in the past few hours than she'd managed in months, and had come out of it with something more solid than the usual regrets and apologies. Her steady collection of goodwill and gossip looked as if it might – just *might* – be lining up for a payoff.

He'd set out to dissuade her, and he'd helped her along. If that wasn't luck, she didn't know of anything that deserved the name.

After hearing the same rumour twice in the space of a few hours, it had all come together back at Charlie's pull-in on the moors; she'd flipped back to some of her earlier notes and there it had been, last March, in one of her routine stop-and-pester interviews. Same haulier, same route, and she was damned sure that she'd been looking at the same driver. He'd told her that he knew nothing and she'd let him pass on by, but maybe her bullshit sensors hadn't been so finely tuned back then. These days, she wouldn't have let him get away so easily.

Especially not when the lying bastard had been driving a cab with a big X of plastic souvenir travel pennants on its grille.

Finding when and where he'd be passing through the region gave her little problem; it took nothing more devious than a phone call to the company's transport manager, and she'd even managed to con him into accepting the charge for the call by pretending to be the driver's daughter with an urgent need to see her daddy. Getting the driver to spill would be something else.

But she reckoned that she had an answer to that one, too.

She checked her watch. It was showing almost mid-day. She'd reset it not too long before, so it was probably about right. From her table by the window, she watched the approach road.

This wasn't a site that she'd visited with Joe even though it was on her list, the reason being that it closed down at eleven and they were really tough on overnight security. There wasn't much here, just a garage forecourt and workshop with a one-storey restaurant building on the side, but it was in a good position on a fast road and, being slightly elevated, it could be seen from a fair distance. As it was close to lunchtime, the restaurant was already more than half-full. She'd bagged a window seat and was hanging onto it, although nobody so far had tried to move her; another reason why she hadn't worked the crowds here more often was that the staff could get a little snotty over a scruffy kid with no money to spend.

But today, she was no scruffy kid. She was in Christine's clothes, and Chrissie's change was more than enough to cover the coffee that served as table rental.

Around twelve-twenty, she saw him arrive.

As his lorry climbed the approach road she stood in her seat and craned for a better look and saw, as she'd half-expected, that the cross of pennants had gone from the front of his cab. In itself, that seemed pretty damning – no other driver had ever reacted in such a way, and it gave her encouragement. Her heart was hammering as she made her way out. She'd lost sight of him as he'd turned in, but she hurried around to the big parking area at the back of the building.

His back was to her as he climbed down from the cab. She remembered him, but only just – she'd seen so many faces in this past year, of all kinds and at all hours, and without her notes she'd have been lost. He was short and wiry, a little rough-looking but nobody's idea of a villain. He was carrying a vacuum flask, presumably to pick up a refill, and there was a folded copy of *The Sun* sticking out of his pocket. He didn't see her until he'd locked up the cab and turned around, and by then she'd stopped, only a few yards away and directly in his path.

He turned. Now he couldn't miss her.

After a moment, she said, 'What's the matter, Billy? Seen a ghost?'

But Billy, jaw dropped open as if on a busted hinge, seemed able to say nothing at all.

It was better than she could have hoped. She actually had to help him inside, and for a minute or so was afraid that she might even have done him some lasting damage. His breathing and his colour were bad, but both improved after she'd guided him back to her table. Having been around for forty-six years, his views on how things ought to be had probably become more or less settled. Seeing the dead raised and walking appeared to have done serious harm to his confidence.

Obviously her self-administered haircut didn't look so bad after

35

all. It was as close to Christine's bob as she could get it, given the circumstances; but then, in the better light of the restaurant's 'Powder Room' – just the usual toilet with the usual tiles, and only an air-freshener and an empty tissue-box to signify its aspiration to be anything more – she'd added her sister's makeup and had to admit that even she was surprised at the result. It was like a transformation. Lucy had looked in the mirror, and Christine Ashdown had looked out. She'd stared helplessly, wanting to speak and knowing that it was nothing more than illusion . . . and then two fat women had come in and broken the spell, and she was Lucy Ashdown again, and it was time to take up her post.

Billy's hand still trembled slightly as he raised his mug. 'I couldn't believe it,' he admitted. 'You're the image of her. Look at me, I'm still shaking.'

There hadn't even been any question of his trying to brush her off as he had the first time; he'd been hit too hard, and so unexpectedly. She said, 'Take your time, Billy. When did you go back onto the Eindhoven run?'

'Just this week. I asked for a switch after . . .' – a nod, because he didn't want to say it – 'you know . . . but it was losing me money. I thought that after a year, I'd be safe. I didn't mean any harm by not coming forward. But I'd broken company rules by picking her up in the first place, and it would have come out. I've got a wife and two girls. I mean, nothing happened, all I did was give her the ride and drop her off . . . but the idea's always there in people's minds, isn't it?'

'That's people for you, Billy,' she said, and she looked out of the window as he fumbled out a big linen handkerchief and blew his nose. *People are the worst*, her mother used to say; *Give me my cats, any day*. After her mother had gone, Lucy had watched the cats and worried for them. It was therapy of a kind, a way of displacing her own grief. The cats, undisturbed, had carried on getting fat and growing old as if no-one had mattered, and no-one was missing. The last one had taken its final basket-trip to the surgery about five years before. It was then that she'd realised that her mother had been wrong; people might vary, but felines genuinely didn't give a shit.

Outside, someone was passing. Then he stopped.

It was Joe who now stood outside the window. He was scanning the restaurant's interior from the forecourt, and he saw her.

Well, it couldn't matter now. If he wanted to give her another lecture about futility, then let him come inside and learn about the value of persistence, instead. His face was like something hacked out of stone. He must have spent the entire morning trailing around all of the previous night's locations, and then been forced to rack his brains to remember any others that had been on the list.

Billy finished honking into his handkerchief, couldn't resist inspecting what he'd produced, and then carefully wadded it and stowed it away with the wet patch in the middle. She felt almost sorry for him, but she was thinking of the long nights and the hard times that his honesty might have saved her. Joe had moved to come inside, and as he was walking down the aisle toward them she said, 'This is a friend of mine, Billy. I want him to hear the rest of it.'

Billy shrugged. Joe didn't even glance at the driver as he slid into the seat opposite. He was staring at Lucy, and his expression didn't change.

Billy said, 'I picked her up at Newport Pagnell. I didn't approach her, she was the one who came to me. And I couldn't say no, could I? She didn't talk much, except to say that she was going home. I got the feeling that she wasn't sorry about whatever it was she was leaving behind. One thing she did say, though. Three or four times she said, *Is there anybody behind us?*'

'Was there?'

'How are you going to tell, on a motorway? Everyone's going in the same direction, nearly everyone's doing the same speed. So I said no, and that seemed to make her happy. Then I asked her where she wanted to be dropped, and she said where she lived, so I said I'd drop her at the services because that was as close as I'd get. I went for a whiz and when I came out, she was nowhere in sight.'

Lucy frowned. Everything had been okay so far, but this wasn't what she'd been expecting to hear. 'Is that the last time you saw her?' she said.

'No,' Billy said. 'Because when I was getting back into the cab I saw her getting out of a car across the way. She must have been talking to the driver for the last five minutes or so. She started to walk away . . .' He swallowed, hard, and looked intently at the table. 'And the car came straight out and ran her down. I've never seen anything like it. She went right up into the air. I thought that's it, she's had it, and I didn't even see her come down. I ran over and looked, but I couldn't find her. After a while, I started to wonder if I'd really seen what I thought I had. And a while after that, I'd more or less convinced myself. Until I read about it and how they'd found her, and by then it was too late.'

'She was alive, then, Billy,' Lucy said, with a control that surprised even her. 'If you'd called someone, she might still be alive now.'

He wouldn't look up. 'If I could bring her back, I would.' And then, head still down, he risked a wary glance at her. 'Am I going to have to tell all this to the police?'

Lucy looked at Joe. His eyes hadn't moved from her.

'No,' she said. 'That's what the police call an accident, isn't it, Joe?'

Joe ignored the barb.

For the first time since he'd arrived, he spoke.

He said, 'I'm going to phone your father, *now*. I'm going to tell him that I'm bringing you home. Now, are you going to give me a hard time?'

But she smiled resignedly, as if all roads had been travelled and a journey had reached its end, and there were no more arguments to be had.

'Not any more, Joe,' she said.

'Good.'

With that he got up and, after a stern look to make her certain that he meant it, stalked over toward the pay phone sign.

She waited until she was out of earshot and then, rising, she grabbed Billy's sleeve and started to pull him out toward the aisle. He looked up at her, bewildered, as with her free hand she reached for her sister's valise.

'Come on,' she said, bundling him toward the exit. 'You've got the length of one phonecall to get me away from here.'

She glanced back, but Joe hadn't seen them. He was going to be most amazingly pissed off when he came back and found her gone.

And with a brief smile at the thought, she went on.

He thought it was over.

She'd barely begun.

PART TWO

On the Town

NINE

It was a crowd like she hadn't seen in ages, and for here it wasn't even anything special. Down on the Underground platform she'd tried to move against it, but in the end she'd found it easier to let herself be carried along. She stood on the rickety wooden escalator, old rubber and brass under grimy striplights, and rode upward into – who could say what?

She'd been to the capital before, but never alone. The first time had been with a school party, the other had been a secret weekend rail-break with Daniel, who at fourteen and a half weeks stood at number three in the longevity chart of Lucy's ex-boyfriends. Neither visit had been much preparation for this. The first had felt like a life sentence in the Science Museum, and the second hadn't been quite so much fun although at least she was spared a stupid questionnaire. Question: Where are the major erogenous zones? Answer: In Daniel's perception, somewhere to the west of the Cayman Islands. Being speedy was one thing, but being proud of it was something else altogether. The relationship hadn't survived.

For the first time, she was beginning to have doubts.

She'd set out to get here with total confidence, certain of her skills in staying afloat. She thought of how she'd made out over the past year, of some of the stunts that she'd pulled, the difficulties that she'd hit and overcome. But that was then, and this was now. Suddenly, she was feeling provincial and disorientated and ill-informed. This was no weekend break, with a hotel booked and a ticket home and her spending money all counted in an envelope. This was open-ended, an unwritten story with no guarantees. Now, as she walked with Christine's bag and in Christine's clothes through a street of bright lights and fast food toward the nightlife circus of Leicester Square, she couldn't drag her mind away from the sight that she'd seen just before she'd reached the Tube Station foyer. At a bend on the stairway, just before the final flight which led to the outside air, a girl of about her own age had been seated on the cold stone floor with her back against the wall and her coat across her knees. On the coat lay some small change, and she'd been holding a piece of torn cardboard on which she'd written something that had gone by too quickly for Lucy to read, but which had been along the lines of STARVING AND HOMELESS, PLEASE HELP. The girl herself was as scruffy as the card, and stared dully into the space before her as if oblivious to the people walking past.

Someone behind Lucy said, *'It's all an act, you know. They make a fortune like that and then they spend it on drugs.'*

But she couldn't drive the image from her mind. Drugs, maybe – but a fortune? Who was trying to kid who? She looked back as the crowd spilled out into the street, but the speaker could have been anybody. The teenaged beggar was already lost from sight.

Now, as the high neon-blocked walls of the square opened out before her, she tried to fight down her anxiety. One step at a time. She'd Christine's money, and what she had to do now was find herself a place for the night in a hostel or in one of the cheapest of the cheap hotels. It was mid-evening already, and there was no time for kicking around and being indecisive.

At the far corner of the square stood Piccadilly Circus, this much she remembered; more lights, more traffic, and as many kids, drunks, deadbeats and tourists as could fit themselves onto the wide steps around the base of the Eros statue. The statue itself perched high above everything, newly spruced-up but still resembling, as Daniel had termed it, a small flying faggot in a big tin hat.

The numbers around the plinth were fewer than before but that was only to be expected, because her last (and only) visit had been on a warm summer night and this was something else. She circled, scanned faces, eavesdropped. Where the ground seemed safe, she ventured further.

The responses she received varied from the pig-ignorant to the suggestions of a bunch of Goths who racked their brains but whose goodwill wasn't exactly a currency that she could use. The best suggestion sent her out of the Circus and into Shaftesbury Avenue, where the glitz of theatre marquees was outshone only by the migraine brilliance of a big MacDonald's that had shouldered in about halfway along. Cars and taxis were jammed nose-to-tail, and she saw more Japanese within ten minutes than she'd seen in her entire life so far. Under the frontage of the Palace Theatre, like a half-restored cathedral complete with ply boards and scaffolding, she talked to a saxophone-playing busker who was in between numbers. The busker was a skinny-looking girl of around twenty, with a wire-grey mutt curled up by her feet. The dog, which was long-legged and as skinny as its owner, looked up as they talked; the busker pointed to send Lucy on her way again, and the dog lost interest as Lucy nodded her thanks.

She wasn't sure how she felt. Scared – yes. Rootless, apprehensive

– certainly, but not in any way that made her want to turn her back on the city and run. There was something more to it, like an electricity that fed through the streets on invisible lines and charged some pit of excitement that lay deep within her. She couldn't describe the feeling. As if something big was about to happen, and everything had become somehow sharper and more meaningful in its shadow. Others went by her, and obviously felt nothing. But every now and again, mostly in those who were around her own age, she recognised the signs and knew that they were wired into the feeling, too.

A couple of them stood by the entranceway to the Centrepoint hostel.

The hostel's red iron gates were closed and locked.

'They're full,' the first kid told her as she began to read the notice on the ironwork. The gates were tall and heavy, and off the street beyond them lay an unlit passage. She couldn't see any immediate evidence of the hostel itself, or any way of catching the attention of anyone inside; just the passageway, and the red-wrought barrier that kept her from it.

'Already?' Lucy said.

'It's always the same. You have to get here really early.'

The youth was underdressed for the weather, as was his companion. They'd shoved their hands into their pockets for warmth, not so easy in such overtight trousers. Both were pale and had bad skin, and the one who'd spoken had the accent of a Tynesider.

Lucy said, 'What will you do?

The boy shrugged. 'It's either this, or sleep rough.'

'Or get friendly with someone who's got a floor,' the other added.

A few doors away, in the light thrown by the designer frontage of one of a chain of pizza restaurants, she paused to consider her options. They seemed few. What had seemed like the best, the no-worries home-and-dry solution, had just been blasted with a cold dose of reality. After checking her cash, Lucy dug out the last of her caramels. She was hungry, but money was tight and she was going to have to be tough with herself. As far as she'd been able to establish, even the cheapest of hotels would cost her all that she had and more – her thinking had been geared to the kind of truck stop prices that were charged back home in the sticks, and it was sadly out of range. A few hours on the road had brought her into a different league altogether, and she was going to have to adjust to it.

She tossed a screwed-up wrapper in the direction of a wastebin across the pavement. It was a half-hearted effort, and the paper fell short and rolled.

'Needs more practice,' a man's voice said.

TEN

He leaned on the wall beside her, with just about enough distance between them. Lucy looked at him warily, not about to run but not immediately ready to offer her trust, either. It wasn't a night for it, this wasn't the place for it, and she wasn't the type for it.

She'd have placed him in his mid-thirties, although he obviously saw himself as younger; his haircut was the expensively-streaked perm of the disco haunter and he was wearing a suit . . . but under the jacket he wore a pullover with no shirt, and a glance at ground level revealed grubby training shoes that seemed about to fall apart. Borderline respectable or borderline weird, depending on the viewpoint of the observer.

Indicating the gates behind them, he said, 'No luck back there?'

She shook her head. She was still sucking on a caramel, and continued to watch him. She wasn't certain. Wasn't it always the way? After a year of fine-tuning her radar, her first big-city encounter had to be with someone who didn't even fit within the spectrum.

Moving a little closer, he went on, 'It's not the only place in town.'

Lucy backed off a more or less equal distance. 'It's the only one I know of.'

'Loads of others,' he said with a tilt of his hand, a gesture that took in the rest of the busy thoroughfare and beyond. 'You know the area around Charing Cross, at all?'

She shook her head.

'Victoria?'

'I just arrived tonight.'

He looked around, seeming to think it over for a moment. And then he made an elaborate show of looking at his watch, which Lucy recognised as one of those throwaway plastic Swiss affairs.

'Look,' he said, 'I'm on my way to a business appointment. If we get a move on, I've just got time to see you fixed up.'

She frowned. 'Why?'

He started to move out.

'You want to find somewhere to stay, or not?'

The answer was an obvious *yes*, but every instinct told her to beware. She was on strange ground, and she was thinking that the specimens didn't come any stranger than this one; but even as the thought was passing through her mind, a bunch of geeks with concert tickets were going by and they made her new acquaintance look almost like a bank manager.

He'd stopped, and was looking back at her. 'Well?'

If they stuck to the main streets, they'd always be in a crowd. What could he do?

And she was desperate.

So she followed him.

They backtracked over ground that she'd already covered, and then carried on toward the river. He seemed to be leading her off the tourist beat, although there were still people around. The fact was that she had no idea of where she was going. She'd been confident of her geography when she'd arrived, but nothing was exactly as she'd remembered it. Down by the embankment gardens, a brief shower sent them running for the shelter of a bridge. It was a paved underpass with about half a dozen shops, well-lighted although none was open for business.

'It won't last,' he told her, looking back at the rain, and they walked on toward the square of night at the far end of the pass. He hadn't told her his name, but he'd been telling her about his three houses and the cars that he kept in different garages all over London, one of them a Ferrari that was under restoration.

'I've got lots of different business interests,' he explained. 'I know a lot of people in the record industry. Do you sing, at all?'

She shook her head. She'd glanced around them and seen that, counter to everything that she'd intended, the two of them were now alone. Somewhere – about a thousand miles away – there was a steady rumble of river-crossing traffic. She tightened her grip on her bag, and held it close.

'I'm actually thinking more of producing films,' he was saying. 'I'm a close personal friend of David Puttnam. He's always ringing me for advice about finance.'

He stopped, and made a great show of looking at his watch again.

'Oh, no,' he said. 'Don't tell me that's the time. I got so wrapped up in giving you a helping hand that I've gone and missed my appointment. Would you believe it?'

In a word? No. Lucy said, 'Sorry,' and increased the distance between them by a couple more feet; they were about halfway through the underpass and she wondered how much Christine's valise was going to slow her down when the time came to run.

'Listen,' he said. 'This friend of mine who runs the hostel, he charges an introduction fee. I was going to pay it for you myself, just as a friend, but this means I'm out on my expenses. I'm going to have to ask you to pay it yourself. If you want to give it to me now, you can . . .'

Lucy said, 'I don't know what you're talking about. You never mentioned this before.'

'Say, ten quid?' There was a hopeful pause, and then he said, 'I'm going to have to talk him down, to get it so cheap. But it's the only way I'm going to get you in at an hour like this. Just a tenner?'

'I don't have it,' Lucy said.

'How much have you got, then?'

'Seven.'

He stopped, and faced her.

'And some change,' she added.

'You're kidding me.'

'I wish I was.'

His face narrowed unpleasantly. 'If I'd thought you were one of those kids who came hitching down with nothing, I wouldn't have bothered with you. But they always look like shit, and you look like class. So fuck you, bitch, I'm not taken in. Open that fucking bag and let's see what's inside.'

'All right, but don't touch me,' she warned, fumbling at the zip of the valise and back-pedalling nervously as he stalked towards her. It opened a couple of inches, jammed, and then jerked a few inches further. 'You can look in the bag, but just don't touch me.'

'Touch you? I'll fucking strangle you if you don't come across.' And he grabbed her by the arm to prevent her from retreating any further, and she winced in pain as his fingers dug in through the sleeve of Christine's coat. He was expecting her to try to pull away, but she didn't.

One second later, he screamed.

The sound made a shocking echo in the enclosed space of the underpass. He fell back, staggering for several steps and holding out his arm. His sleeve had been opened from the wrist up.

So had his forearm.

'You cut me!' he said, incredulous. His sleeves hung in layers from the elbow of his suit. A single red line spiralled the length of his arm in a neat slice; and as he held it out, the line blurred and began to run.

He looked from the wound to the switchblade that Lucy now held in the air before her, as if he couldn't quite bring himself to believe in the sequence that bound them together as cause and effect. His arm was beginning to drip, streaking down his hand and forming droplets at the fingertips.

Lucy said, 'As a bullshit artist, you're strictly painting-by-numbers. Walk away.'

'You cow!'

'Walk away!'

The blade was the key. The blade was her equaliser, a line drawn across argument that said, *no further*. He looked at it, squeezing his injured arm at the elbow, as powerless before the knife as Lucy would have been without it.

And, his face clouded with a fury that almost had him in tears, he did as he'd been told.

She watched, not wanting to turn or take her eyes from him, as he back-pedalled toward the edge of the lighted area. She was trembling. She all but counted the yards as he covered them, but then he paused for a moment. He stood, framed in darkness, clutching his arm like a moody Dane playing Hamlet on some giant stage, and called out to her for one last try.

'*A quick blowjob, then?*'

He was probably mad enough to be serious. She made no reply.

So then he turned and shambled off, away from the river and into the night.

At least he'd been reliable on one count. The rain hadn't lasted.

The embankment paving was wet and slick, but the air was clear. Lucy hugged the suitcase tightly as she walked back, as if it was her anchor to reality; she'd never hurt a living thing before, ever, but the use of the knife had come to her with frightening ease. She didn't know what was worse, the idea of what she'd done or the thought of what might have happened if she'd failed to defend herself. She felt sick, she felt weak.

She had no idea of what she was going to do next.

She'd followed the river. She'd only covered a few hundred yards but it wasn't so deserted here, and there was an Underground station across the way in the shadow of another of the Thames bridges. She wondered about buying a ticket, riding the night away . . . but didn't they close the system down around midnight? That could be even worse. She might be dumped out in the suburbs somewhere. She could maybe spin out what money she had in an all-night café, if she could find one. Or a bus station waiting room; if nobody came around asking to see tickets, she might even be able to get some sleep across three or four seats with her bag under her head. As

Lucy, a scruffy teenager in a scruffy coat, she'd never get away with it; but with Christine's style, the story might be different.

Maybe she could sit for a while, think it over.

The Tube station's entranceway didn't hold much appeal; here a large number of youths and young men were sitting around on cheap suitcases and duffel bags, and seemed to be waiting uncertainly for nothing in particular. A small railed park along from the station didn't exactly thrill her, either; no lights showed, and as far as she could tell it seemed at this hour to be the exclusive territory of older down-and-outs.

Her step was dragging. Her chest was feeling tight, and her head had started to buzz. Her asthma hadn't troubled her in years, not since she'd left school, but she could remember the danger signs. An attack would be the last thing that she could need right now.

There was some kind of Egyptian monument overlooking the river, a tall stone needle with a towering sphinx on either side. Beyond the needle stood a wide stone platform, from which a flight of river steps descended to water level. The platform itself was effectively screened from the road, and the stairway lay in shadow. Nobody was around. Holding onto the railings for support, she descended a couple of steps and then sat.

Her breathing eased a little. Here, in the angle between the stairway and the embankment wall, she felt safe for a while. No-one could see her, nobody could interfere. *Think*, she told herself, *Make plans*, but her mind seemed to have been stripped of its edge. Best not to rush it, she thought; you've had a bad shock, it's bound to have had an effect. The dark sphinx towered above her, backlit by a streetlamp so that it seemed to glow with an eerie golden halo. The river before her was breathtakingly beautiful, reflecting the floodlit city as if with a surface of molten bronze. At the foot of the stairway the river bucked and battered, lifted and splashed, swilled, folded and turned.

She wasn't fooled. The surface might glow like hot metal but it was cold, cold, cold. She pulled Christine's coat lapels more tightly together, and tried not to shiver. Life could be a real bastard sometimes, when you tried to hold it down and it refused to co-operate. But she was sick of being told that she had a lot to learn, mainly by people who'd used up a lot of years and seemed to have gone nowhere. She was learning all the time. That's what mistakes were for.

But maybe, she thought, it wouldn't hurt to space them out a little more.

Out over the water and some way upriver, a train was crossing a rail bridge. Its lit windows were a flicker show through the trellised

iron of the bridge's sides, and the *sound* . . . along with the swell of
the river the sound seemed oddly heightened, a rolling steelworks
of a noise. She shook her head, and felt for the wall. She ought to
be resting, but her heart raced. None of her feelings seemed to
match, a disjointed mess of awareness that was both intensified and
unreal, and instead of it getting better she was beginning to feel
worse.

It hurt.

Oh, bitch, she thought. It *is* an attack.

She had an aspirator, and a lot of damned good that would be to
her now; in its box, with its cartridge probably well past its use-by
date, in the back of a drawer in her father's house. They'd tried just
about every kind of therapy for her, but the only truly effective one
had been time.

Relax, she told herself. Give it a chance, it'll pass. And she stared
down at the moving water, concentrating and trying to lose herself
in the surface patterning.

The lights danced. They danced for her, and nobody else. They
seemed to take form around a shape that had been there all along
but which she could only now begin to see, and which became firmer
as it advanced up the steps toward her. It was like a hole in the stars,
but then it came up into the overspill light from the embankment
above.

'Hello, kid,' it said.

Eleven

She reached the top of the steps, turned, and sat down beside Lucy on the cold and mossy stone. Lucy was still holding onto the ironwork. Recognition had come right away. But acceptance . . . well, that was another matter.

'Well,' Chrissie said. 'That's life in the city. How do you rate it so far?'

Lucy stared at her. The pain had gone. 'This is unreal,' she said.

Chrissie gave a shrug. 'That's one way to look at it. Don't be too surprised. You've gone two days and a night without sleep and you've had a tough time, it's bound to have an effect.'

'I can take worse.'

'You think so? Already you're seeing things. Do something for both of us. Go home.'

'No.'

'Come on, Lucy. I know you. You're not up to this.'

Any doubts that she'd had were instantly forgotten. 'You don't know me at all!' she said angrily. 'The only time you ever noticed me was when I got in your way. You didn't even like me.'

'Is that what you think?'

Lucy didn't answer. Chrissie was watching her closely with what might have been tenderness, but Lucy looked away. Another train rolled across the bridge, static sparks making lightning around it. Like a real-life ghost train, bound straight for hell.

Chrissie said, 'There are no friends out there, kid. There's just bright lights and dirt and hustling and deals.'

Lucy looked at her then. She didn't seem so much older. And the gap that had always been between them . . . well, now it was as if it wasn't even there. Wasn't life a lousy deal, if this was what it took?

Lucy said, 'Is this what it was like for you?'

'Well,' Chrissie said, taking a look around at their surroundings, 'I got a better start than you did. And I never had to doss on any embankment. But it wasn't a whole lot different, no. Go home.'

'I can't. It's too late. Some doors you open, there's just no closing them again. Why are you so against me?'

'I'm not against you.'

'So why try to stop me?'

'Because if you blow it, you'll get hurt. Or, say you don't . . .' Chrissie looked down and her face was in shadow, impossible for Lucy to read. 'Then I can tell you, I don't think you'll like what you find.'

'I'll take the chance,' Lucy said. 'I'm not going back, Chrissie. I'm not going back for anything.'

Christine raised her head again. 'So I can see,' she said. Her faint, seen-it-all smile was back in place, but for once Lucy didn't have the perverse feeling that she was being put down.

Christine started to rise, and went on, 'I'll say one thing for you. Nobody's going to give you low marks for guts.'

'Thanks.'

She started down the steps again, toward the deepest of the shadows between the embankment wall and the water's edge; but before she'd left the light completely, she stopped and looked back.

'Promise me something,' she said.

'What?'

'If you make it. I mean, if you get to the truth. Promise that you won't think less of me.'

Lucy nodded, slowly. 'All right.'

'I'm serious, now. It matters to me.'

'I promise.'

Chrissie watched her for a moment longer; Lucy could see her in a sharpness of detail brought out by the harsh sodium light. The texture of her hair, the fine peachy down on the angle of her jaw, the faintest of age lines that had brought strength into her features . . . and Lucy felt something deep in her heart move, as if a sleeping grief had stirred and turned over.

Then, with a slight nod, Christine turned and descended again, into darkness.

This was all wrong.

The cold paving against her face. Odour of damp and dirt. The voices.

'*What happened, then?*'

'*I dunno. We were walking along and just talking, and she went like this.*'

'*Where were you taking her?*'

'*Nowhere, we were just walking.*'

'*You wouldn't have been trying to shake her for money, would you, Rollo?*'

'*Why would I need her money? I've got six cars.*'

'*You don't own a shirt with six buttons on it. You're totally predictable, Rollo. You picked her up on the street somewhere and told her you'd help her find somewhere to stay. We've had you in and out so many times, we need a revolving door put in the nick. So, what really happened?*'

There were hands on her shoulders, helping her to sit upright. She felt the wall at her back, saw a uniform. A hazy sense of a woman's face close-to, watching her own and asking her something that she didn't catch. *Chrissie?* she thought, but no. A policewoman, it had to be. Young, maybe twenty, twenty-one, little or no makeup.

Beyond her, the underpass. Lucy's weird friend in the suit and ragged trainers was in earnest conversation with a policeman, and the policeman had a tight grip on the man's arm that was strangely at odds with everything else; it gave the scene an almost operatic touch. The man was protesting, but weakly. As he gestured with his free hand, his arm seemed unimpaired. Lucy couldn't be sure, but from here it seemed that his sleeve was uncut.

Had she actually carved him, or not?

'*Christine Ashdown,*' the policewoman was saying, cutting straight through the fog to secure Lucy's attention. '*Christine Ashdown, is that your name?*' She was holding up some library tickets from the suitcase. They were way out of date.

Lucy tried to explain the misunderstanding, and found that she had no breath at all.

The policewoman was looking away from her.

'*I think we need an ambulance for this one.*'

'*Give her a shake, see if that wakes her up.*'

Her face was tilted by a gentle hand. She strained for air.

'*She doesn't need a shake, she needs a doctor!*'

And Yeah, she thought, I expect I probably do.

Twelve

Most of the rest of the night was a blur, clear enough when it had happened but not so clear to her now. She'd vague memories of the ambulance ride and the admissions procedure, and a vision of two young doctors in a whispered huddle at the foot of her bed at some ungodly hour; but then whatever they'd given her had done its stuff, and her final thought upon drifting away had been, Hey, hadn't she come through and made a soft landing yet again?

It was morning when she awoke, and stretched out under the covers in a state of near-bliss. Her hospital nightgown was scratchy and creased and she didn't even want to *think* about some of the things that must have taken place in the history of the bed, but compared to her weevilly old mattress on the floor of the squat it was paradise. It reminded her, with the usual regretful twinge, of home; not so much the dull and run-down house that she'd left, but of how it had been when they'd all been together. Jesus, she thought, what a comment on what her life had turned into. One of the partition curtains alongside her was half-drawn but she had a sense of the air and space of a public ward beyond, with pastel colours and plenty of light and the inescapable scent of antiseptic. At a rough guess they'd have put her either into Accident and Emergency or Women's Medical, depending on where they'd been able to make space, and as soon as the curtains were back she'd probably be able to tell which by the proportion of breaks and stitches to little old ladies.

Stitches . . .

That brought it all back to her. Over her breakfast tray, which she cleared like a chainsaw going through softwood, she tried to work out exactly what had happened to her the previous night. She couldn't decide, for sure. The easiest answer to it would be that she'd imagined something; the rational part of her mind endorsed this one immediately, only to find that there were other certainties which ran much deeper.

What it came down to was that she knew what she'd seen, and no amount of argument would be able to shake that knowledge. She could tell herself that it was a heresy, demand a recantation – and be certain, even while repeating the words, that the truth would remain unaffected. She'd already decided that she was going to say nothing about it to anyone else.

Whatever the explanation, something now had to happen. There was no question of her giving up or going back, and she'd encountered enough omens in the past twenty-four hours to convince her that she was unstoppable. Her main concern now had to be to get herself discharged and back out into the world, where – before tackling the seemingly impossible job of tracing Christine's year-old path through the city – she'd have to ensure that the previous night's problems didn't repeat themselves. Getting hospitalised was okay for a one-off, but it was hardly a reliable standby.

She was feeling fine. A little spacey in the head and dry around the sinuses, but these were probably side-effects and should wear off soon. Her arm was stiff when she bent it to sit herself upright, and she guessed from the sticking-plaster in the crook of her elbow that they'd probably put her on some kind of a drip for a while.

Feeling a little furtive, she crawled down the bed and reached for the chart at its end.

'You're showing your behind,' a voice said.

She dropped the chart and scrambled back under the covers, tucking the hospital gown underneath her as she went and blushing in spite of herself. The speaker stood with the bedside curtain partly drawn back, and an expression of weary sympathy on his face. He was tall and almost awkwardly bony and wore the blue shirt-sleeves and dark trousers of an orderly, although he was almost half the age of the porter who'd wheeled her up to the ward the previous night. His colour was West Indies, his accent was pure East End.

'Well, you seem lively enough,' he said, and he drew the curtain the rest of the way back in order to be able to get the standard-issue wheelchair in alongside her bed. On the chair lay a single, newly-laundered blanket. 'Apparently you were all blue and wheezing when they brought you in.'

'I used to be asthmatic,' she said. 'I haven't had an attack in ages. I feel okay now.'

'Famous last words,' the young porter said, and picked up the chart clipboard that she'd dropped onto the bedcover in her haste to return. 'You shouldn't try to read this stuff,' he said. 'It'll only confuse you.'

'I only wanted to know what they put me on. I used to get Ventolin.'

He looked at her notes, and shrugged. 'These people don't write like human beings,' he said. 'Who knows?' And then he studied the clipboard for a moment longer. 'What do I call you?' he said. 'Christine?'

Something pulled together, making a cold spot deep inside her. She said, 'What?'

He turned the chart so that she'd be able to see the entry on its top sheet. Leaning forward, she saw Christine's name. He returned the board to its place at the foot of the bed.

'There were library tickets in your bag,' he said. 'That's how come they found your address. The police have been trying to get hold of your dad.'

'Oh, great,' Lucy said, dropping back heavily into her pillows.

He seemed to read her without much problem. 'You run away?'

She nodded.

'That rough?'

'Other reasons,' she said. 'What did they do with my stuff?'

'Dunno. Burned it, probably.'

'*What?*'

'Look, your stuff's safe, and I'm taking you down for a chest X-ray. Just get in the chair and don't give me any trouble.'

'What's your name?'

'Gary, and if that's an opener for getting around me, you can forget it.'

He pointed to the chair, and obediently she threw back the bedclothes and slid across into it.

She was able to establish that they'd brought her to University College Hospital, although as an out-of-towner this meant little other than the prospect of having to expose herself in front of medical students if she stayed around any longer than necessary. She explained the confusion over names and then went on to tell him about Christine; who she was, how she'd died, and how no-one else seemed to want to know. He said the right things in all the right places, but after a while she realised that she was doing nearly all of the talking while he appeared to be paying the absolute minimum of attention. How many stories had he heard, she wondered, before he'd perfected the art of tuning out? She couldn't really blame him, but she felt a certain disappointment as she settled into the chair for the rest of the ride.

The place seemed vast and patched-together, not exactly overwhelming in scale at any one point but more so as an accumulation of locale after locale and detail after detail. After broad corridors of grey vinyl tile, they took a lift down to subway level and came out into a dipping passageway that appeared to pass underneath the street; the tunnel was decorated with a frieze of oriental scenes, bright colours applied in a childish hand.

'Do one thing for me, Gary,' she said as he pushed the chair along. It was standard NHS issue, old-fashioned and heavy, and it steered like a cow.

'No,' he said.

'Why not?'

'Because I'm soft, and you're trouble. I don't know what your problem is, and I don't want to get involved.'

This stretch of the journey was less appealing; the lighting was poor and it flickered as they entered a subterranean complex of long and windowless tunnels. The tunnel they were in seemed empty, echoing, and endless. Traffic rumbled somewhere overhead, as she said, 'They'll take me home.'

'Best place for you,' Gary said, undented.

'Just listen out for me, that's all I'm asking. Let me know if there's anything on the cards.'

She couldn't look around at him, but she heard him groan. 'Don't do this,' he said. 'You just met me. I got a hundred jobs today. You probably won't even see me again.'

And that, it appeared, was going to be that.

She spent a dispiriting hour waiting around outside the X-ray department, unable to get out of the wheelchair because her gown was so gappy at the back that it would probably fall open again at the first step. Others were waiting as well, some in chairs, one on a tilting trolley, and three or four who were allowed to come shuffling in under their own power. Before the hour was over, she knew that she'd have to get out or go mad. She didn't want to hear one more case history, one more detailed account of someone else's treatment, or even one more word about hospital food. No wonder she'd failed so dismally in enlisting the porter as an ally; this kind of company could burn off a person's tolerance like jet fuel.

The line moved along. To the middle-aged woman in the next chair, she said, 'Do you know where they keep all the patients' clothes and stuff?'

'You might well ask,' the woman said morosely. 'I had a bottle of Lucozade when I came in. And have I seen it since?'

The line moved again.

After her brief appearance in the invisible spotlight, she was returned to the ward by a different orderly who took her by a slightly different route. They didn't exchange more than two words in the course of the ride. Instead, Lucy slumped low in her blanket and made plans. She was beginning to work out the basics of a strategy, but nothing could be accomplished without the initial stage of the Great Escape. Back in her bed, she'd barely begun to check out the local situation when she had a ward visit from one of the junior doctors. He had a clean shirt and a good haircut, and he wasn't one of the two that she remembered from the previous night. He asked a lot of questions about her medical history, and then he pulled the curtains around and listened to her chest. Then he shone a penlight into her eyes and asked how she'd been sleeping, and she explained that, while she and sleep weren't exactly strangers, they didn't always get together as regularly as they might. Then she asked him about her clothes.

'Try checking your locker,' he suggested as he wrote up his instructions for her medication.

Which she did, as soon as he'd gone; and, damn it, there they were, and the valise as well, in the cupboard right next to her bed.

He'd said nothing about letting her go; not that it mattered, because she was going anyway. Two nurses were working their way down the beds in the doctor's wake, checking notes and handing out dosages, and Lucy received two tablets, a glass of water, and a jab in the behind which made her wish that she'd made her break earlier. As the ward opened for morning visiting and the nurses were occupied elsewhere, she curtained off the bed again and began to dress.

She was pulling on Christine's shoes when the curtain twitched open, and a face looked in. She froze, guiltily.

'I'll probably get shot for this,' the porter named Gary said, and from the look on his face he hardly seemed to be joking.

She said, 'Why?

'Have you got any mental history?'

'No.'

He glanced around and then, opening the curtains wider, indicated for her to follow him. Quickly pulling on her other shoe, she picked up her bag and moved after. Whatever happened, she planned to go straight on out without returning.

The numbers in the ward had more than doubled with the arrival of the day's visitors, and nobody paid the two of them any attention as they walked down the wide centre aisle toward the door. Gary was staying several paces ahead, as if pretending that they weren't really together. Well, that was fine by her.

The end of the ward let out into a corridor of offices and smaller side wards. Gary stopped by an unmarked door, signalled for her to stay quiet, and then opened it in silence for the two of them to go through.

It was a small store room of some kind, its shelves filled with stainless steel instruments and polythene-bagged linen and sterile packaging. He closed the door carefully, again without a sound. Now there was no light or ventilation other than that from a narrow fanlight high on the back wall, a wide strip of frosted glass under the ceiling that stood open with a gap of no more than an inch. At a guess it gave onto some office on the other side of the partitioning, because she could hear voices coming through.

The first that she heard belonged to Joe Lucas.

She looked at Gary, but the young orderly was looking elsewhere. What he was doing seemed to go against his every notion of what was wise or advisable, if not against his sense of what was right. Because as she listened, she heard Joe Lucas saying, 'I think we've already seen that she's a danger to herself. How do you think we'd stand for a Section Three?'

'For asthma? You wouldn't get it.' The second voice, she was pretty sure, belonged to the junior doctor who'd examined her within the last hour. 'We're not talking about severe mental impairment or a psychopathic disorder.'

'Talking to dead people?'

How did they know about that? She must have been rambling as they'd brought her in. The doctor said, 'She was confused. The most you're going to get is a twenty-eight day assessment under section two. She could commit herself, no problem, but it's not that easy to commit someone else.'

Committal? They were talking about locking her away? You bastard, Lucas, she thought, And who do you think you are? She ran hot, she ran cold. Hot with sudden fury. Cold with sudden fear.

Because from the way that Joe Lucas was sounding, the prospect didn't seem entirely unreal.

He said, 'What about her previous behaviour?'

'Not enough on its own,' the doctor said. 'But if you're right about the paranoid delusions and they come out during the assessment, then it's a possibility. Under Section Three she could then be admitted for a maximum of six months, renewable. But it's all down to the nearest relative.'

Her impulse was to scramble up and through the narrow fanlight, protesting loud and long. She wasn't a child, she knew what she was doing. They had no right even to talk about her like this, let alone consider what they were proposing.

But instead, she yawned.

Gary looked at her, sharply.

Over in the next room, she could hear that Joe was moving. 'I know what this has to be like for you, Jack,' he was saying, and Lucy realised with a start that it wasn't only Joe, but her father was in there as well. And again she thought, You *bastard*, Lucas!

'No offence, Joe,' she heard her father saying evenly, 'but I don't believe that you do.'

She put a hand on the nearest shelf, to steady herself.

Joe said, 'Believe me, it's the only way to turn her around. I thought a lot of Chrissie, once . . . only I missed the chance to show it. Let me handle this for you. There's no way I'm going to do what's wrong by Lucy.'

He sounded so plausible. He was probably even sincere.

But she didn't want to be dubbed a mental case and locked away.

She heard her father speak, almost wanly.

'I want to see her,' he said.

There was some movement, and the sound of chairs being pushed back. Within a minute they'd have found her empty bed, and the search would be on. She'd never been so scared, not even on the road.

She yawned again.

Gary was looking at her with an annoyed expression that seemed to say, What's the *matter* with you? and Lucy tried to shake her head to get it clear. Keeping her voice low, she said, 'I've got to get out.'

Gary glanced heavenward. 'Why me, God?' he pleaded in a whisper.

'Look, there's nothing wrong with me. They're just trying to fit up an excuse to get me banged away.'

'So, walk. You don't need me now. I gave you the warning, I shouldn't even have done that, and you were going anyway. It's a big place, lots of exits, they'll never find you. Just go.'

'I'm not sure I can,' she said.

'Meaning what?' Gary said suspiciously.

'They gave me something. Nobody said, but I think it must have been a knockout shot.' She tightened her grip on the shelving, but still she could feel herself sliding away. She was two years old, her head on her father's shoulder, coming home from the fair. 'I can hardly stand up.'

Gary was looking at her now, his face giving nothing away.

'Please,' she said desperately. 'I'm over eighteen. I've been around. I hitched down here without any cash and I knew it was going to be tough but I had reasons. I'd rather be back on the embankment tonight than let them take me away. I won't go, Gary. If they get me now, they'll mark me for life. It's not about treatment, it's about making me behave. I know their intentions are good. That's the worst of it.'

The drug was well into her now, washing all of her thoughts before it. She felt like a falling stone, daylight receding as she hurtled back into a bottomless well.

And Gary said, 'Wait here.'

After he'd gone, she slid to the floor and sat, heavily. She was vaguely aware of some kind of a commotion in the next room, questions being asked and phonecalls being made. She wondered, in a detached kind of way, how she was going to get past the offices unseen to reach the lifts or even the stairs.

Maybe Gary knew a way.

Gary would help her.

He'd been drawn onto the hook, like others before him.

THIRTEEN

I feel like a sack of shit, she was thinking when the door opened
again. She looked up, wondering if this would be the end of the
road and knowing that there wasn't anything she'd be able to do
about it.

But it was Gary.

'They're looking for you,' he said.

'I know.'

He bumped the door open and pushed in a stretcher-length trolley
that almost filled the space between the shelves. It was a long metal
gurney with a hinged flap on the side, and he lifted this and said,
'Get in.'

'What's it for, the laundry?'

'Just get in.'

She needed his help, but she managed it. He was skinny, but he
was strong. As he slid in the valise above her head and closed up
the flap, she sighed. Even though the gurney was unpadded and
carried the scent of some powerful disinfectant, the opportunity to
stretch out was more than welcome. She'd been fighting sleep hard,
but she didn't know if she could carry on the battle for much longer.

The trolley wasn't sprung for comfort, but that hardly mattered.
She felt as if she was ready to sleep on a rope. A knotted rope. A
knotted rope with razorblades in it . . .

'Knock it off,' Gary whispered fiercely, snapping her back to
awareness.

She made a noise which was the closest that she could get to a
question – at least, until Gary spoke again.

'Dead people don't snore,' he said.

'Dead people?'

'What do you think the wagon is? A hostess trolley?'

She lay with her eyes wide open.

She could see a thin slice of light running around the flap, but that
was all. She was aware that she was moving, but she could only
guess at where. They stopped, she heard powered doors, she felt
the bump of the gurney's wheels as she was pushed headfirst into
what she hoped was a lift.

The light shut down to a feebler level. They began to descend. Someone else must already have been inside, because now he spoke.

'Can you get over to Men's Medical?' she heard him say. 'There's a pipe burst and it's messier than a dance hall toilet. We've got to shift everybody out.'

And then she heard Gary say, 'Soon as I've handled this.'

'For the mortuary? I can take it.'

'I'm okay, it's no problem.'

'No, go on. It's a bit of an emergency.'

And then Gary said, bleakly and uncertainly, 'Right.'

The doors opened, the trolley began to move.

Only now, as she knew for certain, someone other than Gary was pushing it.

She tried to clear her throat, as a preamble to explaining that a mistake was being made, but she couldn't utter a sound. To make herself known now wouldn't only dump her rescuer into the deepest of deep shit, but would also probably deliver her to the fate that she was trying to avoid. She didn't know what she was going to do. She felt that if she opened her mouth, she'd squeak like a mouse.

Sounds were few and echoed weirdly out there, and the light flickered. She was being taken down one of the long underground tunnels.

She could feel her nails digging into her palms.

Maybe she ought to talk to Joe and her father, ask for the chance to explain. Wouldn't that be the best thing? She tried desperately to assemble her arguments, trying to find some loophole that would save her from something that she saw as scarcely better than what she was facing now . . .

But then her eyes began to close. She fought, but couldn't help it. She was going to fall into a drugged sleep, and they were going to put her among the dead, and . . . what if something were to happen before she woke up? In a place of extinction, who would think to check for signs of life? She might be heading for a locked drawer in a big chilled cabinet with a dozen other stiffs. Or worse. She'd never liked to think about what they did in those places, especially not since Christine's legally-required autopsy. They'd probably seen everything, wouldn't even blink if she was warm to the touch.

She raised her hand, to rap on the metal side of the box.

And as she did, the trolley was jarred as its leading end hit something; double doors, from the way that they bounced, and the trolley rolled on through into somewhere off the corridor where the lights were much brighter.

Her knock had gone unheard.

She was desperately weary, but she had to try again. Outside, a new voice was saying, 'Wheel it in this way. Give us a hand onto the table?'

'I can't,' said the other man, the one who'd brought her, as the trolley came to a halt. 'I've got a bad back.'

'You want to get it looked at.'

'In this place? Do me a favour. I'd rather suffer.'

The quality of sound had changed, from the aching emptiness of the subway tunnel to the hard reverberation of a fair-sized bathroom. The two men were moving away; and as she tried to call out, they'd already gone.

So then she pushed at the metal flap on the gurney's side. It gave half an inch, and jammed. She pushed again, but that was as far as it would go. She looked for a catch, but saw none.

Not on the inside, anyway.

There was just enough room to get her fingers through the gap. The lid's edge bit into her skin as she worked her way along to find the catch, about halfway down its length. By the feel of it, she was trapped by a simple hasp and staple. Please, God, she thought, don't let there be a padlock in it. She tried to get it loose, but nothing happened; by pushing at the flap to get her fingers through, she'd jammed the hasp.

She withdrew her hand, losing a little skin. It didn't matter. The pain helped her to concentrate, helped to keep her awake and ticking; holding off sleep was like trying to stop one of those descending ceilings in a haunted cellar. She let out her breath. She hadn't even realised that she was holding it in. How was she going to manage this? To release the hasp, she had to reach it. But in reaching it, she as good as locked it into place.

Defeated, she let her head drop back onto the unpadded metal. That hurt, as well. Again she was lying in darkness in the corpse wagon, with just a laser-long slit of light to mark the outline of the door. In a couple of minutes, they'd probably come back.

And in that couple of minutes, she'd probably have lost the fight.

She reached for the valise.

It was as awkward as hell in that confined space, but she got it unzipped and worked her hand inside. Obviously the dead weren't expected to bring luggage. She had to stop, yawn, and give herself a shake. Then she held the switchblade well away from her – or at least, as much away from her as she could – and heard the spring and click as it flew open. A sinister sound. Given that they weren't even legal, she'd often wondered how Christine had come by it.

This had to be the answer. If it didn't work, she was out of ideas. She might as well just let go of the rope, and fall into darkness. She put the blade into the gap, and slid it along until it stopped at the hasp. Then she withdrew it until just the tip of the blade was out, and started to hunt around.

She could see something of what she was doing, but only just. About a half-inch stripe of the blade showed up in the light from outside. There was something on it which looked like rust, although it couldn't be – she'd cleaned and oiled it a couple of times when she'd tried it and found it stiff from disuse, and the last occasion had been only a few weeks ago.

Maybe not rust. Maybe something else.

Maybe from last night, after all . . .?

The hasp flew open, the lid swung loose. Lucy scrambled out so quickly that she almost landed in a heap on the floor.

The light hurt her eyes for a moment. She tried for balance, missed it, then managed it. She was in some kind of an antechamber that looked like part of a big restaurant kitchen that was beginning to show its age; white tiles from floor to ceiling, more tiles on a floor which was angled slightly toward a central drain, and a big stainless steel table with nothing (thankfully) on board. On the opposite wall hung a coiled hose, alongside a low square basin with a bucket grille. There were two ways out, and she grabbed the valise and guessed at the nearest.

Wrong.

She ducked back from the sight of more than a dozen medical students clustered around a well-lighted buffet table, almost before anyone had noticed her; three or four heads were beginning to turn, but already she was out of there. And then, belatedly, she realised that it hadn't been a buffet at all.

She went out through the other doors as if with her pants on fire.

This was grim. She was under the street somewhere in a vast complex with no idea of the way out. Total collapse was being held at bay only by combined adrenaline and determination, and her supply of both was beginning to fail. She swayed like a drunk, uncertain of which way to head.

Someone grabbed her arm from behind.

He held on as she swung around to face him.

'I should've known you were going to be trouble,' Gary said.

'I want to be somewhere else.'

'Yeah, and the sooner the better. This way's out, and goodbye.'

He began to guide her along. She allowed herself to be led, her concentration fading even further. She wondered, if she could stick it out for long enough, whether she could simply walk off the drug's effects and come through it back to reality, like someone re-emerging from a hall of mirrors.

But the drug said, Why bother?

They walked on. Either it was her, or the climate in the tunnels changed radically between one section and another. It was powerfully warm in places, almost tropical. The corridor widened and they passed a spot where piles of mattresses and bed sections had been stacked up together in a still life, along with a heap of rubbish that had been swept this far and no further.

'Walk,' Gary said urgently, and she realised that she'd been stumbling.

'I'm trying.'

'Try harder. I swear it, I'm just going to dump you on the street whatever state you're in.'

'I'll be okay in the fresh air,' she promised gamely, just as she lost her grip on the valise. It slid to the floor, and she all but tripped over it.

'Oh, shit,' Gary said miserably.

'Sorry.'

'At least give me a number I can call.'

'There's nobody,' she said, getting a firm hold on the valise again, and then she remembered. 'Yes, there is. I need a debt collector.'

'A what?'

'A debt collector.' There was daylight ahead as they came into a large, dimly-lit warehouse bay where several hundred colour-coded gas bottles stood in the gloom like a silent army.

'Try Yellow Pages. You're not making any sense, girl.'

'I know. I'm sorry about this, Gary.'

'Not half as sorry as I am.'

Which was probably true. She was aware of them passing a watchman's hut, actually a garden shed in new-looking pine, just inside the entrance to the loading bay, and then they were out into a side street somewhere around the back of the main hospital building.

The fresh air hit her, and she was gone.

Darkness.

Then a vague awareness of the inside of a taxi.

Then darkness again.

FOURTEEN

Nothing much else happened to Gary between loading the Ashdown girl into a minicab and the end of his shift, for which he was profoundly grateful. Leave all that caring stuff to the nurses, he was only here to punch a time clock and do what they told him, which mostly involved transporting the meat from one place to another. The truth of it was, he had a distaste for many of his charges. Maybe he was too sensitive, but if he paid too much attention to their stories he'd inevitably get depressed. As it was, he got by. Like most of his co-workers (except for those whom he classed as terminally stupid, and who seemed to amble through life as happily as anyone he'd ever known), Gary had certain strategies for getting him through the day. They were ways of letting himself drift without the fact being noticed; ways of pulling the main plugs and coasting on through.

Somehow, the Ashdown girl – Christine, Lucy, whatever her real name was – had blown all of these. He wasn't sure that he actually believed what she'd told him and he'd had no plans to do anything about it, until he'd seen her father and the other man being shown into the Ward Sister's office. Her father seemed okay. If he'd arrived alone then Gary would have carried on thinking Fine, if it's commit-tal that she needs then it's what she ought to get, let the nuthouse boys straighten out the fantasies that she obviously can't handle for herself, but then he'd seen the big guy who'd been tagging along behind.

There was no easy way to define it. But the man's presence made everything wrong.

Almost as if they'd over-reacted, and brought in the law.

Even so, he wished he'd resisted the impulse to tip her off. What had begun as a no-cost exercise in brotherly goodwill had rapidly escalated into a severe instance of the lost-dog syndrome – you pat some sad-looking mutt on the head and then somehow it's following you home and then everybody's looking at you when it bays at your door so you have to let it in. One kind thought becomes a lifetime commitment, and wouldn't it have been wiser to kick the little fucker at first sight instead? At least, then, everyone would know how they really stood.

The problem was, Gary had never kicked so much as a pigeon in his life.

And he *really* hated pigeons.

So it was with some relief that he headed down to the locker room when the little hand on the clock hit the magic number. For most other people the day would only be half over but that was their problem, not his. Gary had been up and around when the streets had seemed to be populated entirely by a sparse few of the walking dead, and now he'd be out of it before the homeward rush. He'd only his jacket to grab, throw it on over his uniform, and he'd be away.

Whoever came up behind his opened locker door, he moved without a sound.

'Hi, there,' a man's voice said.

Gary gave a start, but he quickly recovered. He'd thought that he was alone. The door swung about halfway shut, driven by the gentle pressure of a finger against the metal just below the plastic window which carried his name.

Oh, great, Gary thought.

It was the man who'd come along with the Ashdown kid's father.

He was reading what had been written in the plastic window, making more of it than he really needed to. Then he looked up pleasantly and said, 'Garfield, is it?'

'Just Gary,' he said. Garfield? Garfield was a fucking cat in the comics.

The man nodded and said, 'And how was your day?'

'Why?'

'Just curious.'

Don't react, Gary told himself. *Don't let him see that you're nervous.* Give nothing away, and that's exactly what he'd have – nothing.

Gary said, 'I don't even know you.'

'That's right.' His smile died, like the glow of a disconnected heater. 'So why are you so bent on messing me around, Gary?'

'How?'

'On the Women's Medical, this afternoon. Lucy Ashdown, that girl you were seen talking to. Fancy the white girls, do you, Gary?'

There was only one answer to a situation like this, and that was to walk away from it. He glanced around. Apart from the two of them, the locker room was empty. It was the end of a shift, damn it, where *was* everybody?

'This is hospital property,' Gary said lamely, and it sounded desperate even to him.

'Where did you send her?'

'I don't even know what you're talking about . . .'

But before Gary could finish the man had reached out and given him a slight push – nothing violent, just enough to surprise him and set him off-balance, and Gary had to grab at the edge of his locker to keep himself from stumbling.

The man shut the locker door on his hand, and leaned on it hard.

'I talked to the watchman,' he explained. 'He saw you put her in a taxi. There's no point arguing about it.'

For a moment, he couldn't believe how much it hurt. Couldn't even believe that it was happening. It was as if he'd plunged his hand into a bowl of white-hot lava and he watched, still almost off-balance, as the locker door crunched into his fingers. He opened his mouth to scream, but nothing came out.

'You see,' the man said reasonably, 'I know that she isn't familiar with the way things are around here. She doesn't know where she is or where she's going. And she uses people, Gary, she's *very* good at that. Most of the time they don't know it's happening, and I don't even think that she's aware she's doing it. But what I'm saying, Gary, is that I'm not blaming you.'

He didn't even dare to try to pull away. The pain was so intense, he was afraid that he might unstring his hand completely. Ten thousand volts of agony poured through his arm. He took a swing at the man with his free hand, but his swing was as feeble as a child's and the man flipped it aside almost without noticing. Again, he tried to yell. All that came out was a thin, keening sound.

The man said, 'Did she get you to give her any money?'

He lowered his head, and shook it.

'Saying nothing? That's a real pity, Gary. Because I can't walk away from here until you tell me where you sent that taxi.'

Teeth gritted, tears running down his face, Gary managed to say, 'I didn't send her *anywhere*!'

The man bounced gently against the locker door a couple of times.

'Am I making my point, here?'

In a single rush of breath, Gary gave him an address.

Nothing happened for a moment.

Then the pressure eased.

'Good boy,' the man said approvingly, as he removed his weight from the door.

It flew open.

Gary hit the floor, barely protecting his shattered hand in time. He didn't dare to look at it, but looked for his torturer instead. He'd already gone. The locker door was all out of shape and the locker frame had been bent a little, too. The door swung in again with a faint bang. The pain continued, so great that his insides were wound up tighter than a washleather; rather than diminishing it, release seemed to have thrown open the gates of sensation. He lay doubled, feeling as if his balls were trying to crawl up into his chest. His hand felt like something the size of a baseball catcher's glove, incandescent and throbbing.

He rocked himself, gently. For the moment, it was all that he could manage.

He knew what he'd have to do. He'd have to walk. The Emergency department was way across the complex in another building, too far to make it by grovelling along. He could have used some help, but there was never a fucking porter around when you needed one. He'd have to manage this alone.

And maybe a phonecall. Maybe, just maybe, he could also manage a phonecall somewhere along the way. Not for Lucy Ashdown's sake; Lucy Ashdown had suddenly dropped below zero on his scale of concern.

But even under pressure Gary prided himself on a certain kind of grace, and here was his chance to prove it.

He'd already made the setup. All that he'd have to do now would be to ensure that it was followed through.

FIFTEEN

Jack Ashdown slumped low in the car's passenger seat that his
surviving daughter had occupied scarcely thirty hours before. But
that had been in another place, and under different rules. The game
had moved along since then; the rules had changed with the scene,
and the stakes had been raised. Jack Ashdown sat with a paperback
street plan open on his knees and a vacant, distracted look in his
eyes. He'd put on his best clothes to come to town. The fit of his
collar betrayed the weight that he'd shed since he'd worn them
last.

Which had probably been at his firstborn's funeral, at Joe Lucas's
guess.

As a navigator Ashdown was proving less than useful – every now
and again he'd look down at the map as if discovering it for the first
time – and so Joe was mostly handling that side of things for himself.
Ashdown's lap was somewhere to park the book, no more. Joe could
think of a hundred other things that he'd rather be doing than facing
this kind of traffic, but first he was going to settle the Ashdown kid's
problem for good. This was how he should have approached it in
the beginning, ignoring her father's plea that he shouldn't go in
heavy and simply laying it out for her – she was either going to
behave, or be forced to behave, because the road that she was
following led in only one direction and that was down. Instead he'd
approached it like a social worker, playing along and listening to
her.

And the result? Wasted time, wasted breath, wasted energy.

But no more.

The road was way out to the north-east, somewhere in the urban
sprawl that was differentiated from the rest of the city only by name.
In the shadow of an overpass stood an area of badly run-down
Victorian terraced housing; most of the houses were still occupied
although a few were bricked and boarded up. Joe cruised a little,
looking for numbers.

'Doesn't look promising, Jack,' he said as they passed a place with
old furniture stacked high out front and so much grime on its
windows that the glass was no longer visible.

70

'You didn't see the last place she lived in,' Ashdown said. 'Cockroaches like rats. Rats like . . .'

'I get the idea,' Joe said, seeing a space and pulling in about four houses short of the one that he wanted. 'You wait with the car.'

'In case the wheels get clamped?'

'In case the wheels get stolen.'

Joe walked the last few yards, counting the doors. They'd been imposing entranceways once, carved stone around the casings and a wide set of steps; many were the original timber, a hint of the better times that had gone before. None carried fewer than five separate doorbells – except, he noted as he drew level, the one that he was looking for. This one had no doorbells at all. Nor any glass. Nor, apparently, a lock, because it stood open a few inches.

The steps were strewn with litter from a couple of split trash bags at the top. Beside these, a stack of old newspapers had been left to go pulpy in the rain. The house looked like a dead thing, rot already taking a hold, but that was no guide. He'd walked into worse – sometimes by invitation, mostly without. He ascended the steps, stopped before the door, and gave it a push.

An empty hallway in an empty house. The place stank of mildew, and other things not so pleasant. Rubbish had poured down the stairs in an avalanche, making them impassable; bathroom lino, plasterboard, the remains of a mattress burned down to its springs. At the far end of the hallway a door stood open into a daylit room at the back, but a quick glance showed only the illicit signs of a long-ago party and a lot of mess where house wiring had been chiselled out of the walls and taken for scrap.

Even if the cab had brought her here, she'd have no reason to stay. What seemed more likely was that the address was simply false, and he'd been set up. He wouldn't have supposed it, considering the persuasion that he'd been using, but anything was possible.

He paused in the doorway, and shook his head. I'm not a hard man, he thought. I do hard things, but that isn't the same.

And as he turned, he saw a blur that was the first of them coming for him.

Ashdown appeared in the doorway, about a couple of minutes after the three young men had gone. They'd run out into the street, and Ashdown had probably seen them as they'd emerged. There was a puzzled, rather worried look on his face. Joe had raised himself and was sitting at the foot of the messy stairway, showing little external sign of damage apart from the dust that he'd picked up as he'd dropped to his knees under the first blow.

'Joe?' Ashdown said, squinting to adjust to the comparative shadow of the hallway. 'What's going on?'

Joe stowed his handkerchief, into which he'd just coughed a couple of penny-spots of blood. He took a deep breath and stood up straight, using all of the control that he could summon.

'Nothing,' he said, a touch unsteadily. 'She isn't here.'

Ashdown frowned, took a step closer, and almost lost his balance on something slimy underfoot. 'Are you all right?'

'I tripped on the stairs. Just winded.'

They went outside.

Joe had known within seconds that they were amateurs, their hearts not in it. The one with the taped-up cricket bat had done little more than slap at him with the flattened side, and as for the kicking . . . anyone setting out with serious violence in mind would do it in something other than trainers and plimsolls. They'd got a couple in around his sides that might have been worth worrying about, but he'd kept his arms up and protected his head and otherwise suffered nothing worse than he'd expect out of a fit-of-pique pummelling from a drag queen. Thirty seconds, tops, and then they'd scared themselves away. Amateurs. He didn't doubt that they'd been sent out by the porter that he'd leaned on – in a literal sense – at the hospital, but he wasn't going to let himself get over-excited about it. He should have expected something like this, perhaps – on home turf, he'd never have made so simple a mistake – but it was no big deal.

His main concern was that she'd slipped away from him, again. This was supposed to have started out as something simple, a favour for the old man in Christine's memory, the kind of job that could make a person sorry they'd ever said those simple words, *if there's ever anything I can do* . . . but the kid was turning out to be tougher to pin down than a snake on speed.

Something in his side twinged as they approached the car. He said, 'You drive, Jack.'

Ashdown said, 'Where to, now?'

'You're going home. She might call, and I'll need to know what she says. Drop me at the first Tube that we see and I'll head on back into town, see if I can go at it from another angle. Don't worry, I'll find her. She's got no money and she knows nobody. How far's she going to get?'

Ashdown didn't argue, but he made a wry face as he reached to catch the keys.

'She's going to surprise you, Joe,' he said.

SIXTEEN

For the second time that day, Lucy awoke.

But this time it was from a drugged sleep, thick and bitter and unsatisfactory. Her head hurt, and she felt as if her body had been on loan to someone else for a punishing workout.

Somewhere in the house below her, she'd heard a door slam.

She sat up, and took a look at the room in which she found herself. She had no recollection of how she'd come to be here, only of the taxi and of its driver shaking her and demanding to be reassured that she wasn't going to throw up. She'd been lying fully clothed on a single bed, up against the wall under a cinema poster for *Purple Rain* that appeared to have been removed, inch by painstaking inch, from a pasted billboard. The curtains had been drawn, but the material let through some of the afternoon light. Just by the window she saw books, a few hundred of them and mostly paperback science fiction titles, in tall sideways-on stacks which filled the alcove by the chimney breast. She saw a bass guitar on a chair, its neck leaning on a stack of carefully pressed designer jeans, and a sound system the size of a suitcase with several boxes of tapes and albums lined up alongside. Where the light wasn't so good a little Hitachi fourteen-inch portable TV stood on the table along with an electric kettle, a snack toaster, and half of an opened Wonderloaf. On the wall behind the table was another poster; she couldn't tell if it was Eddie Murphy or Olivia Newton-John, at which point she stopped trying to make shapes out of the deeper shadows and moved to open the curtains.

One-handed, she rubbed her eyes. She was looking out of an average kind of a house at the back of a row of similarly average houses. She could have been anywhere. Looking back into the room, she saw that her valise was lying on the floor alongside the bed. The rug was threadbare, the shapes of the floorboards all but visible through it.

Remembering the sound of the door, she moved to go downstairs.

She'd half-expected to find that Gary, her latest unwilling recruit to the Christine Ashdown memorial crusade, would be waiting in the kitchen; but it was the faces of three strangers, their conversation stilled, that turned to her as she stood in the doorway. They were all of Gary's generation, if not exactly of his age. She'd already reached the conclusion that this was a shared house and these, she assumed, would be Gary's room-mates. One was tall with lank, shoulder-length hair, another was a bearded ginger teddy bear in a checked shirt. Standing over by the sink with its ill-assorted stack of crockery, the third man had the furtive, apologetic look of a failed shoplifter.

They showed her no hostility, nor did they move to welcome her. They simply watched her, neutrally, and as she tried on a nervous smile and wondered what they were expecting, the Bear said, 'Feeling better?'

'It's wearing off,' she said. 'Actually, yeah, I feel fine.'

With a little more confidence, she approached the table at which two of them were sitting. 'Who paid for the taxi?' she said, and she was aware of the failed shoplifter sliding around and out of the room behind her like a ghost.

'Gary did that,' the Bear said. 'He's too soft for his own good, sometimes.'

'I'll pay him back when I can.'

'I think he'd rather write it off to experience.'

The Bear hitched his chair back to give her some room to sit, and the other man moved his own chair a couple of inches as a token gesture even though he was nowhere in her way.

Lucy spotted their tea mugs and said, with what she hoped was a meekness appropriate to a stranger on someone else's home ground, 'Could I have some of that?'

The Bear slid his own mug across. It hadn't been touched.

There was an uneasy silence for a while. Lucy had never been too hot on small talk; for the past year she'd had only one topic which had become the focus of every conversation, and she couldn't think of any way to introduce it right now. She glanced around the kitchen. Not exactly poverty row, but not exactly the mark of a generous-hearted landlord either. Over by the door which would lead into the house's tiny rear yard, someone had propped a cricket bat that had been bound with tape. Just above the bat was a wall-mounted pay phone.

Lucy said, 'Have you got a Yellow Pages?'

The Bear looked at the other man, and nodded. The other man unfolded himself from the chair and crossed the room – he had to be at least six-four, and with his lank hair he had the look of a mournful scarecrow – and rummaged in a dresser drawer. Somewhere upstairs, a board creaked as the third man moved around.

The scarecrow brought her an old Yellow Pages, its cover almost completely obscured by doodles and jottings and yearning sketches of big-chested women. 'Thanks,' she said, opening it up and starting to flick through the pages. 'I'll only need it for a minute.'

'Keep it,' the scarecrow said. 'We've got a newer one.' And he returned to his seat.

Lucy said, 'I'm being a lot of trouble, aren't I?'

The other man smiled, briefly.

'Not for much longer,' he said.

She ran through the categories. *Damp proofing, Dancing schools, Debt collectors* . . . she looked up and was about to ask if it would be okay for her to tear out the page, when she realised that the third man had returned and that he wasn't empty-handed.

He placed Christine's valise on the table beside her.

They were watching her again, as they had when she'd first appeared; still no open hostility, and still no welcome.

The Bear said, 'Gary doesn't want you to be here when he gets back.'

Lucy didn't know what to make of this. 'Did he say so?'

'He doesn't have to.'

She hadn't exactly been comfortable, but now she suddenly found that she was embarrassed. Nobody offered to explain. She tore the flimsy pages out of the book and, rising, quickly folded them and stuffed them into her pocket. Once again, she wanted a sharp exit line that would save her dignity.

And, as usual, she didn't have one.

The Bear followed her down the hallway, and waited as she opened the front door to let herself out into the street. When she glanced back at him, he said, 'Nothing personal.'

'You think so?'

'Gary's had about as much of you as he can handle,' the Bear said from the doorway. 'Some people get together, and there's trouble waiting to happen. It's not something anyone can help, but there it is.'

'I don't even know where I am.'

'Nearest Tube's that way,' he said, pointing, and then he stepped back inside and closed the door on her.

The road seemed endless and strange, like something in a weird dream. So many houses, one after another without a break in style or atmosphere, going on and on for miles. A person could walk into one of them and as good as disappear, just another worker in some undifferentiated cell within the hive. Who *were* all these people? How did they live?

And exactly how, in their midst, was she going to pick up the faded traces of the path that Christine had taken?

Unapproachable as the job seemed, Lucy's confidence was undiminished. Her only hesitation came at the thought of those last, haunting words that Christine had spoken before walking down into the darkness of the river steps and out of her life again.

If you make it. I mean, if you get to the truth. Promise that you won't think less of me.

What did that tell her? That the truth of Christine's life in this city was nothing to be proud of, for one thing. Something had stuck in Lucy's mind from that first night of her arrival, and she was beginning to wish that it hadn't; in the bright side-streets leading west out of Shaftesbury Avenue, in the area that she supposed must have been the one they called Soho, she'd seen a billboard standing out on the pavement that read:

GIRLS WANTED FOR PEEP
No experience required

and behind it had been a shopfront resembling a rough-and-ready carnival booth with bulbs all around its window and blackout paper behind the glass. Lucy knew how a peep show worked, if only from third-hand information; coin-in-the-slot booths with peepholes like letter boxes, men crouched in the darkness while girls disco-danced on the other side of the partition wearing little more than a set of beads and a butterfly tattoo. Lucy hadn't even approached the place, but its image had stayed with her; not least the fact that the billboard had been such a neat and respectable-looking piece of signwriting, clearly a permanent feature of the street. Not that she thought that Christine would ever have gone in for something like that, even at her lowest, but it was a depressing indication of the ease with which a certain kind of world could be entered.

They knew a few things from her autopsy. That she hadn't used drugs. That she'd been sexually active – though not, as far as it was possible to determine, in the hours leading up to her death. No diseases, no scars; a few inexplicable scratches, nearly healed, but nothing to suggest that she'd been leading a hard or arduous life. She'd been fit, she'd been healthy.

She'd been murdered.

The inquest hadn't said so, but Lucy had known it from the beginning; she'd realised after Christine's reappearance that it had been something more than intuitive, that she'd been driven along by something greater than an obsession even though, until she'd tracked down her witness, it had been based more in faith than on evidence. Now everything had changed. Emerging from Christine's shadow, she'd become Christine's instrument.

Christine's hammer.

And whatever happened, she'd be going the distance.

SEVENTEEN

Joe Lucas didn't realise it, but if he'd hung around on the Underground stairs for another ten minutes he'd have been able to grab Lucy as she arrived and entered from the street. They'd approached from different directions, Lucy from the shared house and Joe from the abandoned squat that the room-mates had previously occupied, and after waiting at either end of the platform with a growing crowd between them they'd boarded the same train to be carried back into the centre of town. They'd left at different stations, each still unaware of the other, and gone their separate ways – Lucy in search of her debt collection agencies, Joe in search of an affordable hotel.

This wasn't how he'd planned it, but now he didn't intend to go back without her. After their near-miss at the hospital he'd have to be systematic and professional in his search, and that would take time. Lucy's problem was that she didn't seem to realise how vulnerable she really was. She'd survived so far with a little nerve and a lot of good luck, but now it was as if she'd moved from a paddling pool and into a piranha tank. If persuasion wouldn't work, she'd simply have to be grabbed and carried home. And if Joe had to lean hard on a few more people along the way, then no problem, he'd do it – he needed quick results because the longer it took, the further she'd work her way into the city's wormy heart and as the dangers were increasing, she'd become even harder to find.

Part of him wished that he'd never become involved – especially the part of him that hurt when he took too deep a breath after that pansified slap-around at the hands of the make-do revenge squad. He'd originally offered a few hours of his time to deal with Lucy Ashdown, no more. But when he thought of his empty flat, of the letters that were waiting to be answered and of the difficult issues that he knew he would soon have to face, this seemed almost like an escape. Joe wasn't a greatly fulfilled man. Sometimes he looked at his life with a sense of growing panic, wondering at which point he had made the insignificant-looking decision that had begun to steer him toward this. Was it his so-so exam results? His choice of career?

Or was it, as he sometimes suspected when lying awake on the

78

deepest and darkest of nights, that missed chance with a teenaged girl that he'd never quite been able to forget?

Now, as he looked around his hotel room, he found that he'd become almost certain of it. This feeling dated from his arrival at the truck stop, and what he'd seen as he'd looked in through the diner window. The illusion had been almost perfect. It wasn't simply like seeing Christine again, resurrected and breathed into life; it was like seeing her as she'd been, with the years turned back and all of the closed avenues of possibility opened wide again. Closer-to, the nature of the trick had been more obvious.

But still, a little something had lingered . . .

The room was one of several hundred in a hotel that wasn't as cheap as he'd have liked, but which was certainly central. The place had a long, deep Art Deco foyer lined with shops; the staff were sharp and slightly spivvy looking and the main concourse seemed to be full of coach parties that milled aimlessly and appeared to have been abandoned by their couriers. He'd picked up some aspirin and then gone two floors up and about a half a mile's walk from the elevator while following a numbering system that defied human comprehension. By the time that he'd arrived, his side was hurting like a bitch. The key was a piece of punched plastic that worked on the third try and had already earned his immediate dislike.

It could have been better, could have been worse. It was as if someone had tried to make a good room out of an old and shabby one, but couldn't completely disguise its origins. He noted new curtains and carpet, brass fittings, mahogany furniture . . . but the walls were old and rough, to an extent that couldn't entirely be concealed by a layer of Artex plaster. There was no Gideon Bible, but the fattest commerical directory that he'd ever seen. He took the glass from by the washbasin and, after waiting for the water to run cold, washed down a handful of the aspirins without bothering to count them.

The glass still in his hand, he moved to the window. He had no view of the street, just an open-air courtyard that had been roofed-over with wire like the main stairway of a prison. Directly opposite in some other building he could see into a trendy office foyer – or maybe it was even an art gallery, to judge from the impractical-looking lampshades and the welded sculpture on display. A woman was moving through, unaware that she was being observed. Sharp-shouldered and expensively made up, she resembled some exotic bird of prey.

Wincing, he turned and moved to the bed and stretched himself out. He set the glass on the bedside table, almost missing because his eyes were already closed. Somewhere outside there was the

79

constant, low-level drone of an air pump. He needed rest. He needed relief.

And he hated to admit it, but he needed inspiration.

When he awoke, it was well into the evening.

He switched on the reading lamp, and resisted the impulse to do the same with the TV. While hovering on the edge of sleep he'd turned over a scheme in his mind to start working his way through a list of the main hostels and relief agencies. He'd have to step carefully because some of them would be more concerned to defend their charges than to give him any help, but it would be a start. Also, places where young kids slept rough. And where they gathered. And where they begged.

Still feeling a little blurred, he reached for the phone.

'Jack?' he said a minute later. 'Any word?'

'I've heard from her,' Jack Ashdown said.

Suddenly, he was fully alert. 'When?'

'Within the last hour. She wanted me to know that she was all right, and that she won't be sleeping rough. She'll be in some bed and breakfast place.'

'Did she say where?'

'I tried to get her to tell me, but she wouldn't. Not even the area.'

'Where did she get the money?'

'She wouldn't tell me that, either, but she said it was straight. She said she could only scrape up enough for one night.' Here he paused, and sounded embarrassed. 'I said . . . I said I'd let her have more.'

Joe was silent for a moment, to let the older man squirm.

Then he said, 'Why?'

'What else could I do? I want her back here . . . but if I can't have that, then I don't want her walking the streets and getting into trouble.'

Joe eased himself a little more upright. Across the way, the uncurtained gallery windows were going dark, one after another.

He said, 'You're only encouraging her, Jack.'

'She doesn't need encouragement. She'll go her own way, whatever I do. Haven't you seen that, yet?'

'How are you getting the money to her?'

'I'll go into my bank in the morning, and they'll telex it through.'

Joe sat up so fast that the pain almost brought tears to his eyes. But he ignored it. 'To which branch?' he said, and Ashdown told him.

Everything clicked into place, with perfect precision.

'That's it, then!' Joe said. 'We've got her!'

As Joe lay in his room, Lucy lay in hers.

She was on the upper level of a set of bunk beds. The frame was of bolted metal, and creaked when she moved. There were seven of them sleeping in the room, three allocated to folding metal cots that took up nearly all of the floor space. The sheets were thin but clean, the single blanket was scratchy. She hadn't undressed, but had brought her shoes and her valise up with her. It wasn't that she didn't trust the others – they all seemed to be backpacking tourists on rock-bottom budgets, three of them American and the others speaking no English – but she felt that, with so little privacy, she wanted to bring everything into the space that was hers alone.

It was mid-evening. Unwinding time. People were chatting out in the hotel corridors, hurriedly wringing out wet clothes in the bathrooms, smuggling supermarket food back to their rooms in order to picnic on their beds at less than restaurant prices. Lucy had bought an apple and some biscuits. She felt safe enough here. They probably didn't come any cheaper than this, a big old house with unpainted plywood fire doors and mismatching carpets, no locks on the rooms and a perfunctory breakfast of cornflakes and tea, but compared to the streets it was fine.

In the light from the strip over the washbasin mirror, she carefully went through her papers.

She'd dumped all of the stuff about drivers and routes and the ways of the road; it was history now, no longer of relevance. This was a new phase. She'd spent the main part of the afternoon tracking down addresses, ducking into bookstores to check on street plans when she seemed to be losing her way, and finally she'd found a tacky-looking back-street agency near to the Westminster County Court that seemed to be more or less what she was looking for. She'd spent about a half-hour explaining what she needed them to do, they'd dodged and shrugged and given her a few maybes, and she'd left feeling reasonably sure that she'd started something useful. Then, as the evening had started to gather, she'd spent her entire cash reserve on long-stemmed roses at a Shaftesbury Avenue flower stall and then taken these across the way into Chinatown, where she'd hawked them from table to restaurant table at a surprising profit.

And as soon as she'd known that she could buy herself one day's worth of security, she'd phoned home.

The first couple of times the phone had rung out in an empty house, but on the third try about an hour later her father had picked it up. He couldn't have been home for very long. When she heard his voice it was with a rush of feelings of love, regret, and relief. She'd been afraid that he and Joe might stay in town, like hounds on her trail, so that she'd have to waste energy watching her back whilst trying to push her way forward. But he didn't try to do a number on her, and she reassured him that she was managing fine, and he even offered to wire her some cash rather than see her at greater risk. Maybe he'd finally come around. Or maybe he'd accepted that, no matter what he said, she would go ahead anyway.

She turned the page on her latest notes, uncovering her sister's photograph.

Sometimes, she wondered if the photograph was really all that remained of Christine. More and more, whenever she thought of her, it was the photograph's image that she saw – just a paper front, with the reality fading behind. The clock was ticking. She didn't have forever.

She wondered if she'd see her again, before she was lost completely.

Jack Ashdown sat in his empty lounge. The house was cold. The car that belonged to Joe Lucas stood out on the drive, steam rising from the bodywork over the heat of its engine. He'd hit rain twice during the long drive back. When he'd arrived there had been no welcome, no sense of homecoming.

At least he'd had the chance to speak to each of them. For a few moments, there, he'd come alive. But then, when the phone had hit the cradle, he'd died again.

This was the time of his life when everything should have been coming together. Retirement, the house finally paid for, the children grown and off his hands, maybe even the odd grandchild to fuss over and spoil. Instead, what did he have? Nothing but a trail of bereavement and loss, and his own best efforts conspiring to make the situation worse. It was as if the ice had broken, and he'd fallen through. Others skated by, believing they were safe; all they had to do was look down, but somehow they never did. Ashdown had always been sensitive to that kind of thing. He couldn't explain it, he just was. He could remember walking into Christine's bedroom when she'd been about two years old, and looking down on her as she'd slept in the half-light that reached her cot from the inches-open door. She'd been a breathtaking child. No father could have loved a daughter more. And yet, without invitation, without any conscious impulse at all, the notion had dropped into his mind: *Someday, My love even you will die*. He was shocked. Christine had stirred a little, her child's breath fluttering the curls that lay on her teddy-bear pillow.

82

He'd told no-one, ever, knowing that no-one would understand. They were the skaters who never looked down. He was an ordinary man, no deep thinker, but he knew what would happen if he tried to share the burden of his insight; at best he'd be called morbid, depressive at the worst, and the truth would still be the truth however he tried to unload it or to push it out of his mind. All that he understood was that he'd been put into touch with something commonplace but terrible, perhaps the most terrible thing in the world, and the rest of his life could never be the same thereafter.

Hardly a week went by, as Lucy came along and then the two girls began to grow up, without him thinking of that night at least once. It would come like a gentle stab from something way down inside, as from the nucleus of some disease buried far too deep for any knife to reach. The worst of it was that, when Christine had actually been snatched from him, the years of awareness had been no preparation at all. If anything, they made it harder.

But he'd come to understand one thing. It wasn't a simple matter of life's a bitch, and then you die. Because there were places of warmth, and they shone out as welcoming as any campfire in a hostile forest; and even if no fire burned forever and the welcoming spots were few, this was all the more reason to give them full value for as long as they lasted. Without knowledge of the darkness outside, the warmth could so easily be taken for granted. It was never easy but it was better than being a skater who never looked down, complacent and stupidly happy and never more than half-alive.

Lucy was all that he had left. He wanted her back. He wanted her home.

And the harder he tried, the further he drove her away.

Nothing made any sense.

Suck on *that*, he thought, and he shambled through into the kitchen to brew up some tea.

EIGHTEEN

They kept her hanging around for a while at the bank, but it was going to be worth it. The simple fact of money by wire seemed like a kind of miracle. There was a problem when they asked her for some form of identification because everything had Christine's name on it and nothing had hers, but after a couple of phonecalls back and forth they sorted it out and gave her the cash. She walked out into the street carrying the plain envelope; her biggest fear now was that she might lose it sometime during the next few hours, somewhere between here and the agency that she'd visited on the previous day.

The actual danger was one that she hadn't anticipated at all.

She was stepping out. One hand grabbed her arm, another jerked the envelope from her. Her first thought was that she was being mugged, but even before it had formed completely she'd seen the face of her assailant and realised the truth.

'Joe!' she said. 'No!'

'Don't push me, girl,' Joe said, jerking her aside and away from the doorway; she looked back helplessly, hoping that someone from inside might see and intervene, but it was a waste of time. Joe was walking her onward, forcing her along the street. He said, 'I just spent the night in a dump with whores working the landings, and I'm in no mood to be messed about.'

'Give me my money,' she said, making a grab for it, but he jerked her back and out of reach.

'It's your father's money. If I'd been there when you'd called, I'd have stopped him. Now I'm going to take you home and you can pay it back.'

He hustled her to the pavement's edge, and started to scan for a taxi. 'Joe,' she began, and he jerked her arm again, roughly, to silence her.

'No arguments,' he said.

'You're hurting me!'

After a beat, he seemed to calm a little. The pressure on her arm eased as he relaxed.

'I'm sorry,' he said, and he seemed to have made a conscious effort to scale down his anger. 'But whichever way we do it, this is going to happen. Hard or easy, it's down to you. Well?'

'I don't seem to have much of a choice.'

'Now you're getting the idea.'

A black cab made a U-turn against the traffic and pulled in to pick them up. They got in. Joe didn't release his grip on her until they were moving, probably in case she should get any ideas about diving out of the opposite door. She sat with her bag on her knees, and Joe slid her money envelope into an inside pocket of his jacket.

He told the driver to take them to the station. The driver said, 'Which one?' and as they were working it out, Lucy looked through the window at the street outside. The best course would be one by which she could retrieve her money and make an escape. Failing that, escape alone would be better than nothing; the loss a terrific setback, but a long way from being her first. But then whenever the cab slowed, for lights or for heavy traffic, Joe was ready. He didn't paw her. But it was clear that if she should make a grab for the door handle, she'd be pinned again before she could get it open.

She looked at Joe. He hadn't been lying, he looked as if he'd had a lousy night. His clothes were rumpled, his hair uncombed. His skin had a greyish tinge and as he settled back into the seat he seemed to wince, as if in pain.

'Are you all right?' she said.

And he said, 'Didn't sleep so well, that's all.'

Little more was said until they arrived, about ten minutes later. Joe paid off the taxi, and they took an escalator up from the subterranean dropoff point.

The mainline station was a huge cavern of wasted space, a vast marbled floor with nowhere to sit. Joe clamped her arm again as he walked her across the concourse, pushing her a little faster than she wanted to go. They got a few strange looks, but nobody seemed inclined to interfere. Stopping under the big electronic board, Joe scanned it and said, 'I can never read these things.'

Lucy gave it a quick look. There was one train due to leave in about twenty minutes and another, different service less than an hour after that.

'The next train's in two hours,' she said.

And he bought it.

He didn't seem happy at the idea, but nor did he question it. Instead of checking out the information on the board, he looked around the concourse and spotted a car hire booth. They recrossed the floor, but even before they'd reached it Lucy could see that there was nobody in attendance. There was a courtesy phone with a printed invitation to pick it up, which Joe did. He listened for a while, seemed to get no response, and finally hung up with a look of disgust.

'We'll wait it out,' he said. 'And you're going to behave, you understand?'

Lucy nodded.

'I have to pee,' she said.

This seemed to catch Joe from an unexpected angle.

'Now?'

'When you have to, you have to.'

He took a deep breath, and sighed. The way he'd been behaving, it was as if he'd spent the best part of the last few hours psyching himself up for the encounter. Now, after grappling with practical details for a while, he seemed to be coming down from his manic high. She didn't quite know how to take it. In spite of the fact that he was dragging her home against her will, she seemed to represent something that mattered to him. It wasn't a feeling that she'd known very often.

He was calmer now.

'All right,' he said.

So easy? 'You're not going to watch,' she warned.

'What do you think I am?' He released her arm. He seemed to want to say *sorry*, but it hung unspoken between them. They started back across the concourse, walking side by side like normal people. He said, 'I'm not trying to punish you for anything. But God Almighty, you should see what this is doing to your father. You *would* see, if only you cared enough to look.'

'I know,' she said.

'So you're not going to mess me around?'

'No,' she said meekly.

The Women's Room was in a side-passageway by a tie shop and an instant photo booth, away from the main concourse and close to the platforms. There was constant foot traffic along here, some coming, some going, some waiting around for others to reappear. Joe stopped one woman and said, 'Excuse me. Is there more than one exit inside?' The woman said that there wasn't and then hurried away, glancing back at Joe as if she was sure that he was a pervert but couldn't quite work out how he was getting his kicks. Joe, seemingly unaware of her, was steering Lucy toward the entrance-way.

'I'm going to be waiting right here,' he said.

'I'll need some change.'

Joe almost asked why, but then understood. He dug around in his pocket, and brought out a handful of coins. 'What does it take?'

'I don't know yet, do I?'

So he handed her all of it, and said, 'There should be something you can use.'

'Thanks,' she said. 'I'll pay you back when I can.'

'Don't worry,' he said drily.

It was a busy place. There was a waiting line, easily visible from the outside as the double doors banged to and fro; that was good, because it meant that Joe wouldn't expect her back in too much of a hurry. Lucy joined for as long as it took the doors to close behind her, and then bypassed the line. One or two heads turned quickly, ready to put her back in her place, but she ignored them. She was more interested in the presence of a cleaner who was mopping down the tiling in the right-hand aisle.

At the end of the row of stained-wood cubicles, a narrow green door stood open. It led into the cleaners' walk-through store cupboard; from here she could see that the shelf space was crammed with toilet rolls, packs of paper towels, drums of liquid soap, plastic flagons of disinfectant. She could hear the cleaner calling out behind her as she entered, but she took no notice. She saw a plug-in heater, some spare mops, and a single chair with a magazine on it. On the opposite side of the tiny room was a mirror-image door; this was locked, but it was a Yale and the latch was on her side. She sailed straight on through and out into the Men's Room.

The door slammed after her. There was no time to mess around. There seemed to be building work going on in here, because half of the area had been screened off with plywood sheets and the urinals were makeshift-looking steel troughs. Jesus, it was even worse than the Women's Room. About a dozen men stood with their backs to her, too preoccupied to be aware, but as she headed for the exit she saw sudden looks of panic on the faces of those coming in . . . were they walking into the wrong place, or what? But she bypassed them, leaving them to work it out for themselves, and only slowed when she reached the end of the screened entrance passageway.

Here she stopped, and took a cautious peek around the corner.

Joe was still waiting, about twenty yards away from her now. He seemed to be studying some pattern in the dirt on the station floor but every time some woman emerged, he'd glance up quickly.

She took a breath, counted to three, and launched herself out and away.

She didn't dare to run. Nor did she dare to look back, in case she caught his eye and ruined everything. The tension was almost overpowering as she set out to lose herself in a crowd that wasn't as dense as she'd have liked, almost as if she could sense the shadow of a gunsight between her shoulder blades. She forced herself to walk steadily, do nothing that would give her away. Some distance ahead were the escalators that would take her down to the station's Underground link.

She let the escalator carry her, rather than push her way through. Less conspicuous. Only when she'd reached the ticket hall did she feel the pressure beginning to ease.

Joe's change bought her a ticket at one of the machines. The fear of recapture was steadily being replaced by the exhilaration of having pulled off her escape. Losing the cash was a pity but, what the hell, she'd scam it up some other way; the main thing was that she'd come through yet again. She was beginning to feel that there was nothing she couldn't achieve.

But her elation, she quickly realised, was a touch premature.

She was through the automatic barriers and boarding the second level of downward-moving escalators when a cry of outrage caused her to glance back; she caught a flash-impression of Joe Lucas in midair as he hurdled the turnstile and then she stayed to see nothing more. She threw herself into the descent, ramming through the solid crowd on the moving stairway with her bag held high. She pushed, she clawed, she ignored the shouts of protest as she fought her way down. Somewhere behind her Joe would probably be doing the same, but he was bigger and less agile and wouldn't be able to move quite as fast.

She hit the lower level at a run, and took the first tunnel toward the Northern Line; dodging the crowds and clutching her luggage, she was half-expecting to feel Joe's hand on her shoulder at any moment. She could hear the whine of airpumps over train thunder as she hopped down a short flight of stairs and out onto the first available platform.

If only she could get on a train – *any* train – just far enough ahead of Joe, timing it so that the doors closed only moments after she'd boarded, then she'd be away and with no chance of recapture. She hadn't much liked the expression on his face. Anger wasn't a strong enough word for it.

The train had just left. The platform was almost empty.

She couldn't go back, so she went on; a clear run almost halfway down the length of the platform to the next available exit where she made a sharp turn and, seeing a NO ADMITTANCE sign, took this route in preference to the public tunnel. Why not, it was worth a try. What was the worst thing that could happen?

Lucy found herself on a wide spiral staircase, grey-painted and dust-covered. The upward steps were barred off with a slide-across metal gate and a blackboard that she didn't have time to read, so she went down. It seemed to be a little-used service route with drains and air vents running down the central well of the spiral; there were drip stains on the walls, and water stains on the floor. She came down into an area scattered with old newspapers where a big flood door had been propped back and chained to allow passage through.

She came out of the flood door, made a turn, and found herself in a linking tunnel between two back-to-back platforms.

One was almost empty, which suggested a recent train with nothing imminent. The other wasn't. One or two faces glanced incuriously toward her as she emerged, breathless and panting, but nobody reacted.

She slowed, moved into the middle of the crowd, and waited.

This was harder than anything. Please, God, she thought, send me a train; I'll believe, I'll go to church, I'll stop swearing, I'll never sleep around, but send me a train and send it *now*.

The rails began to sing.

A breeze came up, lifting her hair and cooling the perspiration glow on her forehead. Leaning out to look into the darkness of the tunnel, she could just see the moving, glistening line of a train light caught on the angle of the rails in a distant bend. The train itself was not yet visible.

Anxiously, she checked back along the platform.

Which was a mistake.

Joe had emerged from the furthermost access point and was scanning the crowd; he locked onto Lucy immediately.

'Police business!' he roared, and started to charge down everyone in his way.

The song of the rails was louder and the approach of a one-eyed light was visible in the tunnel at the end of the platform, but Lucy knew that she no longer had a chance – not here, not now. Before Joe could reach her, she turned around and dived back into the subterranean warren of service tunnels.

She climbed some different stairs and crossed a track bridge, tugged by another cool breeze as the train behind her sucked air through the system. There was another thundering rumble from somewhere ahead as she came into a much older stretch of corridor, its ceiling a dusty mess of cables and piping. Lucy wondered how much further she could go; fear was a powerful fuel, but it tended to run the engine to destruction.

And she wasn't exactly planning her way. There were no signs, and she was lost. The tunnel was dim and dusty, old paint flaking away from the arch of its roof, and hardly seemed filled with the promise of escape . . . but unless she was mistaken, there was another train on some other line ahead of her. The sound came echoing down like that of some hellish engine, as if offering a journey into darkness where she might look down upon the birth of monsters.

She broke into a run again. The breeze reversed direction, became a wind, raising her hair once more and rustling the debris along by her feet.

There was light, there were stairs.

The carriage waited, almost empty, with its doors standing open. Lucy boarded, breathing hard.

She couldn't imagine what state Joe might be in; he'd a good ten years on her and hadn't been looking so great when they'd started. Lucy had gone about as far as she could go, the long hard sprint having run her down close to exhaustion. The carriage lights were too bright, and sounds were no longer clear. Even the powered sliding of the automatic doors as they closed was no more than a far-off whisper.

She waited. The train didn't move.

The doors abruptly opened again.

She was stretched like a wire as she waited for them to close, and the movie poster on the curving wall of the platform had burned itself into her memory by the time that the edge of a door wiped it out of view. The carriage jerked, and they started to move.

Lucy counted off three stations along the line before she stood up to leave the train.

This place seemed older, the entire station darker and gloomier than most. A few people alighted further down the train, and left the platform by some other exit. Lucy walked alone. *It hasn't turned out so badly*, she was telling herself as she climbed a stairway to cross over the platform. *You got a scare and lost the money, but you still came out ahead.* Somewhere on another level of the complex, a busker was playing solo saxophone. It wasn't *Pennies from Heaven*. The sound drifted along to her, distorted and given extra distance by the tunnel network that carried it.

She was still considering the tradeoff when a four-ton ram hit her from behind.

Nineteen

She went down hard, throwing out her hands too late. Her valise came down heavily and skidded for a yard or more. The macadam flooring bounced on her teeth, and she tasted grit and blood.

Joe had pushed himself too far. As Lucy rolled over to face him, he tried to rise and failed. He lay there panting, his eyes red-rimmed and fixed on her. His lips were bloodless, his skin almost blue.

The floor beneath them began to shake as their train pulled out.

Somehow, he found the breath to speak.

'I went in the toilets to look for you,' he said. 'I never heard such a racket.'

'Do you want an ambulance?' Lucy said, scrambling to her feet. He didn't look good at all.

But he said, 'No,' and with an extra effort managed to lever himself up so that he could sit with his back to the wall. This was something more than exhaustion; he seemed to have been damaged.

She said, 'How did you get hurt?'

'Nothing that matters,' he said, and he put out his hand to be helped up. Lucy hesitated, and then didn't take it.

Despite the obvious pain, he managed a brief grin.

'He said you'd surprise me,' he admitted.

'I'm not doing this to spite you, Joe,' she said. 'Not you, not him, not anybody. I just have to go on.'

'You don't even know what you're saying.'

'But I do.' She started to move around him, circling at a safe distance. 'What's to go back to? I've no friends left, no future, the house is like a grave. Time stopped there when Chrissie died. If I go back then life might as well end, right now. There's only one way, and that's the way I'm going.'

'For the last time . . .'

'No, Joe. I have to leave, now. I'm sorry you're hurt.'

He was off-guard. She quickly stepped in and reached across him, and had the bank envelope out of his jacket before he'd realised what she was doing. She skipped back again, out of reach, but he was too far-gone to grab at her anyway; he sat with his back against the tunnel wall, eyes red and burning into her as she backed away.

'I'll tell someone you're here,' she said as she picked up her bag. And then, difficult as it was to do, she left him.

She phoned her Debt Collectors from a callbox nearby. They'd done the work that she'd asked for, and her account was ready. Having risked enough on the Underground for one day, she walked all the way.

It went under the name of a business services agency, with an office in a street of restaurants and car showrooms and one, off-the-beaten-track backstreet theatre. It had taken her a while actually to spot the doorway, which was of solid timber with a couple of locks. It was impregnable-looking, and appeared to have survived at least a couple of attempts to storm it. There were no business signs and no glass, just a line of bellpushes and a tinpot speaker alongside the frame. Each buzzer was marked by a slip of typewritten paper behind clear plastic; the other names included a computer services company, a firm of solicitors, and a market research bureau. Most of the other places that she'd looked at had been too upmarket – bleached wood porticos, tinted glass reception areas with uniformed security guards – but this one had seemed appropriately seedy. The door gave onto a stairway that resembled something from an underlit Victorian public toilet.

The woman at the reception desk went inside and then returned with an envelope and an invoice.

'Thanks,' Lucy said.

'Don't spread this around,' the woman suggested. 'Tracing by VAT number isn't strictly kosher.'

'But you do it anyway.'

The woman shrugged. 'Business is business.'

'Yeah,' Lucy said, her eyes widening slightly as she read through the invoice. 'And business isn't looking so bad.'

As soon as she was on the stairway, she seated herself on the top step and opened the envelope. Firstly, out came all of the year-old receipts that had been amongst Christine's effects. Then, a single typewritten sheet listing an address to go with each.

Reading through them, Lucy nodded to herself.

The search could continue.

Joe took a cab back to his hotel. In the foyer, the same coach-party crowds waited in their groups; different faces, the same look of uncertainty and abandonment. He struggled through, and then had to wait in line to speak to someone at the desk.

'Another night?' the desk clerk asked him.

He slid his plastic key across the counter. 'Another room. I didn't much like the ambience in the last one.'

'Well,' the clerk said doubtfully, 'I don't know. We're pretty full.'

Joe leaned forward. 'Tell you what,' he said. 'You don't disappoint me, and I won't tell the Vice Squad about the tarts and backhanders that go back and forth of an evening.'

The clerk's face hardened. 'I don't need this.'

'Me neither,' Joe said. 'Let me have the room.'

TWENTY

The list was pretty varied. Lucy put the names into some kind of order, the most promising-looking at the head. She spent most of that afternoon following it through; firstly to an upmarket clothes store near Covent Garden, where the 'fifties lived again and the Utility mark was a major cultural icon, then to a jeweller who specialised exclusively in watches that nearly nobody could afford, and then to a comparatively down-to-earth chain store near Oxford Circus. She showed around Christine's photograph, she asked if it was possible to trace back the receipts to learn anything more. But nobody recognised the face and nobody could help; she reckoned that the jeweller might have been able to do more if he'd wanted to, but he clearly hadn't wanted to.

As the afternoon fizzled out and the evening began to take over, she stood in the electric darkness of Oxford Street with the homeward-bound crowds and the traffic roaring by. There were tiny lights in the trees along the pavements; Christmas lights, she realised with some slight surprise, out early but Christmas lights all the same. They didn't exactly bring her any sense of seasonal cheer. What had started out as a promising strategy was leading her nowhere. Once again she was almost out of cash, and once again she was almost out of options. Only one address on her list remained and it was for a take-away coffee shop down on the fringe of Soho, so minor and unlikely that it was barely worth pursuing.

She actually felt that, in a perverse kind of way, she knew less now than she'd known before. There had been no designer clothing in Christine's luggage, no Rolex or Cartier on her wrist; the under-wear that she'd died in had come from Marks', her dress had been off-the-peg with probably a thousand like it on the streets, and her watch had been the one that she'd been given by their parents on her eighteenth birthday. Lucy was wearing it now, and it kept no better time than her own.

People kept on going by, heads bowed to their own problems. Lucy felt like the one momentary point of stillness in a world that was shifting; a world that was hitting and running and leaving its victims a long way behind.

94

She could feel that she was getting light-headed. As usual, she hadn't eaten since breakfast in the flophouse, and that hadn't been anything spectacular.

But at least she knew where there was a coffee shop, cheap.

It wasn't hard to find. She'd passed it once on her very first night in town, but hadn't noticed it then; squeezed-in without much in the way of frontage, it was narrow and cramped and had half of its area taken up by a big glass-and-stainless-steel counter with a claustrophobic working space behind. The lower part of the walls had been panelled in yellow formica, the rest in mirrors that gave an illusion of greater depth; customer seating was on splitting vinyl bar stools at a narrow lunch counter along one wall, no room for tables at all.

It had the claustrophobic ambience of the inside of a Wendy house but business, if the turnover in perishable stock was anything to go by, had to be terrific. As Lucy joined the line for service she could see that every inch of the wall space and counter top was crammed almost to the ceiling with sandwiches, salads and cake. Where space ran out, stock hung in wire baskets. The staff appeared to consist mainly of two youngish men with shaving-brush haircuts, one of them in a sports sweater and the other a striped shirt and apron; impossible as it seemed, the kitchen area behind them had been arranged to fit in a big expresso machine, two microwaves, a deep-fat fryer, stacks of napkins and carry-out cups, and several large glass bowls of fruit. They had help from an old guy, who sat motionless in the main part of the shop and slowly got to his feet, cloth in hand, to clear up when some sit-in customer walked out. He wore a cap and was unshaven, his stubble a pure white.

The line moved. Just ahead of Lucy was a greasy-looking kid in black with a haircut so close that the back of his head was just a dark stubble from the ears down. He ordered sandwiches and Cokes to feed half a dozen people, and when the price had been rung up he grabbed it all into his arms, said 'Fuck off, Stavros,' and dived out of the door.

The man in the striped apron reacted with hair-trigger speed, ducking under the hinged counter flap without even stopping to raise it, but by the time that he'd crossed the floor and reached the pavement the youth must have disappeared from sight because there he stopped, and bellowed his anger down the busy street. Everything around him carried on without missing a beat, business as usual, and with a face as dark as a bruise he stalked back inside. The old guy at the back said something, but it was nothing that Lucy could understand.

'You know,' Lucy said seriously as the younger man came up again on the other side of the counter, 'I think that's one of the lowest tricks that anybody can pull.'

'They think it's funny,' he said, with a passionate flick of his hand in the air as if throwing something away. 'Can you believe that? I'd be ashamed!'

'I blame the parents.'

'And the teachers.'

'Especially the teachers.'

Lucy was trying to think of some way to spread the blame even further, to the Welfare State perhaps, when the other young Greek from the back of the working area said, 'I don't blame anybody but him and the other thieving bastards who are like him.'

And the old guy at the back said something else, which again Lucy couldn't understand.

The counter man said, 'So, what can I get you?'

'Just a coffee,' she said, 'and one of those chocolate donuts.'

It seemed pretty futile. She thought of the numbers of people who'd pass through in the course of a single day and evening; office workers, shopgirls, tourists, construction workers, ticket-takers, taxi drivers, and hundreds, maybe thousands, of plain ordinary types with no obvious story behind them. At some of the other places she'd hoped that there might be some more detailed customer records, but here she was going to look pretty stupid when she produced the last of her faded till receipts and asked them the same kind of questions.

But she wasn't deterred. She held up Christine's photograph and said, 'Did you ever see this woman? It would have been a year ago, at least.'

There was nobody in line behind her, so they were able to take a moment to give it a look. The two young men stood together, studying the picture over the counter flap.

The one in the striped apron, who was slightly older than the other and seemed to be the senior employee, shook his head.

'Nah,' he said.

'I know she used to come here,' Lucy said. 'This was in with her stuff.' She passed across the slip of paper that had led her to the place. The man studied it and shrugged, as if there was nothing that could possibly be learned from it.

'Biggish order,' he said. 'Maybe an office or one of the show places. We do loads of these. Sorry.'

The old guy had shuffled up in silence; he was beside her at the counter, and the younger of the two men had turned Christine's photo-graph for him to see. After a moment he started to speak, and Lucy tensed as she waited for a translation; there was some exchange back and forth between him and the younger man, and then the younger man said, 'Uncle Panos thinks he remembers her. She used to come in most nights about nine. That could mean a backstage order from one of the shows. Interval time, see? That happens a lot.'

Lucy looked at the old man. His eyes met hers, blue and watery and utterly sincere. 'He wouldn't know which one?'

They asked. He shrugged.

'If she said, we probably wouldn't remember. It was ages ago. Sorry.'

'Tell him thanks anyway,' she said.

She took her stuff over to the lunch counter. Show places. That had to be progress of a kind, didn't it? But somehow, it didn't feel like much. The field wasn't exactly narrow.

But at least, she told herself, it's now narrower than it was.

People came and went as she stalled over her supper, in no rush to be anywhere else right now. She wondered about having something more, but she'd already pushed her cash reserve to the limit. She could afford to go back to the same bed for the night, but only just. The real problem would start in the morning; most of her schemes for raising more money called for seed capital, and by morning she'd have none. Rock bottom, and no way to raise herself from it. She really ought to be spending a couple of hours at a coach terminus, maybe, showing her bankroll and explaining to the unsuspecting how she was just a small amount shy of her fare home, and could they perhaps help her out? Looking at a more or less respectable young woman with money in her hand, most people wouldn't take it for a con. By the end of the evening, she'd have picked up enough to keep her going.

She thought of the girl, on the stairway, in the Underground. The memory came to her like a spectre of possibility.

Starving. Homeless. Please help.

Rock bottom.

Weary of the day as she'd become, she slid from her stool to face the prospect of a return to the battle.

'Wait a minute,' the man in the striped apron called to her.

She'd been aware of him rummaging around in the back of the till drawer, and he'd brought out what appeared to be a bunch of foreign banknotes and other paper. He was checking through, apparently with something specific in mind, and as she approached the counter he pulled out a printed card that resembled a dance ticket with an airbrushed tint around its edge.

'Can't guarantee it, but she might have left this,' he said.

'What is it?'

'Dunno, some kind of complimentary. We get some for the clubs, but not many. Mostly they're just a come-on to get you inside and paying the bar prices. We never use them. Take it and try it, for what it's worth.'

Uncle Panos held the door open for her as she left.

'He says she was pretty, and that's why he remembers,' one of the boys called out. 'And he says you look very much like her.'

'Tell him, she was,' Lucy said. 'And tell him thank you.'

She knew almost nothing about night clubs – not of this kind, anyway. She knew about discos and some of the town clubs at home, bear pits with tacky floor shows and bouncers like steroid-inflated penguins, but this seemed to be something different. At least it was something classier than a peep show. She hadn't wanted to admit it, but the spectre of the *Girls Wanted* board still haunted her a little. But this place seemed more or less respectable.

It wasn't a Soho club, but stood in a narrow lane in the area west of Regent Street – not quite the vice zone, not quite Mayfair, not quite anywhere with a specific identity of its own. It was mid-evening now, and the club was open although business seemed slow. Lucy stood aside to let a few people pass, but they didn't exactly constitute a stampede. Studying the entranceway, she saw a lot of brass and marble crowded into a small area of frontage, along with a backlit plastic sign and a few hundred tiny copper-tinted mirror tiles. The sign carried the club's name, The Gilded Cage, and under the legend of *London's Finest Nightspot* was a big colour photograph of a dancer in cutaway costume and pasties and a bandmaster's hat.

She moved to the door. Most of the glass was obscured by credit card stickers; if it was plastic, they appeared to take it.

'Here goes,' she said to herself, and went on through.

A carpeted stairway led down to a corridor that was arched-over with beaten copper above gold flock wallpaper. Heavily turned brass handrails were probably a leftover from some earlier style of decor. The lighting was feeble, but enough to reveal that the carpet had a tasteless floral pattern like a sicked-up pizza. At the corridor's far end there was a big framed picture on the wall, but she couldn't make out what it was.

The usher looked her over, but she didn't back down. She waited as he gave her ticket a long, frowning inspection, but he couldn't fault it and pointed her toward the cloakroom. She passed it by. She didn't want to part with her bag, and she certainly didn't want to part with a tip. She went straight through an archway and onto the main floor of the club.

Wow, she thought. What an armpit.

No more than a third of the tables were occupied. The music was canned, and no-one was dancing. Low shaded lights on the tables themselves meant that the decor was barely visible, which was kind of a blessing. A thrust stage backed by a golden curtain and lit, disco-style, from underneath brought a promise of some form of floor show.

A waiter with an accent and an oiled-castor walk seated her and left her with a drinks menu that made her eyes pop with shock. She knew people who'd bought cars for less than the price of a bottle of house champagne. Lucy closed the menu and looked around.

There were a few couples. One party of six might as well have hoisted a banner reading Married Men On The Town. A few men sat alone, all of them middle-aged or older, but no women other than herself. As she was scanning these singles tables, one of the men caught her eye. He was smiling pleasantly.

Oh, shit, she thought wearily, and slid out of her seat.

There was an upper level which overlooked the stage, and she retreated to this as the sound system switched to a loud warmup for the cabaret. She didn't want to add complications to the evening by giving anyone the idea that she was touting for a pickup. Like everyone she had her stories of persistent encounters, and didn't want to add to them. Moving around a pillar, she stopped to watch the beginning of the show. This was hardly more than a shallow balcony, tables for two up against the rail, but it was empty and she felt a little safer above the main action.

The curtains parted, the Showstoppers came on. It was a mimed routine, no sign of live music anywhere, and was more or less the kind of dinner show that she'd have expected to see on a cruise liner; a little more skin than would suit a family audience, maybe, but hardly sleaze-palace stuff either. The music was loud, the costumes glittered, the dancers were well-built and good-looking and unapproachable in their stage makeup. She counted eight of them. Midway through the number they were joined by a male dancer over whom the routine required them to go ga-ga. From the way that he moved, Lucy guessed that he looked in the mirror every morning and saw Robert Redford. Probably had to climb onto a box to reach it first, but there you go.

The opening number ended to a spattering of lacklustre applause, but the taped track bulldozed onward. The lighting changed and the dancing midget came on again after a fast switch of costume, carrying a toy golden gun for a Bond Movie routine. Lucy wondered how much of this she could take.

Not much, she suspected.

She scanned the house for employees. One approachable-looking face would have been enough. But already she had the place nailed as a ruthless machine for stripping money out of people before turning them out into the early hours, and the waiters were merely a part of the process. She needed an angle, and right now she didn't have one.

At the back of the stage, the golden curtain shimmered as it moved. She thought of the city's lights, and how they'd played across the heaving surface of the river. Christine had urged her to give up and go home, but Lucy had sensed her approval under the warning. She'd show her.

Even in death, she'd show her.

'Can I help you, at all?' a low voice said close to her ear.

She looked up, startled. A big man in a dinner jacket stood over her. He was the kind who could shave three times a day and still show a five o'clock shadow. Behind him was her waiter, looking cool and unimpressed.

'I don't think so,' Lucy said.

'Perhaps I could just check your ticket.'

'Why?'

He put out his hand. 'Please?'

Reluctantly, she handed over her cancelled complimentary. He checked it, both sides, before shaking his head in regret.

'I'm afraid this isn't quite in order,' he said.

'It says I get free admission.'

'And it's dated for last year. We'll have to charge you for drinks.'

Lucy glanced at the waiter. 'I haven't had anything.'

'We'll have to charge you anyway,' the big man said. 'We're on a club licence here. You understand.'

Lucy understood. A small stone had somehow made its way into the machine, and the machine had to spit it out or risk endangering the smooth running of the process.

She said, 'How about if I just leave?'

And the big man shrugged, as if he was broad-minded and open to any suggestion. 'If that's what you'd prefer,' he said.

She was escorted across the floor to the exit. Behind her, a solo dancer was high-kicking in a French maid's costume. The venue might be third-rate, but the dancer was giving it everything. Lucy knew that half the audience or more would be looking her way instead of at the stage, but she refused to slink out. She'd been ejected from better places than this, and with less grace.

100

As they were passing, she caught the usher's eye.

'When I first arrived,' she said, 'you thought you recognised me.'

'I made a mistake,' the usher said, and returned his attention to the updating of his Rolodex.

It was then that she knew it for sure.

Christine, somehow, had been a part of this.

PART THREE

Christine's Hammer

TWENTY-ONE

She returned to the club about a half-hour later, but this time she was changing her approach. This time, she had her angle. She'd circled the block until she'd found the side alley where the stage door was located, and then after hiding her bag in a dark spot behind a big wheeled trash hopper she'd turned around and headed back to the coffee shop. Now, carrying a cardboard tray loaded with teas and coffees and soft drinks cans, she stepped in again from the street and felt the silence of the alley as it clamped in around her.

At the far end was a place where the backs of four high buildings came together to form a small courtyard. There was a single overhead lamp in cast iron and, looking up, by its light Lucy could see warehouse-style windows fitted with the exterior boxes of air-conditioning units, more windows with rotting frames, iron galleries, fire escapes, and a couple of high railed terraces with a hint of greenery in silhouette against the night sky. Down at ground level, all but two of the courtyard's doorways had been roughly sealed with cinderblocks. One of these was the loading bay for The Gilded Cage – or, as it apparently had once been called, the Ambassador Club – and the other was its stage door.

The loading bay had old roll-across galvanised doors, twisted and battered out of shape and just about held together by a new-looking chain sheathed in blue plastic. The stage door was of plain wood, and carried a couple of handprints in primer where some impatient builder had once slammed it shut. There was a buzzer to the side, nothing much else. She pressed the button, heard no sound, and waited with her tray held level at shoulder height.

Nothing happened for a while.

(And as Lucy was shuffling tensely and waiting for someone to respond, Joe Lucas was in his hotel room and trying to prise the cap off a fresh bottle of painkillers that he'd picked up, along with some disposable razors and a few other essentials, from a late-opening pharmacy on Piccadilly. The cap had a childproof seal, and it was proving to be pretty Lucasproof as well. The harder he worked at it, the less success he seemed to be having; his pain and frustration were combining to make him angry, and he flung the bottle down onto the

bed. A gentle voice behind him said Easy, Joe, *and he spun around in terror and surprise. The room was empty. He put a hand to his head, and wondered what the hell was happening to him. He could have sworn that the voice had been that of Christine Ashdown.)*

The stage door opened.

She'd wondered who would answer. The door was opened by a nondescript man in his forties wearing a brown overall. He'd obviously walked some distance to respond to her buzz, and right now he was wondering why.

'Don't hang about,' she said. 'The stuff's going cold.'

He looked at her cardboard tray, and his face cleared a little.

'I thought Charlie had put a stop to all that,' he said.

'Are you kidding?' she said. 'Most of this is Charlie's order.'

He moved back and, only a moment later, she was inside.

The adrenaline was really pumping now. She had a bad moment as she heard the alley door closing behind her, but she was already on her way down. She'd entered a rough-looking hallway in which two flights of concrete stairs descended to a fire door. Loops of wiring and cable ran overhead, loosely tacked at intervals to the unpainted ceiling; it was the kind of *Who cares, no-one'll see it* protocol that had applied behind the scenes in the shopping mall where she'd landed her first Saturday job.

The next ten minutes would be critical. Like a shark, she'd have to keep moving to survive . . . and some shark, Lucy thought as she shouldered her way through into some windowless corridor which echoed with the tinny sounds of the show playback, coming through on a cheap relay speaker. She had to look as if she knew where she was going, move as if she had every right to be there; one challenge could ruin it all. Ten minutes at the most to get the measure of the place, to get some idea of its layout and how it all ran, and to use the information to work out her next move in the game. Not for the first time, she was going for broke; she tried to tell herself that nothing much bad could happen, at the worst she could be discovered and thrown out, but somehow the stakes seemed much higher.

Second chances didn't come by too often. Mostly, they didn't come by at all.

Holding her tray high, she moved on down the passageway. It was hot, airless, badly lit, and generally had a cramped below-decks feel to it. There were no signs on the doors, no markers or anything, but fortunately most of them stood open. The area was strictly functional, no frills and no great obsession with tidiness either; crates of empty bottles half-blocked the way by a storeroom, and there was a bicycle under the punch clock. Two small offices and a staff locker room, all unoccupied; she gave a quick once-over to the noticeboard just inside the door, but it told her nothing. She could hear ventilators pumping somewhere deeper in the complex, but they didn't seem to be equal to the job.

Wherever the action was, it was all taking place somewhere other than here.

So go for it, she told herself, and pressed on.

The grey vinyl floor gave way to carpet tiles. Some stairs, and then around a corner where a staff pay phone hung under a grey plastic hood on the wall, and she was looking down what she guessed had to be the dressing-room corridor.

The paintwork was black, the walls covered in silver foil; each of a line of doorways blazed with about a thousand watts of brilliance and there was a smell of greasepaint and cleansing cream that she hadn't encountered since having a couple of bit parts in school plays. She squared herself, and moved along to look into the nearest of the rooms.

The light came from a long mirror surrounded by unshaded bulbs. She could feel their heat from the doorway. On the table before the mirror stood half a dozen wigs on red velvet stands, the wigs themselves all Barbie-doll perfect and in colours unknown to nature. The walls had long ago disappeared under a solid mass of posters and playbills, some of them so old that they'd faded completely. Two young women were in the room; one was reading a magazine, the other was stuffing herself into a tight corset of black vinyl that appeared to be a part of a stylised nun's costume. It was cut low across the top and high above the thighs, and for a moment Lucy was stopped short by the thought that Jesus, it looked hell to wear, but wouldn't it just kill 'em on the disco floor back home?

They both looked her way. The one with the magazine, who appeared to be wearing a bathrobe over nothing, looked at her tray and said pleasantly, 'Who's all that for?'

'You, if you want it,' Lucy said, and moved in.

Neither of them seemed to find her presence remarkable or unusual. She slid in and around the one who was dressing, and set a couple of coffees down in what limited space she could see on the table. Close-to and without their performance wigs, these two hardly seemed to connect with anyone that she'd seen out on the stage less than an hour before; then they'd been all front, carnival vamps, not so much real human beings as fantasy figures with hidden human operators. Back here, they seemed pretty approachable. One of them said, 'What do we owe?'

'On the house.'

'On *Charlie*?' the one in the bathrobe said incredulously, from which Lucy gathered that whoever Charlie might be, his reputation rested on something other than his generosity.

Well, kid, she thought. It's time to shit or bust.

'Not on Charlie,' she said. 'It's on me. I want to ask you about Chrissie Ashdown.'

Their faces were polite, slightly puzzled blanks.

'Christine Ashdown,' Lucy said, feeling her heart begin to sink. 'I think she may have worked here just over a year ago.'

'We wouldn't have been here then,' the one in the nun's costume said, snapping the last of her buckles. 'There's quite a turnover. Go see the show from out front, and then work out why.' She smiled, briefly. 'But it's work,' she said, and she put on her head-dress, checked her black stockings, picked up her whip, and went out to prepare for her cue.

The other dancer said, 'Thanks for the coffee,' and returned her attention to the magazine.

As Lucy moved back out into the passageway, she met the returning tide from the last ensemble number onstage; they arrived in a rush, panting like horses and shedding their quasi-military costumes as they moved. Everyone was in a hurry as they squeezed by; no-one seemed to notice her, and she didn't see much chance of getting their attention right now. They charged into the other dressing rooms, gabbling as they started a quick change for another number. Over the relay system Lucy could hear the filtered strains of *Ain't Misbehavin'*. Every now and again the music would cut for a couple of seconds and there would be some faint, whispered phrase that would haunt its way down the wire, but she couldn't make out what was said.

Her depleted tray cooling fast, she moved on to see what else she could find.

Time was running out.

A couple of the doors further down the corridor were shut, and appeared to be locked. The biggest open room was a wardrobe area with hundreds of costumes on moveable racks, two sewing machines and a makeup chair, but for the moment it was unattended. The costumes were an assortment of the bright, the bizarre, and the impossibly sequinned. Shower cubicles were steamy with recent use, but also unoccupied.

But then she saw an office at the corridor's end, and it was occupied. A man sat with his back to the open doorway. He was using the phone. As she was approaching she saw his head turn slightly in awareness of her, which meant that there was no going back.

She went in. Like everywhere else down here it was cramped and lightless, and there were books and files and heaps of dusty papers wherever she looked. There was a shaded desk lamp by the telephone, and that was it.

Lucy wanted to back out, and now. Immediately she'd sensed that this was wrong, that there was nothing for her in this office, and that she'd be at risk if she stayed around a moment longer than was necessary. She reached over by the man's shoulder to set a styrene cup on his desk, and saw him look at it sharply.

'From Charlie,' she whispered as she turned to make her getaway, but he was fast.

He grabbed her wrist, and spun her back to face him. His chair swivelled around to meet her.

'*I'm* Charlie,' he said. 'Now, what the fuck do you think you're playing at?'

TWENTY-TWO

She swallowed, totally wrong-footed. He was a big man in an unbuttoned dinner jacket, someone who could probably shave three times a day and still show a five o'clock shadow.

In fact, he was the man who'd escorted her to the door to mark the end of her first visit.

And he had pigs' eyes, was all that she could think as he said, 'Let me call you back,' into the phone and then cradled it before standing and, still holding her arm and not much caring about how it would hurt, moving to close the office door. The tray went, along with her balance. She had to twist around to follow him, and still her elbow and shoulder screamed; she fell back as he let her go, pushing her slightly to make her stagger.

'Well?' he said.

There was only the one way out, and he was blocking it. She was in a trap within a trap, and she had no-one to blame other than herself. She felt desperate, she felt empty.

And all that she could say was, 'I'm Christine Ashdown's sister.'

There was silence for a while.

Then he eased away from the door, and back to the desk. Lucy watched him uncertainly, turning with him as he moved. He seemed to be out of scale with the rest of the room, as if his size and all of its angles had somehow been exaggerated. He reached out and turned the lamp so that it shone onto her face, seating himself on the edge of the desk so that he could study her.

She winced when the unshaded light hit her, but she didn't look away.

'I reckon you are, at that,' he said, and there was a slight sense of wonder in his voice. 'So what's the game?'

'Turn the light away, and I'll tell you.'

He grinned. Already she liked him even less. If he'd broken her arm, she doubted that it would have altered his tone or his attitude in any way. He reached out and gave the lamp a push, and it swung away from her to shine onto the wall. Charlie stayed where he was, now mostly in shadow.

She said, 'Have you seen much of Chrissie, lately?'

It wasn't easy to make out his expression, but she was watching him as carefully as she could. She saw no change, no glimpse of an unguarded thought before defences could go up; in fact, he seemed pretty well relaxed.

'Not since she walked out,' he told her. Lucy wouldn't have staked anything on it, but he didn't appear to know that Christine was dead. Lucy wasn't about to educate him, at least not yet.

'Well,' she said, 'I just got into town and she said if ever I was here, I should look you up.'

Another moment went by, as he considered the thought. She saw him glance down to where her cardboard tray had fallen.

He said, 'And why all this business?'

'She told me you'd be a hard man to reach.'

He grinned again. She could imagine the calculation in his eyes, like dull glass mirrors reflecting the action of some well-oiled clock-work.

'All right,' he said. 'So you've reached me. What do you want?'

'The same deal as Christine got.'

Nothing happened for a moment, and in that moment she started to think that she'd over-reached herself; but then Charlie said, 'This isn't some charity for runaways, you know,' and she knew that she was still within the limits, if only just.

'I know,' she said. 'It isn't charity that I'm looking for.'

'I'll tell you what I'll do,' Charlie said, standing and moving toward her. 'I'll think about it.'

She tried not to flinch as he passed within arm's length, but he reached by her and re-opened the office door. She had to restrain herself from dashing for it, almost in the fear that it would close again and that this time, it would be forever.

She said, 'For how long?'

'I said I'd think about it. Go down to Wardrobe and see Josie. She'll find you something to do.'

'Is this a job?'

'I'll see what I can slip you at the end of the week. You want to call that a job, then it's a job.'

'Thanks,' she said.

'You'd better mean it. If you weren't Chrissie's sister, you'd be out on your arse in the alley.'

'Understood,' she said, and started to slide gratefully toward the doorway as Charlie moved over into his chair and picked up the phone again. He started to dial.

'But clear that shit up, first,' he said, nodding toward her fallen tray and its spillage, and then he swung his chairback around to her as if she'd ceased to exist.

TWENTY-THREE

The shit went into a waste bin, and Lucy went into the Wardrobe room to wait. *Not bad*, she thought with a fierce kind of glee that she knew she didn't dare to show. *Not bad at all.* She sat demurely on the edge of one of the room's more nondescript-looking chairs, knowing that this Josie, whoever she might be, would be her key to success or failure over the next few hours and maybe even the coming days. So far, all that she knew of Josie was that she owned a big handbag.

After about five minutes a middle-aged woman appeared in the doorway and, seeing Lucy, stopped and frowned at her over the top of her glasses.

'Are you Josie?' Lucy said.

'Who needs to know?'

'Charlie sent me to give you a hand.'

Charlie was clearly no big deal as far as Josie was concerned. 'What's he doing,' she said, 'fucking you, or hoping to?'

Lucy shrugged and said, 'He can hope for as long as he likes.'

Which overcame the frown, and even drew the beginnings of a smile out of Josie.

Not a bad start. Not bad at all.

Josie was a solidly-built woman, hefty but fit-looking, whose taste in clothes ran mostly to knitwear and slacks. Lucy was later to learn that she attended lunchtime yoga sessions on three days of the week. She had dark curly hair with no sign of grey, and a certain shyness that could make her manner seem brusque. Her father had been an army officer of fairly high rank, and she'd spent most of her early life in a military environment. Her age was something, Lucy quickly deduced, that one could not enquire about and expect to survive.

There were two shows, at nine and at midnight. The work consisted of laying out costumes in the appropriate dressing rooms in advance of the required changes, rescuing those from the previous number

112

and returning them to Wardrobe, checking for damage, separating out for laundry. On close inspection the various materials proved to be sweat-stained and much-repaired. Josie seemed to be pretty well organised, the work fast and precise without being pressured. The only mistakes were Lucy's own, and she quickly got to hear about them. Her worst was when she got in the way; backstage timing sometimes had to be precise, and it was no place for someone who was still taking in the sights.

Between shows the girls dressed in sweatshirts and jogging shorts; some of them stayed in the dressing rooms and stretched out to sleep or read, others went to another room in the basement complex where they could watch TV. Maurice, the male dancer, went out front to sit on a bar stool and be seen.

Josie seemed okay. Not exactly forthcoming, but not averse to having someone around to talk to, either. Lucy tried not to be pushy, and Josie slowly thawed.

'How is Christine, these days?' she said as she worked along the racks, pulling out the second set of changes for the show that was just about to start.

Lucy hadn't been a hundred per cent sure with Charlie, but here she felt certain. Josie knew nothing of Christine's death. As far as she was concerned, Christine had simply left town and never been heard from again. Given the nature of the business, nobody would have expected her to get in touch.

So Lucy said, 'She's taking it easy.'

'Now, there's bright for you. That's what I ought to be doing. But I've been stuck in this line for twenty years, and I reckon I'll be stuck in it when I drop.'

'All in the same place?'

'Are you kidding? I've done everything. Rep, tours, big musicals . . . though not so many of those. This suits me for now. It's regular and I don't have to travel.'

'Were you ever a dancer?'

'Once, for a while. But you reach thirty in this game, and you're on the way out. Some of these girls are sharper than I was. They're making the money while they can, but they're planning ahead.'

'You seem sharp enough to me,' Lucy said, thinking how hard it was to find a way of guiding someone into telling you things that they'll assume you already know.

Josie looked at her, that over-the-glasses look again. 'Not as sharp as I needed to be, though,' she said. 'I had an abortion go wrong. This was way back before it was legal. End of high kicks and handstands.'

'I'm really sorry.'

113

'I don't mind you knowing,' Josie said, dumping the costumes into Lucy's arms and then picking out more. 'Kids ought to know stuff like that. Maybe you wouldn't get so many of them wasted before their time.'

'It won't happen to me,' Lucy said.

'Glad to hear it,' Josie told her.

So there it was, Lucy's first night in showbusiness. The air heavy with sweat, greasepaint and burning dust, a lot of clutter and small talk, some haste, occasional flurries of panic, and long stretches of nothing much happening while the empty passageways echoed with relayed sound from the house pickup. She saw everything except the show. After the final number, when all the dancers came offstage whooping and whistling with relief to crowd into the showers, Lucy followed Josie around in a final inventory of wigs and clothing and then generally cleared up ready for the next night's work.

It was around two in the morning and most of the performers had now dispersed to waiting cars and taxis. In a great gesture of trust, Josie let her switch off the lights unsupervised. When Lucy came out, Josie was on the pay phone at the corridor's end. Seeing her, she covered the receiver and said, 'Will you need a taxi?'

Lucy, feeling awkward, said, 'I don't think so.'

'Where are you staying?'

'I'm not sure, yet.'

Josie turned away and finished her minicab booking, and then hung up and faced Lucy again. 'You've got nowhere lined up?' she said.

'I've managed before. It's not a problem.'

'It's two o'clock in the morning. You've got jailbait written all over you and you're proposing walking the West End without a place to stay. Are you demented, or what?'

'Do you think anyone would notice if I crashed out here? I don't mind being locked in.'

'There's a man with a Doberman comes around two or three times every night. If you've ever fancied your chances as dogfood, go right ahead.'

'There's other places.'

'Name one.'

'Hostels.'

'They're full by nightfall, and you know it. The kids they turn away end up sleeping in cardboard boxes by the river. I can't *believe* that Chrissie would let you come down here without setting you up better than this.'

'Chrissie's not involved,' Lucy said stubbornly. 'This is just me.'

'Looking for what?' Josie said, facing her squarely. 'Good times and glamour? That's just bullshit. Go back home.'

'I will. But not just yet.'

They were almost shouting at one another, and both seemed to realise it at the same time. Embarrassed, each looked away.

'You'd better come with me,' Josie said then, with resignation.

'I don't want to be a problem,' Lucy said.

Josie met her eyes again. Her gaze was dark, and hinted at some impossibly deep sense of pain; and for a moment Lucy felt a certain regret, if not shame, at the way that she seemed to be ready to manipulate any situation for whatever advantage she could get.

But only for a moment.

TWENTY-FOUR

During the minicab ride to Josie's place, Lucy did a little mental stocktaking. On the minus side, she'd blown a lot of money and received a couple of scares. She hoped that she hadn't made an enemy out of Joe Lucas; she knew that what he'd done, he'd done for her and for the memory of Christine. Lucy was no saint, but she could forgive him the rough handling. She could even forgive him the talk about having her committed, now that that possibility was safely in the past and she was making progress on her own. She'd show them. She knew nothing of the future other than that it was an inhospitable fog that no-one had any choice but to enter, but she was certain that there was a scene all laid-out and waiting for her where she brought in the name of the man – or woman – who'd first talked to Chrissie and then run her down. The fog would clear, and some daylight would enter. Life would be different.

Christine could rest.

Lucy wondered if Christine was watching her now. Wondered if she could see how well she was doing.

Because that was the plus side – the progress she'd made, on the slenderest of evidence. Better than the police, better than anyone. She was Christine's hammer, and she was unstoppable. From here she'd get to know those whom Christine had known, perhaps find out where she'd lived; enter her skin, almost as if Christine were to walk again while Lucy became the ghost. The two of them, closer in death than they'd ever been in life.

She'd rewrite Christine's story from the inside. And this time, the ending would be different.

The cab made a turn through a narrow archway in a row of buildings. She hadn't been paying much attention to the journey, and didn't have any idea of where they were; the archway led into a long courtyard with a cobbled surface and small, squeezed-in houses to either side. It was a mews; she'd never been in one before, but she knew what it was. The buildings would once have been the stables to the bigger houses out on the street, but now the bigger houses would all have been subdivided long ago and the stables leased off and converted. Simon Templar had lived in a mews. Lucy had been reading *The Saint* from her father's shelves when all of the other girls had their noses in *Black Beauty*. The thought of living in a mews cottage had been one of her daydreams, like living in a penthouse. Modesty Blaise had lived in a penthouse, and Travis McGee lived on a boat called the *Busted Flush*. Nobody, but nobody, had ever seemed to live in a boring house in the suburbs with a swing in the back garden.

She looked the place over while Josie was paying off the cab. Beyond its roofline, the backs of the big houses looked down. An exterior stairway led to the entrance at first-floor level, with another storey above; these would have been the groom's quarters over the stable itself. In some of the other houses the stable was now a double garage, but in this one it had been blocked in and a window installed. It looked impossibly quaint, although nothing like as appealing as those far-off places of her imagination. It wasn't a big place, but it didn't look cheap. She wondered how Josie could afford it. Perhaps The Gilded Cage was a better employer than it appeared.

A lantern burned above the stairway, in the same wrought iron as the handrail. Josie stood under it as she fished out her keys and then, as she opened the door, signalled to Lucy for silence.

They went in.

A couple of low lights were burning in different rooms, lit as if in anticipation of Josie's return. Lucy wondered by whom . . . a husband? But Josie wore no rings, and had talked of nobody. Boyfriend or lover? Yeah, perhaps, Lucy thought. Who could say for sure? Maybe old people could still get up to that kind of thing. Still in silence, Josie beckoned to her to follow.

The carpets were deep and expensive, and they made no sound as they moved to the end of the hall. Lucy glanced into a couple of the rooms as they passed. The house was immaculate and had been furnished, as far as she could tell, like something out of a design magazine.

She caught a movement in the corner of her eye, and looked up.

Someone was watching them from the top of the stairs. Lucy's first impression was of the robe that she wore; it was either silk or satin, she couldn't be certain. She was tall, slender, thirty-plus; she had long hands, red hair, and the kind of class that could make a shopgirl weep with envy.

The woman looked down on them for a moment; not seeming to see Lucy at all, she was looking at Josie. Her face was hard to make out in the half-light. After a moment she turned abruptly, and moved away.

Lucy glanced at Josie, wondering what the story was and what her place in it might be. Josie was watching the space where the woman had been. The light was soft and one-sided, Josie's eyes were bright and clear. Lucy saw sadness in them. A sense of inevitable damage, inadvertently done.

And then Josie whispered, 'Follow me,' and started down the carpeted stairway to the lower level.

This was the spare room, the room that had once been a garage, and it was noticeably colder than the rest of the house. It had books, records and unsorted bric-à-brac, and a foam chair that folded out in three sections to make a single bed of sorts. Josie disappeared for a couple of minutes and then reappeared with some pillows and a duvet.

Lucy said, 'Did Chrissie ever stay with you?'

Josie glanced over the arrangements, as if checking for anything that she may have missed. 'No,' she said. 'Chrissie could afford better than this. I'll see you in the morning.'

'What time?'

'Not too early.'

When Josie had gone, Lucy closed the door and looked around. It didn't much matter that she was in the junkroom of someone else's home and that her position here was uncertain. At least for tonight, she had privacy and she was secure. The months since she'd left her father's house had been tough in a number of ways; she'd known loneliness a lot of the time, solitude hardly at all. Opportunities to relax and let her guard down, even if only for a few hours, had been rare.

She wondered what they were saying about her, up at the top of the house, as she undressed and laid her clothes out before sliding under the duvet in her underwear. Kind things, she hoped. It wasn't only because she didn't want to trail damage amongst those who'd helped her; partly it was that calculating element in her mind again, that perpetual level of awareness that was tuned to seek out and recognise any opportunity that she could take to keep her in the game and moving.

Just like a shark, she thought for the second time that night, and the image didn't entirely displease her.

She hadn't switched off the light. But now she felt too good to move. She'd stir in a while, before she fell asleep.

She thought about Christine.

She wondered where she was. If she was watching, and whether she'd seen Lucy's progress. Her dark sister, the unquiet spirit, everyone's back turned against her but Lucy's. Perhaps, if she waited for a while, Christine might come to her again.

And, still waiting, she drifted into sleep with the light undimmed.

TWENTY-FIVE

Joe Lucas' new room was hardly better than his first. It overlooked the street, it was too hot, and the people on the other side of the wall had been watching the hotel's cable channel late and loud so that he'd had to go around and hammer on their door. The door hadn't opened, but there hadn't been another sound out of them for the rest of the night.

It hadn't made any difference.

Even before it was light, he dressed and went out. The last couple of days had been mild, but at this hour there was no mistaking the imminence of winter. He could feel its bite. He wandered around the streets in the heart of the city, past darkened buildings with odd floors of offices lit, ready, and empty. What life he saw, was all at street level; dawn risers moving stiffly, holding carry-out coffees from early-morning takeaways with the delicacy of rare isotopes. Most of the store windows were already given over to Christmas displays in silver and white, whilst around behind his hotel, down-and-outs were sleeping over hot air vents in the pavement. Outside a big store on Regent Street he saw an elderly woman hurriedly changing old clothes in a doorway.

Back in the hotel's dancehall-sized breakfast room, he sat alone amongst a couple of hundred empty tables. In about an hour they'd be forming lines in the lobby outside, but for now he had the buffet almost to himself. It was a pity that he didn't have much of an appetite. His bruises were fading, and no longer such a problem; the problems lay elsewhere.

Afterwards he went upstairs, hung out the *Do Not Disturb* sign, and lay watching *Sesame Street* until the world outside had come fully into life.

He had a few contacts in the Metropolitan force. He'd attended courses, and on a couple of occasions he'd travelled down with another officer to collect prisoners. It hardly made him a frequent visitor, but it gave him a few numbers to ring. When he started phoning around, he played it straight in every respect apart from one. He let everyone think that he was calling from his own area, and not from the middle of their territory.

'No, nothing specific on the cards,' he'd tell them. 'It's just background I need at the moment.'

Most of what he heard he already knew, but still he made notes.

They weren't encouraging.

Young kids, some of them not even teenagers, were arriving all the time, mostly for reasons that they hadn't thought through or couldn't express. The juveniles could be brought into a place of safety and passed along to one of the agencies for intensive counselling, but the rest of them – those over eighteen, and who were neither obviously offending nor mentally ill – were free agents. Mostly they'd make for the West End and meet others like themselves; they'd pick up survival information, get oriented within the subculture that they'd entered, and learn where the free food could be picked up. They'd haunt the alleys behind bakeries, they'd help themselves from uncollected deliveries, they'd stick around on the embankment for midnight handouts from the Salvation Army and the Krishna Temple. Some slept rough, the more streetwise would find their way onto somebody's floor or into a squat . . . Hackney or Lewisham, somewhere not too far out. They never went too far out. The centre of town seemed to draw them back like a magnet.

Certain doors stood open, particularly for the girls. It might take a while for the contacts to happen, but they'd happen. Drugs were a bigger hazard than sex. Hostess work in some of the clubs involved little more than chiselling money out of tourists for fake champagne, and the money that changed hands for street assignations almost invariably led to an instant disappearance with no follow-through. But hang out for long enough, and something illegal was bound to be made available. Most of the kids would be pretty unworldly, and unequipped to deal with what was on offer. They'd see a free sample and a temporary escape, and only later would the outlines of the cage become apparent. That was how many of them got into the peep shows, selling off their self-respect in order to finance their habit.

After Joe had hung up, he stared at the window for a while. He heard the housekeeper's cart go by outside the room.

Then he called Jack Ashdown.

'Jack,' he said, 'it's me.'

'I tried to get you. Line was busy. Any news?'

'Nothing since last night. Has she called you?'

'Not yet.'

'That's it, then,' Joe said, and he lay back on the bed with the receiver to his ear and the handset held on his chest. 'She's got her money, what does she care? We'll hear nothing until it runs out, and then she'll put the tap on you again. God knows when that will be.'

120

'She's not like that, Joe. She's not a bad kid.'

'No?' Joe said. He'd been beaten up, lied to, and left flat on his back in the Underground. He reckoned he'd earned the right to be cynical.

'No, she's just obsessed. She promised that she'd keep in touch and I know that she will.'

'All right, Jack, point taken. But look at it from my angle. I'm on the spot, here, and I'm making no progress. You've got to give me something to work with.'

'I won't set her up in another trap. One time was once too often. There's got to be some trust involved.'

'Christ, Jack, whose side are you on?'

'I didn't know it was a matter of taking sides, Joe,' Ashdown said with a gentleness that was almost a reprimand.

Joe held back his anger. It wouldn't help. 'Do one thing,' he said. 'If she calls you again, persuade her to meet me somewhere.'

Now it was Ashdown's turn to be disbelieving. 'I can see her going for that,' he said.

'Persuade her, Jack. It'll be above-board, the whole thing. She can pick the time, the place, she can set it up however she wants. I'll talk to her and we'll try to work something out.'

'What if she won't?'

'You'd better make sure that she does, Jack. You're not doing it for me, you're doing it for her. She's so damned intent on following in Chrissie's footsteps . . . do you want to see her end up in a box, as well?'

'There's no call for that kind of talk,' Ashdown said, clearly hurt, but Joe didn't back off.

'No?' he said. 'You ought to be where I am. You ought to hear what I've been hearing. If you really don't think she's in any danger, then I don't know what else I can say to you.'

There was silence on the line.

Then Ashdown said, 'I'll try.'

'Trying's not good enough,' Joe said. 'Do it. I'll call again later.'

And then he hung up.

TWENTY-SIX

Lucy crawled out of bed around lunchtime, found her way up to the shower while Josie could be heard moving around in the kitchen, and couldn't resist leaving aside her own hard soap and super-market shampoo in order to freeload a few squirts and squeezes of the gels, mousses and lotions that stood on the tiled windowsill. The bathroom was tiny, but well-designed. Her last bathroom back in the squat had been mouldy, iced-up in winter, and mostly decorated with the husks of dead bugs in spiderwebs. Water would some-times come through the one working tap and when it ran, it ran brown.

Josie was alone in the kitchen, reading a trade newspaper at the breakfast bar over a glass of hot lemon juice and some wholemeal toast. She'd said something about being careful with her blood sugar; nothing as serious as diabetes, but something she had to watch. Lucy reckoned that it was just some middle-aged woman's thing, and left it at that. Josie waved toward the refrigerator and Lucy took her at her word, beginning with a plate of leftover ham. Until Charlie paid her at the end of the week, Lucy would again be in her usual flat-broke condition.

Josie's mood seemed okay, which suggested to Lucy that any problems that her presence may have caused must now have been smoothed over. The woman that she'd seen last night at the top of the stairs was nowhere around, and Lucy knew better than to ask. At a guess, she owned the house. Beyond that, it would be tactless to enquire.

Over the countertop, Lucy said, 'Did you ever know where Christine lived?'

That look, over the glasses. 'Didn't she tell you?'

'You know how it is. Unless you're familiar with a place, the name means nothing. She probably told me and it didn't stick. I'd never been to London then.'

'Whereas now,' Josie said with the trace of a smile, 'you're an old hand.'

'Right.'

'Well,' Josie said, turning her page and then refolding the newspaper to keep it manageable, 'I couldn't tell you for sure. It wasn't cheap, though, I remember that.'

'I didn't realise Charlie paid so well.'

'Charlie pays as little as he can get away with. Look, I've arranged for you to stay with us a while longer. But do me a favour. Don't be tempted to look on it as anything permanent.'

This was a better start to the day than even Lucy could have hoped. She said, 'That's great, Josie. Thanks. And don't worry.'

Lucy spent most of the next couple of hours in the ground-floor utility room just behind the room where she'd slept, sitting on the tiles against the wall and reading back numbers of magazines while her washing tumbled around in the Zanussi. Her fringe had a tendency to fall over her eyes, and she had to keep blowing at it to knock it aside. Tonight she'd try to find out which, if any, of the other employees had been working at the club when Christine had been there. Also, she wondered if the taxi firms kept any kind of record of their more regular late-night destinations; if she had to rely on drivers' memories then there wouldn't be much hope, since on the evidence of the previous night they'd mostly be part-timers with a high turnover.

They set out for the club toward the end of the afternoon. Josie said that she didn't usually get in until around six, but that there were a few extra jobs that she wanted to finish off; Lucy had the feeling, but didn't say so, that the main point of the exercise was probably to get her out of the way before the slender red-haired woman arrived home.

If that was the case, she didn't mind. Whatever they had going, it was their business and none of hers, and if it wouldn't lead her toward Christine then she wasn't even interested.

(And then she thought, But how do I know that for sure? How well had she known her sister in adult life, after all? And with the vague, uneasy sense that, having forced the door open a little way, the country on the other side might prove a lot stranger than she'd ever imagined, she walked on in subdued silence for a while.)

But the silence didn't last.

Out through the archway at the end of the mews, a couple of turns, and Josie told her that they were on Harley Street. Harley Street, the Mecca of big-money medicine. To Lucy it looked drab and overdone, lined with cars bumper-to-bumper like every other London street that she'd seen since she arrived. The only difference was that many of the cars were big limousines, in contrast to the bikes and the pieces of bikes chained to railings that were her last, hazy recollection of the hospital. She spotted a couple of receptionists in designer whites, coats slung around their shoulders against the chance of a late-afternoon shower; and then, because she was looking more closely now, she spotted a couple of doctors in conversation on the steps before their town house offices. They *had* to be doctors. They wore expensive suits and had the general air of men who'd found the secret key to the money pump and were cranking its handle for all they were worth.

Now they were crossing Oxford Street, according to Josie. The distant city of Lucy's dreams was becoming steadily demystified. She felt an unaccountable sense of loss.

'Boyfriend?' Josie said when Lucy returned from the pay phone at the end of the corridor. They were midway through the first show and just about everyone was out on stage, giving ten minutes of comparative quiet before another storm of quick-changes and running repairs. Just enough time for a reverse-charge call, and an excuse for getting away if the conversation began to get awkward.

'My dad,' Lucy said.

'I'll bet he's worried about you.'

'I told him not to.'

'Yeah,' Josie said disbelievingly, 'and that'll make all the difference in the world. Does he know where you are?'

'Not exactly,' Lucy said evasively. 'He doesn't much approve of what I'm doing.'

'Working backstage in a tit show? Now what on earth could be wrong with that?'

'I don't mean this. I mean being on my own, travelling down here the way that I did. He sits thinking about everything that could go wrong and I suppose it just eats him up.'

'The man is no fool.'

'I know he isn't. But neither am I.' Lucy sat on one of the big property baskets. It was old and well-worn, and it creaked under her weight. 'He wants me to meet somebody and I'm not sure I should.'

'Why not?'

'Because the last time I did, he tried to drag me home. I'll go home someday . . . but in my own time. And not like that. What do you think I should do?'

Josie fluffed out some of the tail-feathers on a costume for the upcoming number, and gave the matter some thought. Without actually giving her the details – and still keeping back the crucial fact of Christine's death, which would have changed the tone of their conversations completely – Lucy had been able to give Josie some idea of her home situation and of the problems that she'd caused with actions that she'd felt to be right. Working closely as they were, it was almost inevitable. But consideration apart, Josie's answer was the one that she'd probably have given anyway.

'If it was me,' she said, 'I'd meet whoever he asked me to. You're giving him a tough time, it's not fair to make it tougher. Pick somewhere public and stay out of his reach, if you're worried about being forced. But I don't know why I'm telling you this, because you're going to do exactly what you want to anyway.'

Lucy's first reaction to her father's pleading had been *No chance*. More than anything, she remembered her feeling of helplessness, the total loss of control, as Joe had dragged her along toward the station. And yet . . .

And yet, even though her father had talked to her like one adult to another, as if at last he was ready to acknowledge that she'd grown up and was making her own decisions, she'd sensed the undercurrent of despair in what he was saying. She didn't know how to make him understand that, in a sense, she was doing this partly for him. The last thing that she wanted to do was to add to his pain. But how could she make him aware of that, let him hear from someone else how well she was doing, without putting herself at risk again from Joe?

It was too risky. She wouldn't consider it.

And as the house playback signalled the end of the number, she picked up a pen and some scrap paper and went out to collect orders for interval food and coffee. It had been a forgotten tradition, but Lucy's availability had revived it.

She'd made her decision.

So now she had to stop thinking about it.

TWENTY-SEVEN

Lucy wasn't entirely sure what to make of Josie. In years she was senior to everyone including the infrequently seen Charlie; as mother hen to the dancing girls she'd taken Lucy in and allowed her to feel at home in a matter of hours. She'd even given her a bed in her own place, brought her in like a waif from the streets in a gesture of stern and unsentimental charity. Hadn't given her a key, but Lucy supposed that there were limits. She talked freely, didn't treat Lucy like a child, and told her stories of old times in long-forgotten venues.

But something was being held back. It wasn't just some inevitable reserve because of the age difference, and it wasn't just that she was an intensely private person whose public persona didn't tell the whole story. Lucy knew it because whenever she started to talk about Christine, she'd realise after a couple of minutes that they'd moved on and were now talking about something else.

As time went by, she grew more certain. Josie knew more about Christine than she was saying. Ask the wrong questions or apply the wrong kind of pressure, and she'd close up like a clam; Lucy only wished that she could have more of the patience required to play a waiting game.

After she'd returned with the coffee shop order and sorted out everybody's change, Josie said to her, 'Take a seat in the chair.'

'Why?'

'If you flick your hair out of your eyes once more, I'll scream. Who cut it for you?'

'I did,' Lucy said, neglecting to add that the job had been performed in front of a dusty mirror with rusting scissors and in the worst kind of light imaginable.

Josie said, 'The term that springs to mind is "self-inflicted". Get in the chair, and I'll tidy it up.'

Josie switched on the lights for the department's makeup mirror, and Lucy winced as the brightness hit her. She sat in the chair, and Josie slung a nylon barber's gown around her.

Lucy said, 'Have you done hairdressing?'

'I've done a bit of just about everything there is,' Josie said, lifting sections of Lucy's hair and watching to see how it fell. Then she took out a comb, and began to set it into some kind of order.

Lucy, resisting the temptation to blow at her fringe, said, 'You sound like you've had a great life.'

'You think so?'

'Yeah. All your stories.'

'There's some old Chinese curse about living through interesting times, isn't there? The best stories always come from the worst experiences.'

'But say you had to do it all over again. What would you change?'

Josie laid down her comb, and picked up a couple of big plastic clips from a box on the makeup table. 'I'd probably do everything exactly the same. But I wouldn't go and see *Ziegfeld*.'

She swept back a handful of Lucy's hair and pinned it up, first on one side and then on the other; but before she'd reached for the scissors to begin, Charlie's face appeared around the doorway.

'Josie?' he said. 'Got a minute?'

Then he disappeared.

Moving around her, Josie said, 'Don't mess about with this. It's all kind of raggy, but I think I can get it to look like a hairstyle again.' And then, leaving Lucy in the chair with the gown around her, she followed Charlie.

Lucy gave it a moment, tugged the gown free from underneath, and then moved in silence to the doorway.

They'd gone into Charlie's office, at the end of the corridor. He'd closed the door behind them, but he hadn't closed it all the way. It stood open about an inch. Lucy glanced back. No-one was watching.

She moved closer, and tried to listen.

'If it's a problem,' Charlie was saying, *'get the kid to lend you a hand.'*

'It's no problem,' she heard Josie say. *'And I want her left out of it.'*

And that was all she heard, because abruptly the door began to open.

Lucy scooted back to Wardrobe, dived into the chair, and fumbled with the gown to get it tied. She was panicky and totally unco-ordinated. Josie walked in before she'd finished.

'Too tight?' she said.

And Lucy said, 'A little.'

So then Josie retied the gown, and said, 'Now it's decision time. Do we go with the black roots, or the bleach job?'

Lucy looked at her own face in the mirror.

'I want it how Chrissie had hers,' she said.

Spooky.

Lucy stared at herself in the mirror. Something like this had happened to her once before, but now the feeling was even stronger. It would take only a minor leap of faith, a moment of transcendence, to believe that Christine Ashdown stared back. Younger, perhaps, and less well travelled, but there in all her essential details. Josie seemed to sense it, too.

But she turned away.

'That's about as much as I can salvage,' she said.

'It looks great,' Lucy said. 'Thanks.'

Josie glanced back over her shoulder, not at the mirror but at Lucy herself. 'Yeah,' she said. 'It doesn't look too bad. Listen, do you want to knock off early tonight?'

'We'll have all the stuff to put away.'

'I managed on my own before you came along, madam,' Josie said, not really offended but acting the part. 'And I've got to stick around and do a couple of things.'

'How will I get in?'

She hesitated.

'I'll give you the key,' she said. 'And I'll phone Pamela to tell her what's happening. Don't worry, you probably won't even see her.'

'Whatever you say.'

Josie rummaged in her oversized handbag, finally bringing out a set of keys on a ring. She fiddled around for a while, and cursed and muttered before she managed to get one detached. Lucy waited patiently. She'd feel awkward, alone in the house with this strange other woman who tolerated her presence at best and to whom she hadn't spoken, but she'd handled worse. The little that she'd been able to piece together was that Pamela was a barrister, that the house did, as Lucy had suspected, belong to her, and that she and Josie had been together for at least five years and probably longer.

Josie held out the key.

'I'm trusting you, now,' she said.

'I know,' Lucy said. 'Thanks.'

And all that she could think about was, why did Josie want her out of the way?

Shortly after midnight, Josie handed Lucy her taxi fare and told her to scram. Lucy collected her stuff together and put on her coat and said goodnight, but she didn't leave. Once out of Josie's sight, she turned and pushed her way through the double blackout doors leading directly into the backstage area. Non-performers were supposed to stay out, but as far as she could tell nobody paid the rule much heed.

This was great. You could see everything that wasn't visible out front; the braced wooden frames of the canvas flats, the angle irons and stage weights that held everything in place, the fact that the ceiling was hollow and the space went on up to about another fifteen feet above, the gap crossed by a catwalk and a lot of cabling. The sound system's speakers were like upended steamer trunks, one on top of another; standing so close, the volume gave her a sensation in her ears like that of tearing paper and she experienced a few moments of sensory overload before she recognised the tune as *New York, New York*. Behind the golden curtain was a four-foot gap, and then the back wall of the basement. It was kind of exciting to realise that another three strides would put her out in front of everybody, almost like looking over a low rail at a mile-long drop.

Someone waited in the wings. One of the artistes, as she'd heard Charlie call them. She seemed to sense Lucy's presence, and turned her head to look; then she smiled, and Lucy's uncertainty diminished. The girl's name, according to the house advertising, was Coco Wunderbar, but everyone in the dressing rooms called her Jeanette.

Lucy found herself mouthing like a mill worker to make herself understood over the noise, which was louder than any machinery.

'Am I okay, here?' she said, and Coco/Jeanette said, 'Sure,' and pointed to a place alongside her where Lucy could stand and see a part of the performance without any risk of being seen or getting in the way.

They stood together, watching the New York routine for a while. Top hats and canes, spangles, lots of high-stepping. The dancers, from what Lucy had seen, were all pretty good in their way; she'd even begun to develop a liking for Maurice, who'd winked at her in the corridor earlier. It was the show itself that was garbage. She couldn't see much of it because the thrust stage ran onward out of sight . . . but you didn't have to down the entire egg to know that it was rotten. Nobody could remember who'd staged it originally; none of the originals were left.

Jeanette leaned toward her and said close to her ear, 'You're Chrissie Ashdown's sister, aren't you?'

Lucy's eyes widened, but she tried not to betray her surprise.

'Can you tell?'

'You look just like her.'

Something in Lucy's heart warmed. 'Did you know her well?'

Jeanette shrugged. 'You know how it is. She had a life outside. We all have.'

They watched for a while longer. Or rather, Lucy pretended to watch as her mind raced. She was seeking the next angle, the next approach, knowing that she'd have at the most a couple of minutes to make her pitch.

She said, 'How did you get into this?'

'Usual way,' Jeanette said. 'Ads and auditions. It's just another dancing job. Worse than some, better than most.'

'I couldn't do it.'

Jeanette smiled. 'It's only showbiz. It comes off with the makeup.'

'No, I mean, I couldn't *do* it. I'm the worst dancer in the world.'

Jeanette gave her a quick once-over. 'You've got a good body.'

'Until I move it around.'

And that was as far as she got because the crash-bang music gave the final crash, the stage lights held for a moment and then cut to blackout, and there was a smattering of couldn't-care-less applause from the front of the house. A tiny green bulb winked on, wired to the back of the flat at eye level, and Jeanette McArdle became Coco Wunderbar and stepped out into the darkness.

Lucy was left alone. After a few moments, the dancers from the previous number could be seen filing out from behind the golden curtain, having exited on the far side of the stage; their faces were slack and tired, their breathing hard. Apart from their costumes and the props that they carried, they might have been factory workers anywhere.

The next number was starting. There was a spyhole in one of the flats. Lucy had to stand on tiptoe to use it, but when she did it gave her a partial view of the clientele at their tables. Most of them were watching. Some of them weren't. Almost all of them probably had something else on their minds.

Lucy didn't think of herself as deep. She'd certainly never reflected on the nature of performance before. She'd gone through all the usual phases; rock fan magazines, writing to film stars, sometimes getting back a photo with a printed signature, usually not. But here, for the first time, she realised something essential, something that had never occurred to her when composing those letters; that a performance was something that a person did, and not something that they were.

But not to the faces out there, on the wrong side of the lights. She'd crossed over, they hadn't. She looked at them, and saw dupes. Happy in their illusions, probably, but dupes all the same.

When the show finally ended and the house lights came up, Lucy found herself a backstage corner and waited for a while longer. Out on the dance floor, the evening ended with disco music and strobe lighting. The reflections flickered on her like a distant storm.

And then, when she felt that she'd waited long enough, she quietly made her way back toward the dressing rooms.

She'd almost mistimed. Many of the dancers were already showered and changed and out of the building. Two of the dressing rooms stood empty but the door to Wardrobe had been closed.

She could hear voices in there, one of them Charlie's. But this time the door had been closed all the way, and she couldn't make out what was being said. She retreated to one of the dressing rooms across the corridor, switched off the lights, and set the door to give her an angle of view without much risk of being seen.

Again, she waited.

And about ten minutes later, the door opened. Charlie came out first. Someone came out behind him, but Charlie was blocking her. He was turning to speak to the other person, who appeared to be wearing an evening gown; as her hand moved, there was a glint of dress jewellery. Way in the background, Lucy could see Josie with her back to the door as she cleaned up around the makeup chair.

The woman said, 'Who pays the taxi?'

And Charlie said, 'The taxi's taken care of, don't worry about it. Just watch out for the dress and don't get it damaged.'

Charlie moved on. The woman followed.

For a moment Lucy had thought that it was Jeanette McArdle, but then she realised that it wasn't. She'd seen Jeanette close-to, and she'd seen her scrubbed clean and ready for home. This woman was broadly similar, that was all. Mistakeable at a distance, but only then.

'Who am I tonight?' Lucy heard her say. She barely sounded interested.

Charlie's voice was dwindling down the corridor.

'He'll call you Coco,' he said.

```
**********
FOR SALE
**********

Ibanez Roadshow Bass Guitar. With amp and
practice speaker. Genuine reason
for sale. Gary, Box 24.
```

TWENTY-EIGHT

It was two days later at eleven in the morning, and Soho Square wasn't anything like as crowded as Lucy might have hoped. For a while she hovered in the doorway of a film company building and watched the steady but sparse traffic of shoppers, office messengers and business types who were using the pathways through the square's railed park as a shortcut on their way to somewhere else . . . but then a gold-braided security guard stepped out and asked if he could help her, and it was clear that she was being told to move on.

She was nervous. There were plenty of gates and there were numerous ways out of the square, and the park itself was barely a couple of hundred yards across; just another backstreet pigeon trap with no feature other than a strange half-timbered lodge near its centre to make it unique, but still she hesitated to enter. Her choice of ground, no chance of surprise . . .

But still she hesitated.

Joe Lucas was waiting by the lodge, around on the other side. He saw her walking toward him, but he didn't move. When she stopped, it was with a distance of at least ten feet between them. Call it a safety zone, she thought. Joe noted her caution, and nodded. He didn't seem offended, he didn't exactly appear contrite. But he seemed different.

'Hi,' he said.

'This is as close as I want to get, Joe.'

'Understood,' he said. 'I want to apologise.'

'For what?'

'Grabbing you like I did. It was entirely wrong. All I can say is that it was for the best of reasons.'

She studied him, warily. There was no mistaking his sincerity. She said, cautiously, 'I can see that.'

'It won't happen again,' he said. 'All I want to do now is talk.'

'What about?'

'You. Your sister. Where we go from here.'

'I'm not going anywhere until I find out what happened, Joe,' she warned him, but he was already nodding in agreement.

'Maybe we can work together on that,' he said. 'Whatever you

134

may think, I'm really not against you. And . . .' he looked down at the ground, as if he'd suddenly become embarrassed. 'I think you probably know how I felt about Christine.'

She didn't know what to say. But Joe didn't let the remark hang, as if it was something that he'd felt compelled to let her know but didn't want to discuss any further; he said, 'Are we going to stay here, or move somewhere warmer? Your choice.'

Her intention had been to move nowhere – that everything necessary would be said here, and then she'd back off and disappear faster than Joe could follow. But so much seemed to have changed . . . and Joe would make a much better ally than an enemy, if only he could accept the situation as it stood.

Also it wasn't exactly pleasant right here, with a November sharpness in the air that had arrived almost as a response to the Christmas lights and store displays that were just about everywhere now. So she said, 'We can go somewhere. But you don't touch me, you don't even come near me. And if you start to talk about me giving up and coming home with you, it ends right there.'

'Agreed,' Joe said, and held up his hands as if to say, *See, no deception . . . would I lie to you?* Lucy, still wary, watched him for a moment longer.

After what had happened last time, he'd need to earn her trust before he could assume it.

But this was a start.

Soho at this hour was an area of delivery vans, and of pavements that were wet with hosing-down. Cold as it was, the sun was shining weakly. Conversation was difficult because she walked several yards behind Joe, and always crossed the street at least two cars' lengths away. Joe indicated a corner pub, newly opened-up for the day's business, and asked her if this would be okay. She looked it over, saw that it had at least two exits, and gave him a cautious yes.

Even then, there was a moment in the doorway when he could have reached her. He'd slowed to step around some soft drinks crates – the bar, although open, seemed only half-ready for business – and their arms almost touched as she came up behind him without realising. Her eyes were still adjusting from the brightness outside and she felt a surge of panic at her mistake, but he did nothing. He didn't even seem to have noticed the opportunity.

And so, relaxing her guard just a little, she followed him inside.

Somebody must have forgotten to lock a window one night, and designers had managed to get in. Now the interior was all of artificially roughened timber, raw beams and panelling with a sawdust-covered floor, and the lights were piss-coloured imitation gas lamps that were almost too dim to see by. Joe winced at the look of it. Lucy thought that it looked fine.

They sat at a corner table, a slab of mahogany on an iron base that had once belonged to a Singer sewing machine. Joe toyed absently with the rail around its edge as they talked. He was starting to appear distinctly shopworn, Lucy noted; he seemed to have bought himself a new shirt, but a dip-through in a hotel washbasin didn't exactly make for the best possible finish. His clothes were all out of shape, and so was he.

'You were right about what happened to her,' he admitted. 'I don't know why I held out for so long.'

This wasn't easy for him, she could see. 'It's not the kind of thing you'd want to be true,' she said.

'I'll set wheels in motion,' he promised. 'Get someone to look at the new evidence you turned up. If that happens, *then* will you consider coming home?'

'Perhaps,' she said.

He gripped the rail, so hard it must have hurt. 'I don't know what I can tell you,' he said. 'I'm not making any promises that I know won't be kept. All I can say is, I'll do my best. Even if it means hauling in every driver in the country.'

'It's nothing to do with the lorry drivers now, Joe.'

He looked up, sharply. 'Why? What else do you know?'

'I've found out where she worked. I've met some of the people she worked with. That's what I've been doing over the last few days.'

He sat back. 'Where?'

'I don't want to tell you right now.'

He started to protest, but then he seemed to remember his promise and made a conscious effort to stop himself.

And he simply said, 'You're making a mistake.'

'I don't think I am,' she said. 'There's something more to it, but I still don't know what. I've got to move *so* carefully here, Joe. But if you could see how it's going, I think you'd be proud of me.'

He managed a half-smile, and moved to put his hands over hers.

She flinched. But she let him.

'I'm sure I would,' he said, and she felt almost overcome by a tide of relief because it was all right, at last he understood . . . and then he took his two hands away from hers on the table, and his smile and his entire attitude dropped away like a paper mask.

She looked down at the white plastic loop that now bound her wrist to the brass rail on the table. He'd secured her with practised ease, and so fast that she hadn't even been aware of it happening. He'd used a disposable handcuff on her, a simple self-locking noose that was tough, effective, and impossible to break.

136

'Joe!' she said. 'You promised!'

'That's exactly your problem,' he said, rising. 'You'll believe any old bullshit if it's what you want to hear.'

Leaving her safely tethered, he walked over toward the main door. As he passed the bar he briefly held up what Lucy assumed must be his warrant card. The landlady, a woman in late middle age with a beehive hairdo and a face like fallen stone, gave no reaction, and Joe stepped out into the street and raised his arm for a taxi. One went by, he looked for another.

'Oh, Joe,' Lucy said sadly as she drew out Chrissie's knife and, holding it away from herself, released the blade. One spring-driven second later she'd cut herself free, and two seconds after that she was showing her heels at the side door. Joe was still out on the street at the other end of the bar, arm still raised, already way out of date.

She could almost feel sorry for him, the way that everybody felt sorry for the coyote in the *Roadrunner* cartoons; so singleminded, and with a lack of perspective that was spectacular. She wanted to hand him a killer, he still wanted to play dogcatcher.

Well, he'd had his chances.

She glanced back just as she was about to turn a corner, and saw Joe as he came hurtling out of the side-exit. She hadn't picked up as much of a lead as she'd thought.

And he must have done some healing, because he was no longer moving so slowly.

Lucy broke into a run. They'd moved away from the office district and she was now in an area of sandwich shops, electrical stores and ticket agencies where the traffic was heavier and the pavement crowds more dense. She ran, she dodged, she took a quick look behind her. Joe was scattering people like a runaway truck. Finally she dived through the alley by the Revuebar and into the market on Berwick Street, a drab thoroughfare enlivened by a sudden riot of colour in the narrow sunlight that came slanting down between the buildings – the yellow awnings over the stalls, the bright shades of new fruit, the brilliant white of new cardboard.

And the noise. Dire Straits pounding from a stallholder's ghetto-blaster against strong competition from the shopfronts lining the street. She was hit by the unique scent of the market; powerful, sweet, aromatic.

Joe was still behind her, but Lucy was smaller and she was fast. There wasn't much space along here, and he could no longer rely on people taking one look and then getting out of his way because there was nowhere for them to go. And there was plenty of crap strewn all over the pavement, so he had to be more careful. She could glance back and see him, bobbing his way through a sea of heads. As soon as she saw him look down, she made a sideways dive between a couple of stalls and crossed to the opposite side of the street.

There, she doubled back. From a place of comparative safety she was able to observe as Joe pushed his way onward, unaware of her move. She waited until he was lost from sight, and lifted an apple when the stallholder wasn't looking.

Poor Joe, chasing a wraith.

But unlike Lucy, with no prospect of success.

Twenty-Nine

That evening, she waited until Charlie was in his office and then presented herself in the doorway. He was working through some papers. Lucy reckoned that, for the man in charge, he had some staggeringly dull tasks to handle; she'd seen him in the stockroom once, counting every bottle in every crate of tonic water. Charlie was an employee like everyone else, but in the absence of the owners he was the man at the top . . . all the responsibility, almost none of the rakeoff. Every now and again – or so she'd been told – the owners would call in the books. And as long as Charlie had no particular desire to lie flat and be fed through a tube, it was in his interests to see that these were watertight.

He saw her in the doorway, and said, 'What are you hanging around for?'

'It's the end of the week,' she said. 'You promised you'd pay me.'

'Come on in,' he said, and he drew a bunch of keys across the desk and sorted out the smallest. 'Close the door behind you.'

She did as he said, and took the spare seat without waiting to be asked. He unlocked one of the desk drawers, and brought out a battered tin cashbox.

'Okay, what are you worth?' he said.

'More than you can afford.'

Charlie grinned. Nothing she'd care to trust too far, but it made the atmosphere a lot easier than the last time she'd been in here with the door closed. 'You're all right,' he said. 'You know that?'

'Thanks.'

'I mean it. Especially after the way you worked your way in here. That routine with the coffees, it was pretty good. Shows quick thinking. Flexibility.'

'If you're a kid, people sometimes think you've got nothing going for you.'

'Who says you're a kid?'

'Well, that's what they used to say.'

From the cashbox he took a bundle of notes, and tossed them for her to catch. She didn't miss. It wasn't a particularly fat bundle, but it was still money.

'Aren't you going to count it?' he said.

'Will that get me any more?'

'Not a cent. We're talking petty cash, I'll pay you what I can justify without having to explain it away. But it's strictly smalltime. I get the feeling you're more ambitious than that.'

Lucy shrugged, said nothing. The atmosphere had suddenly changed in the windowless little room, and she was interested to know why.

Charlie said, 'You told me you wanted the same kind of deal that Chrissie had. Were you serious?'

'Of course I was.'

He nodded, watching her. 'You *do* know what I'm talking about?'

'We've always been close,' she lied. 'We've never had secrets.'

'What about experience?'

'I get by.'

'Getting by's not good enough in a game like this. You're either a hundred per cent into it, or let's forget the whole thing.'

'Don't worry about me, Charlie,' she said, wondering for how much longer she could stall around the subject without letting something slip and betraying her ignorance, and hoping that Charlie would give her some further clue. 'Just tell me what you want me to do.'

'Well,' he said, 'I've been let down for tonight. It's a problem, but it doesn't have to be a disaster – that could depend on you.' And he turned away from her to face his desk again, as if everything had been settled for the moment.

Lucy stood, pushing back the chair.

'Stick around later,' Charlie said. 'I'll talk to Josie.'

The rest of the evening was like a ten-year sentence that raced by her in moments; a sense of endless time that ended far too soon. She coasted through it as if dreaming, buoyed by a strange mixture of anticipation and dread. Josie looked at her strangely a couple of times, and asked her if she felt ill. She was having to repeat herself, and even then Lucy was picking up the wrong costume or completely mistaking what had been said.

'Just got some stuff on my mind,' she told Josie, and Josie didn't press her further. Kid stuff, she probably thought. Romance and froth.

When Lucy went around the dressing rooms picking up after the final number, her hands shook.

Charlie had stopped by to speak to Josie as he'd said he would, but Lucy hadn't been present at the time. She'd seen him coming out, but he hadn't noticed her. Josie's behaviour toward her didn't change after that, but again she told her to go home early with the house key and her taxi fare. Lucy could only conclude that, whatever Charlie had been saying, it hadn't included specific mention of her name.

He stopped her in the corridor, and told her what to do.

When most of the dancers had set off for home, and Lucy had given Josie reason to assume that she'd done the same, she sat in one of the empty offices for a while and then returned to the wardrobe department.

Josie was laying out makeup brushes on the table, and didn't look up as Lucy stepped inside and half-closed the door behind her. Alongside the mirror Josie had hung out an evening gown, long and slinky and black as a panther.

'Take a seat,' Josie said. 'I'll be with you in a second. Have you ever worn the dress before?'

'No,' Lucy said, and Josie reacted to the sound as if caught by the tip of a lash.

She straightened, and turned.

'Tell me this isn't true,' she said stonily.

'What's the matter?' Lucy said.

Josie went around behind her, and closed the door fully. 'Are you mad?' she half-whispered with considerable force, and from close enough to make Lucy flinch. 'Charlie said he'd found a substitute, but he never said it was you.'

'I volunteered,' Lucy said meekly.

'Well, you can un-volunteer. Have you any idea what you're getting into, here?'

'I think it's a call-girl racket,' Lucy admitted. The phrase sounded strange and carried a number of echoes, mostly from half-remembered headlines in Sunday newspapers.

'You think? And what are you? You're a child.' Josie started to pace. 'Don't do this to me.'

'I've got to go through with it.'

'It isn't worth it.'

'Doesn't matter whether it's worth it or not. I still have to.'

'For what?' Josie demanded, turning. 'The money?'

'For personal reasons. This is what Christine was doing, isn't it?'

'Yes, but she didn't run straight in like this. At least she took some persuading.'

'That makes a difference?'

Josie tried to reach for some killer of an argument, a real zinger that she could pull out of the air and use to disarm all opposition.

But then she dropped into the makeup chair, all of the steam going out of her.

'No,' she said wearily. 'Nothing makes any difference in the end.' She looked up at Lucy. 'What would your father say?'

'He mustn't ever know. I'd kill anyone who told him.'

Josie looked into her eyes, and saw that this was something very close to the truth.

'You're not entirely beyond hope, then,' she said.

'I can look after myself.'

Josie shook her head, with a hint of a bitter smile. 'We all say that, and none of us really can.'

Lucy crouched down by the makeup chair. There was a suggestion of tears in the older woman's eyes. Lucy said, almost gently, 'Will you tell me how the setup works? There's some special angle, but I don't know what it is.'

'You're unbelievable,' Josie said.

'I'm asking you to give me credit for knowing what I'm doing, Josie. I'm asking you to accept that I've got reasons, and not to ask me what they are. I'll do whatever's necessary, but I'm nobody's fool. I'll come through because in here' – she touched her own chest, lightly – 'there's a piece of ice.'

Josie looked away.

'Why couldn't you just stay in the back of beyond?' she said.

'Will you tell me?'

Josie sighed. It was as if she were the child, cornered and reasoned into giving an explanation, and Lucy the teacher with all of the patience and the pressure working for her. If only she could see what an act it was, how scared Lucy was now feeling deep inside. Lucy wanted to tell her, but knew that this would be wrong. She'd lose her advantage, she'd lose her edge.

As always, she was alone.

'There's a house rule,' Josie said. 'The dancers don't mix with the clientele. They can't even meet their own boyfriends outside the club – they've got to go right outside the area. That's fine by them, they're professionals; they've worked for their Equity cards and they're a cut above the trash that sits out front. But sometimes, the trash drops a hint to a waiter. They'd really like to make it with a showgirl. That's where Charlie comes in.'

'How does he fix it?'

'The trash thinks he's getting a date with a dancer. Charlie's the house manager, who better to arrange it? Only, what he gets is one of Charlie's list of ringers, girls who look enough like the real thing to justify what he charges. And he charges a lot.'

'Does anyone ever catch on?'

'Never. It's fantasy, stage lights and stage makeup. What Charlie does is to extend the performance.'

'And it starts right here,' Lucy said, looking at the makeup mirror and seeing the two of them fixed and framed in its unforgiving light.

'Don't do it, Lucy,' Josie said quietly.

Lucy got to her feet.

'Do I put the dress on first, or after?' she said.

THIRTY

It had to be close to four in the morning. Lucy sat on the tiled floor of a shower cubicle in the bathroom of the most expensive-looking hotel suite that she'd ever seen, hugging her knees, shivering despite the temperature of the water that beat down upon her. She'd turned it as high and as hard as she could get it to go. The cubicle was narrow, and it made her feel safe. The bathroom door was locked from the inside. She'd been in here for at least fifteen minutes, maybe longer. She couldn't bring herself to move.

For the second time, there was a tentative tap on the door. Again, she pretended not to hear.

It was peaceful, under the rain. It helped her not to think too much. Unfortunately, it wasn't enough to stop her thinking completely. Great hunks of recent memory would break loose and surface, turning briefly before sinking again like the unclaimed wreckage of the soul. Charlie, leading her down to the trash and making the introduction (*'I know you've made plans now, and I feel kind of responsible so I talked to one of the other girls. I know you were so specific, but this is a fabulous kid and when I told her all about you, she just begged me to let her stop by and say hello.'*). The trash, getting ready to protest at this change in plans and then his jaw dropping at his first sight of Lucy; getting into the cab with him, knowing what she was doing but somehow feeling that she was watching it all from somewhere else. Looking into the taxi's vanity mirror. A stranger looking back. Then the hotel (*'Charlie sent us,'*) and the assistant manager drawing her to one side (*'I'm putting you in a suite for a couple of hours. It won't show up as a registration, so no phonecalls out and no calling reception or room service, either. You need anything, phone my office and nowhere else. I'll stop by every now and again and listen at the door, just in case there's any rough stuff. Ready?' And she'd nodded, her heart hammering in fear.*).

And then in the suite, scaring herself; not because she played her part badly, but because she played it so well. Even the small talk (*'How did I come to be in the show? The usual way. Ads and then*

144

auditions. There's nothing special about it, just another dancing job.').
And then . . .

It's only showbiz, she tried to tell herself. It comes off with the makeup.

And the water hammered down, and washed her and washed her, and why was it taking so long to make her clean?

He was tapping on the bathroom door again.

This time she reached up, and reduced the pressure a little so she'd be able to hear. 'What do you want?'

'*Are you all right?*' Even through the door, he sounded nervous and uncertain. He was young, dark, bookish-looking. He'd had small hands and flawless skin, very pale. He'd told her that his name was Russell. Even this was more than she'd wanted to know.

She said, 'Yes.'

'*I have to go.*'

She made no response. She didn't want to face him. If she could have wiped his memory as well as her own, she'd have done it without any hesitation, and at whatever cost.

He said, '*I've left something for you on the bedside table. I hope I can see you again.*'

'Speak to Charlie,' she heard herself saying, and turned up the pressure.

She stayed under the shower until she could feel nothing more.

And when at last she emerged, beaten and dull, it was to find that her sister was waiting.

Lucy stood in the bathroom doorway, wrapped in an oversized courtesy robe. Before her stretched the main room of the suite. She'd never before seen a carpet so thick that it showed vacuuming lines, like a lawn. Charlie obviously had some running arrangement with the night manager, getting the use of some part of the hotel that stood empty and could all be set straight again before morning. She'd wondered who'd handle that side of it – somehow she couldn't imagine the night manager himself with a housekeeping trolley piled high with sheets and towels.

By the light of a single dim bedside lamp, she saw Christine. Knew her immediately, even though her face was turned to the window and she was looking out. On the other side of the glass, an infinity of darkness made the window into a shadowy mirror. They were ten floors up, and the suite overlooked one of the big city parks.

'Hi, kid,' Christine said.

Lucy felt at a disadvantage. She was damp, she was sore from scrubbing with the shower mitt, her hair hung in rats' tails. She didn't have to ask if Christine knew what had been going on here. Of course she knew.

Lucy moved into the main room, barefoot on the carpet.

'How could you?' she said. 'How could you live like this?'

Christine half-turned then, and glanced at the room as if some ironic comment had presented itself in her mind; but instead she said, 'Anyone can do anything. It's just a matter of motivation. Look on the bright side, you're braver than I was.'

'How?'

'You had the nerve to go through with it. I didn't have the nerve not to. How do you feel?'

'Cheap and shitty.'

'Well, don't.' Now Christine turned to face her, and Lucy saw that she was angry. 'What about him? You think he feels soiled? You think he feels ashamed? I don't think so. I know what just happened, and it wasn't even any big deal. He probably paid a month's wages for tonight and look, he wasted most of it on the mattress. It changes nothing.'

'That's easy for you to say.'

'You think so?'

'Yeah, you're already dead.'

'Sorry you started?'

'I don't know,' Lucy admitted.

'But you're still going to carry on.'

Lucy's silence was her confirmation. Hate it as she might it would be harder to stop than to go on, almost like riding a tiger. She'd come so far, she'd given so much . . . and all of it would be meaningless without a final context of success.

She didn't care what happened to her, as long as she came through. It would be worth it in the end.

Wouldn't it?

'Listen,' Christine said. 'I'll always be here, you know that. If it's too much to handle, let me help. I did everything a sister could. I tried to talk you out of it but nothing worked. So let me do this for you instead. I'm as good as lost anyway, there's no further down for me to go.'

'I don't understand.'

Christine moved from the window. She seemed solid, she cast a shadow. The warm light of the bedside lamp softened her features, giving her a look as fresh and ageless as that of an angel. Lucy sat on the edge of the bed. Christine looked down on her.

'I've been your mission,' she said. 'Now you can be mine. There are some things that I can deal with better than you. I mean, you could *learn*, but I've been down that road and I don't want you to follow. If you still want to go on, then let's go on together.'

'Why don't you just tell me who killed you?' Lucy said.

But Christine only smiled, more enigmatic than a gallery of Mona Lisas.

'You figure that one out,' she said.

THIRTY-ONE

It was late in the morning, and Lucy was sitting on her fold-down bed with the curtains still drawn when Josie looked in. As far as Lucy could see she was dressed for going out, and her manner was grim.

'Coffee's in the kitchen if you want some,' she said. 'I expect you to be gone by the time I get back.'

Lucy stared at her, uncomprehending. She was still in her night things, and somehow didn't seem able to make the simplest connections in her mind; right hand hugging her left elbow, she'd been rocking herself gently ever since she'd been wakened by the sounds of garage doors opening and cars being started in the mews outside her window. That had been hours ago. There seemed to be a blankness in her that prevented her from going any further; a momentary spark that said, *But wait . . .* and then said nothing more.

Josie seemed to sense that something was wrong.

'Are you all right?' she said, taking a hesitant step forward into the room.

'I'm all stiff and sore,' Lucy said, and then pulled down the shoulder of the oversized *Blues Brothers* T-shirt that she'd bought for sleeping in. 'And look, I'm scratched.' The scratches weren't much, but their unexpected presence was enough of a worry.

She looked up at Josie again. 'I can't remember what I did last night,' she said helplessly.

Josie took her upstairs, and sat her in the kitchen. Wherever Josie had been intending to go, the errand appeared to have been forgotten. She was still mad at Lucy for something, and Lucy was sure that a little time and concentration would tell her what . . . but for the moment, somehow, the knowledge was just out of reach.

Josie gave her a black coffee and then opened a kitchen drawer, bringing out bottles containing just about every prescription tranquilliser known to medical science. She checked the labels, shook her head, tossed the bottles back one at a time. In the end she settled on a stiff dose of Courvoisier brandy poured straight into Lucy's mug. Lucy nearly choked on the stuff, but kept it down.

148

Josie made her go through everything that she could remember, prompting wherever she could.

Some of the pieces came, some didn't. Some remained as gaps in the puzzle, suggestive in their outlines but mystifying in their detail.

'I've got this vague memory of the hotel,' she said after a while. 'And then later on, I remember talking to Christine but I don't know what about.'

'What did you do, phone her from the room?'

'I can't phone her,' Lucy said. 'She's dead.'

This had been a fact of Lucy's life for so long now that she'd almost lost her sense of its shock value, but Josie was hit by it head-on and without warning.

'What are you talking about?' she said.

'Sorry,' Lucy said belatedly. 'I forgot you didn't know.'

So then she had to explain the rest of it, from the beginning. She couldn't feel any direct effect from the brandy, but she felt looser and more able to talk.

Josie brought the bottle out again, and took a shot for herself.

'I know how it sounds,' Lucy said after a while. She'd left almost nothing out, although she'd downplayed Christine's reappearances. 'You think I'm losing my mind, but I'm not. It's just something that happens to me, I don't know why. Perhaps it's like she can't die for real, until someone's sorted it all out. And I'm the only one who's trying.'

There was a certain reserve in Josie's eyes that said Yeah, okay, let's leave the dead-walking issue to one side just for a moment. That was fine by Lucy. People could think what they liked about her mental state, as long as they didn't stand in her way.

Josie said, 'What are the police doing?'

'I've been through all that. The best I can hope for is to be dragged home and given stuff to make me manageable. I won't let them do that, Josie. Christine's world is opening up to me now. I'm finding out things about her that I never could have known.'

'Yes,' Josie said. 'And at what price?'

'Nobody down here seems to know that she died. Nobody except the person that killed her. He's the one I'm finding my way towards. I have to meet all her old contacts, I have to enter the life that she had. Sooner or later, he's going to turn up.'

'You think it was someone on Charlie's client list?'

Lucy could hardly believe what she was hearing. 'There's a *list*?'

'Well, he keeps records. But I don't know where.'

'Does he get names, and everything?'

'The waiter makes a note of the table number, and Charlie digs out the credit slip at the end of the evening. It's his insurance against comebacks. You wouldn't believe some of the people he's got in there.'

Lucy gripped the breakfast bar. Her mind was now as clear as spring water. 'I'd like to see that list,' she said.

'Not so easy,' Josie said doubtfully. 'He keeps the books well hidden.'

'In his office?'

'Or somewhere close by.'

In the cramped space of the mews kitchen, Lucy got to her feet. Suddenly she wanted to be dressed, and out, and running.

'Let's find it,' she said.

Nothing could happen until the evening, but then Lucy got her chance to see the inside of Charlie's office much sooner than she'd expected. The moment he saw her, he called her in. Her heart did a flip when she saw the ring binder that lay open on his desk. He told her to sit down, and then he went around and took an envelope out of his desk drawer which, she noted, was already unlocked. The envelope contained cash, and the cash was for her.

Not too many notes. But mostly big numbers.

Christ, she thought, how good *was* I?

This was something that Charlie now seemed to want to establish. He hemmed and hawed and rambled through a number of subjects before making a sideways approach to what he really seemed to need, which was any useful or memorable detail that would be worth noting about the previous night's client. Any scars, tattoos, birth marks . . . anything odd that he'd done, anything weird that he'd wanted or said. Any unease that Lucy had been feeling now vanished in the face of Charlie's uncharacteristic embarrassment. Charlie, manager of a tit show with a little pimping on the side, couldn't talk about sex without blushing.

She gave him a few things, all invented, and watched as he jotted some notes in the ledger. There was a limit to what she could make out, given the angle and that she was trying to see the page upside-down, but what she saw was enough to confirm that this book, or perhaps its predecessor for the previous year, had the potential to tell her exactly what she most needed to know. It had dates, it had initials, lots of numbers, some addresses . . . she briefly speculated about the possibility of braining Charlie with his own desk lamp in order to get her hands on it, but relinquished the option with a certain regret. Braining Charlie wouldn't be so easy. His head was probably tougher than a brass doorknob.

No, she'd have to rely on other means.

Somewhere outside the world went on turning, but down in the backstage changing rooms and passageways of The Gilded Cage – London's Finest Nightspot, All-New Revue – everything moved to the beat of Performance Time. The dancers arrived, singly or together, wearing jeans and thick sweaters and high-heeled leather boots, and they hung up their fun furs on the backs of dressing-room doors as the showtape was being wound onto the reel-to-reel in the stage manager's control room somewhere above. The tape controlled the entire show, including all lighting cues, and the stage manager would have little more to do than read his newspaper and greenlight the girls as they waited in the wings. First costumes were already laid out, wigs were on stands, the changes were hanging in show order on rails in the wardrobe department. Out on the floor of the house, about half a dozen of the tables would already be occupied.

When there was an opportunity, Lucy slipped up to the control box and borrowed a screwdriver. She didn't much rate her chances of getting hold of the key to Charlie's desk, but the desk itself was so old and the drawer appeared to be so ill-fitting that a touch of leverage might just spring it open.

'I'll bring it straight back,' she promised.

'You bet you will,' said Billy, stage manager and all-purpose house technician, over the top of his copy of the *Standard*.

But when would she get the chance to use it? Charlie would be on the move for most of the night, supervising, troubleshooting, bringing back cash from the tills to be counted and put into the safe, but there was no regular pattern to it and he was liable to show up in his office at any time. It wasn't the risk of getting caught that troubled Lucy. It was the risk of getting caught and then losing any chance that she might ever have of getting her hands on Charlie's ledger information.

Why not just ask him? she wondered as she stepped over the outstretched leg of Polly Inferno, aka Amanda Stern from Lanarkshire, who was using the corridor space for some warmup exercises and somehow, at the same time, studying a book. Lucy could just imagine how Charlie would react; at the first whiff of implication in a murder case he'd probably burn everything. He'd be stupid to do otherwise. Charlie might be lowlife, but stupid he wasn't.

And she owed Christine something more than ashes.

'What are you doing?' she said to Polly/Amanda as she stepped over her again. Amanda was on her back, book held at arm's length above her as she bicycled with her legs. She was in her warmup kit of white tank top, running shorts, red legwarmers, and basketball shoes. She was also chanting softly to herself.

But at Lucy's questions, she broke off.

'Modern Greek,' she said, only a little breathlessly as she scrambled to her knees and began a series of back stretches. 'I speak four languages now. When I'm too old for this line, I reckon Europe should just about be ready for me.'

'The boys in the coffee bar are both Greeks. You should come along and get some practice.'

'Chance would be a fine thing,' she said.

At around ten o'clock that evening, Lucy's chance arrived. If it hadn't been for Josie, she wouldn't even have been aware of it. One of the waiters passed the open doorway of the wardrobe department on his way to Charlie's office.

'Wait,' Josie said to Lucy, who'd been about to leave with an armload of silver lamé for dressing room three, and Lucy waited. Sure enough, the waiter returned a moment later and Charlie was with him, brushing dandruff from his jacket as he squared himself to face the public.

'The waiters only ever come back here for one reason,' Josie explained in a low voice. 'Some trash is sniffing the bait. Charlie's going out to check on the territory and strike up a deal. Unless it's just a runaround we'll have ten, fifteen minutes at the most.'

'We?'

'I'll keep watch for you. Come on.'

Josie stood by the door. Lucy went straight to Charlie's desk and tried the drawer. She had her borrowed screwdriver ready to attempt a little amateur lockpicking, but she didn't need it because the drawer wasn't locked. For a moment she was elated, but that didn't last. There was nothing much in the drawer beyond the cashbox (which now contained only loose change), some rubber bands, a clutch of half-used ballpoint pens, a calculator, a stopwatch with no glass, and a bundle of guest passes identical to the one that Lucy had first used to enter the club. Leaving everything more or less as it had been and closing the drawer, she turned her attention to the rest of the room.

'Any idea what you're looking for?' Josie said from the doorway, and so Lucy explained about her earlier interview and the ring binder that she'd seen.

Josie said, 'What did you tell him, if you couldn't remember?'

'Some old crap. I don't know. He was happy enough.' She opened a cupboard, rummaged through. The ledger was a fair size, and surely couldn't easily escape her. Nothing inside, so she checked

152

between the cupboard and the wall. 'Exactly how many ringers does he have?' she said, spying nothing but dustballs and old mouse turds.

'About a dozen that I know of,' Josie said, 'and I think I know them all.'

'Where does he get them?'

'No idea. His wife used to handle all the recruiting, but then she ran off with someone. They're all kinds. Not one of them's a hard-bitten tom, the kind you'd find on the streets. Some are just housewives, and there's at least one who I *know* doesn't need the money.'

'Why does she do it?'

'She enjoys it.'

'Sick.' She got down on the floor and ran her arm under the bookcase. Again, nothing. 'By when do I have to get out of the house?'

Josie was blank. 'Who said anything about that?'

'You did.'

Josie gave a shrug. 'I don't know. When you're ready.'

'Does that mean I'm forgiven?' Lucy said, clambering to her feet and then looking around for anywhere that she might have missed. Charlie's office was small and poky and lightless and overcrowded, but the number of possible hiding places was limited and it seemed that she'd tried them all.

'I'm not in the forgiveness racket,' Josie said. 'I only handle the Wardrobe. Time's up, kiddo.'

She checked the floor for loose boards. But the floor was parquet, with concrete beneath.

So then, in frustration, she had to retreat.

She bumped into Charlie later on, as she was heading out with her list for the coffee-shop order. He gave a slight raise of the eyebrows and said, 'Same again?'

'When?'

'Tonight, if you can handle it.'

'I can handle it,' she said.

THIRTY-TWO

Jessica had just seen the boys to bed when the call came. This consisted mainly of shutting them in and leaving them be – go in sometime after midnight perhaps, switch off the TV, unplug the Commodore, pick up the comic books and rearrange the covers, but that was about it. When she reached the top of the stairs and turned to descend she saw Simon on the hall phone and hesitated, wondering. He looked up at her, held the receiver out, and then she knew.

'*Can he hear us?*' Charlie said when she'd taken it over.

She watched as Simon wandered on through into the all-white kitchen, the door swinging shut behind him. He never quite seemed to know where he was going, or why. The house was huge, and he seemed lost in it. When they'd moved in he'd made a point of telling just about everybody where it was and how much it was costing – wincing a little at the same time, as if he were telling the story against himself and his own folly – but it had become a sterile kind of heaven, and he sat around in it like some forgotten angel.

'No,' she said. 'He can't hear us now.'

All the books that he'd bought to fill the stripped pine shelves, and never read. Bought them by the yard or by the box, or on a whim. All of the spines looked good. Most of the books were crap. He'd bought a BMW because he'd heard that it was the car to have, and wouldn't admit that he felt uncomfortable in it.

Charlie said, '*There's work tonight, if you want it.*'

'Can I make it in time?'

'*I can stall. It's a party of three. You'll meet at the hotel, then pair off. Don't let them talk you into doing it any other way, I'm not having anything kinky. Okay?*'

'Send me a cab.'

'*It's on its way.*'

After she'd hung up, she went through into the kitchen. The lights were on, but Simon wasn't there. So then she cut through the dining room and into the lounge, where she found him sitting in front of the big Sony TV. He had the remote control in his hand and he was channel-hopping, listlessly. She felt an urge to tousle his hair and say, *Never mind. Back to work in the morning.* At work he had a job title, and his own parking space.

'Callout?' he said.

'Another emergency. They're sending a taxi. I wouldn't wait up.'

He nodded, as if this was what he'd been expecting.

'Will you be all right?' she said.

'Yeah, I'll be fine.' He was running through the cable channels now, most of them showing 'seventies reruns or obscure sports cheaply covered.

'There's all kinds of stuff in the freezer, if you want anything.'

'Don't worry,' he said, skipping on through the amateur boxing and back around to the broadcast channels again.

Jessica had been a dental nurse before they'd married and now she was a dental nurse again, for an average of six hours a week on Tuesday and Thursday afternoons. As far as Simon knew, the late-night callouts were an occasional part of the job that she didn't much like, but said that she felt she had to do. Simon had only the vaguest idea of where she worked and what was involved, but didn't much mind. She went out, she came back. End of story.

I know it isn't much, she used to say. But it gets me out of the house for a while.

Jessica had been getting out of the house for a while since just after the youngest of the boys had begun at school. She'd started with a small ad in a contact magazine, and a box number to keep the entire business at arm's length; she couldn't believe the number of replies that came in. Most of those who were freaks seemed to declare it by their handwriting, and these she ignored. Also any that gave her the wrong kind of buzz. Those who remained, once she'd made allowances for the ways they described themselves, fell broadly within the category of Ugly but Eager. The first couple of times she'd arrived at a rendezvous and then lost her nerve, backing out before anyone could approach her; but then she'd tried getting herself a little drunk beforehand, and from then on the doors were flung open and she was away. Always with strangers, mostly in their cars, always in the late mornings or early afternoons in some remote country spot or shady lane. No names exchanged, no comebacks. The sense of betrayal and the risk of danger only served to intensify the experience, much more so than the most potent of drugs. Once it had been on the top deck of a multistorey car park in town, with shoppers passing only a few feet away on the other side of a layer of tinted glass, and she'd felt like a tight-fitting skin over a multiple explosion that was sounding off again and again and again.

And of course, every now and then, she'd do it with Simon.

Good old Simon, pounding away and probably thinking about his golf handicap to keep himself going. Jessica had no real complaints. She lived in a big house in what they called the stockbroker belt, she had healthy and good-looking children, they took two holidays every year. Life with Simon gave her everything she needed.

Except for a little spice of danger. And the occasional sense of being in total control.

She went up to the bedroom. Everything would be provided, even the underwear, so she didn't need to change; all that she had to consider was the little ritual that she went through every time. She took off everything that could identify her, and stowed it in the bottom layer of her jewellery box. Her wedding ring, as well. Then she pulled on gloves, so Simon wouldn't see that the ring was missing. Not that he was in much danger of noticing.

There was a thin slice of light showing under the door to the boys' room. She listened for a while, heard the low murmur of the TV. All seemed fine. She grabbed a coat, went back downstairs, kissed Simon on top of the head and got a grunt in reply, and then went out to meet her cab.

Less than two hours later, a city-centre taxi let her out under the lighted awning of the hotel by the park. After a change of costume and half an hour in the makeup chair at The Gilded Cage, she was no longer Jessica. She went in through the front door, as always. Further along the bay, it seemed to be taking five flunkeys in grey uniforms a lot of effort to usher one middle-aged man into a chauffeur-driven Bentley.

It was now after one-thirty. The hotel was quiet, but by no means dead. She saw the night manager as the night manager saw her, and he quickly signalled her to go around and into his office.

He took a hell of a risk. But greed seemed to get to people that way. Jessica could hardly have cared less about the money; she'd simply stick it in her purse like always, and when it was spent, it was spent. She'd have done all of this for nothing. She'd found her way to Charlie through another of the contact magazines, back in the days when his wife had been handling that end of the business; she'd had to send along a photograph and that had gone a little against the grain – in all of her moonlighting so far, she'd never let slip so much as her name – but everything had worked out well. Now most of her contacts were out-of-town businessmen, far more scared of comebacks than she'd ever have to be.

Because when she was with them, she was somebody else.

'Wait in the office,' the night manager told her. 'I'm trying to find three rooms on the same floor.'

'Charlie said nothing kinky.'

'Good old Charlie,' the night manager said with a roll of his eyes, and hustled her into the office.

The other two ringers were already there.

One was turning the pages of an old copy of *Hotel & Caterer*, the other was looking out of the window. The one with the magazine looked up briefly and without interest, and then carried on.

But the other one seemed familiar, at least from what Jessica could see of her reflection. But she couldn't be certain and so, tentatively, she said, 'Chrissie? Is that you?'

The woman turned.

On the window, her shadow turned away.

'It's been ages,' Jessica said. 'I almost didn't know you.'

The woman smiled.

'Hello, Jess,' she said. 'How've you been?'

THIRTY-THREE

In the days that followed, Joe felt a growing sense of panic. It was as if the hunt for Lucy Ashdown had spread to take over his world from one horizon to the other and everything else, every essential concern and unanswered question, had been crowded out at the edges. He was running up a huge bill on his credit card, and he was getting nowhere. Back home, he'd missed more appointments. More calls would have gone unanswered. People who wanted information from him were noting his silence and making their judgments accordingly; his life seemed to be funnelling down into a pit like so much waste water, and yet he couldn't stir himself to the right kind of action. He'd try. But then his concentration would slip away from the complexity of it all, and escape into Ashdown country again.

He moved out of the hotel and into some serviced apartments that rented by the week and were slightly cheaper. When he wasn't walking the streets, he'd lie on his bed and torment himself with thoughts of her being somewhere close. Possibly even less than a mile away. What was she doing? How was she getting by? How far had she fallen already? For all that he knew, she could be lying dead and cold in an empty building somewhere. Waiting to be discovered, but in no particular hurry.

Or worse. Joe had been around. He could think of worse.

A bleak thought that occurred to him one night, crossing the Hungerford Bridge on the way back from a check of Cardboard City, was that he might look straight at her and not even know her. Some of these kids were going down fast. They looked back at him with the bright eyes of rats in old people's faces and when he asked them a question, he could barely understand their replies.

Cardboard City, on the south bank of the river. Already an institution, of a kind, and accepted as a fact of life. How long before the tour buses began to include it on their schedules? But then, Cardboard City all but vanished in the daytime, and reappeared like a gypsy camp at night. In the afternoons there was little to see other than the skateboarders who came to clatter back and forth in the bowl-shaped space under the Festival Hall, making a sound that was

158

somewhere between a roller derby and a kendo match; but as evening came on, bags and boxes would start to appear in the best-lighted spots under the concrete. Each makeshift arrangement concealed a human larva that would emerge again at the first signs of dawn.

Most nights he made at least one trip out here, and each time he learned nothing. She was calling her father every couple of days, that much he knew. The cash was probably gone by now, and Joe's guess was that she'd have to beg or steal to keep going. He hoped so. He didn't like to think too much about one of the conversations that Jack Ashdown had reported to him on one of Joe's occasional check-ins.

'Jack? Has she called again?'

'She phoned me this morning.'

'How did she sound?'

'She says not to worry, she's found herself some work.'

'Meaning what?'

'I couldn't get her to say exactly, but she says she's getting by. She's doing the same kind of work that Christine used to do. Joe? Are you still there?'

'I'm still here.'

'That's something reassuring, isn't it?'

'Carry on thinking so, Jack.'

But this was said after he'd hung up the phone.

After that, he'd headed for a street in north-west London that he hadn't visited in over a year. He stood almost on the same spot as before, and watched the lighted windows of a basement flat across the way. This was a Regency crescent, its big houses a shuffled deck of peeling stucco and expensive restoration, and even the meanest of them wouldn't come cheap. This wasn't one of the meanest. The flat was reached by a narrow flight of steps descending into a well between the entranceways of two adjoining buildings, a small pit of private space behind cast iron railings, and the angle of view was limited. Someone down there hadn't drawn the blinds. Probably never even occurred to her that she was observed. Joe could see the end of an ironing board, and somebody moving around.

This had been Christine's place, once. But this woman was nothing like her.

So he'd walked away.

Now, returning across the Hungerford Bridge, those same thoughts came to haunt him a little as the overhead lights stained everything to the colour of dull old parchment. The footbridge section was narrow, but only a couple of feet to his left – within touching distance, in fact – was the steel mesh side of the railway bridge where monsters went battering across, drowning out conversation as their lights flickered through the big crossed support girders.

Christine.

Lucy.

In his mind, they were starting to merge. He'd asked Ashdown to send him a photograph that he could use. He wasn't even sure which of them it showed.

Even on the bridge there was no relief. They sat in the littered corners at the ends, beggars in various states of desperation waiting mutely for handouts. Down below the bridge, he knew, about eight or nine shambling street people would be setting up the plastic pallets and bakers' trays that would keep them off the floor for the night. It was as if his vision had steadily darkened, until he could see nothing else; no brightness, no sunlight, just a public hell into which he felt he was being dragged while others walked by it unseeing. He couldn't even hear faint sounds from the next apartment without his imagination putting together some unwholesome scene of matching action.

If only he could find her.

If he could find her, and keep a hold on her this time, then none of this would matter.

But where *was* she?

At around eleven o'clock, by an all-night snack counter near to Marble Arch, about half a dozen teenaged girls had gathered outside the service window to chat. The specialities of the counter were overcooked pastries and undercooked rolls, and nobody was buying; the place was simply a focus of life at this hour of night, in an area where nothing much else was happening.

Most of the girls were clippers, specialists in stopping men on pavements and taking cash in advance in exchange for a key and an arrangement to meet indoors about half an hour later. The keys were cut by the dozen at an Oxford Street heel bar, the addresses were always false. It was an obvious-looking deception, and shouldn't have had a hope in hell of working; but the girls were mostly young and good-looking, and their prey were mostly out-of-towners, and as long as they kept shifting their ground the money kept on coming in. The group had a perky, schoolgirlish look, and bore a close resemblance to an officeful of typists at a hen party.

One of them, a girl named Marion from Northampton, felt a nudge from one of the others. The conversation was dying all around her as she looked in the direction that had been indicated.

Across the wide pavement, a man was watching them. He was tall and badly shaven, his raincoat collar turned up against the cold of the December night. The girls looked from one to another, but no-one seemed to recognise him. The biggest danger in the racket was to be caught by a client who was angry at his treatment. Mostly, they were never a problem.

But once could be problem enough.

At their silence, he came forward. He seemed to single out Marion, to be looking straight at her.

'Can I ask you something?' he said.

'That depends what it is, doesn't it?' Marion said, glad of the security of the others around her and thus able to sound pretty sharp.

The man brought out a photograph and held it at arm's length, walking toward them. 'I'm looking for this girl. Do you think you may have seen her?'

Marion glanced at the picture, but didn't really bother to take it in. 'Maybe, maybe not. What's she done?'

'I never said she'd done anything.'

'No. But you're a copper, aren't you?'

He stopped. Slowly, he lowered the photograph.

'Not right at this moment,' he said, seeming to choose his way carefully.

'Don't try to kid me that you're looking for business,' Marion said. 'Coppers always want it for nothing.' But then she felt the sudden tension of the others, and knew that she'd pushed it too far.

'You want to watch what you say,' he told her quietly, eyes burning as if with a long-term fever. 'Talk like that could get you a smack in the mouth.'

She didn't answer him, or try to goad him any further. She threw back her head, and yelled for Jerry.

Instantly, three athletic-looking youths sprang from a doorway where they'd been idling just a short distance along the road. Without exception, their hair had been cropped short enough to reveal the scars underneath. The man took a couple of steps back as they headed for him; but then they stopped, as if they'd sensed his fury and found it to be a wall that they hesitated to scale.

'That's near enough,' he said. 'I'm just not in the mood.'

Hands held up in a no-harm gesture, he continued to back away. The three youths waited, debating within themselves whether honour had been satisfied as he took attention from them and returned it to Marion; and suddenly, as his eyes burned into her like a couple of lasers, it was as if the two of them stood alone and everything else was just background.

'You look at yourself,' he told her. 'Just go home to the mirror, and take a look.'

'Up your arse,' Marion said defiantly.

And later she might have sworn, even though the lighting was bad and he was already some distance away, that before turning around and stalking off into the night, the stranger had snarled like a beast.

PART FOUR

Death and the Maiden (II)

THIRTY-FOUR

Whenever he could, Joe would arrange to work through the Christmas period. Christmas on the job was fine. Lots of atmosphere, a few in-house parties, a whole new angle on the people that he spent so much of his time alongside. Wartime must have been a little like this, he used to think . . . routine thinking not allowed, every moment fresh and open-ended. A purer form of existence, somehow, that paid no heed to the conditions that had created it.

This year, he supposed it would be different.

This year he wouldn't even have the fallback option of his sister and her family, something that he always approached with a grim sense of duty and then often wound up thinking, at the end of the day, that perhaps it hadn't been so bad after all. A wild idea occurred to him – why didn't he just get his spare shirts and the few pieces that he'd picked up while he'd been staying here, throw them all into a bag, and jump on a train or a bus to present himself on their doorstep? For a while the notion gripped him, and he prowled the many floors of Hamleys looking for toys. He bought a magic set for Sebastian (although his ideal present for the kid would have been a brand-new name) and a marionette for Louise. He could remember that there was an age for puppets and magic, just as he could remember the time that he'd spent trying to fan a deck of cards or sitting in front of a mirror trying to get the hard consonants down like a real ventriloquist. Never managed either, but there you go. The Hamleys bag sat on the dressing table at the end of his room, the one clean, bright item in the place, and Joe lay back on the bed and stared at it as the daylight outside gave way to the evening.

He began to get the odd feeling of doubt.

Kids were reckoned to be more sophisticated, these days. He'd seen the stuff that was pitched at them through advertising. Much of it was way beyond anything he'd ever been able to dream about. What if they thought his presents were old-fashioned and stupid? They were polite, they'd probably try not to show it. But think of it, emotional charity from a couple of eight-year-olds – how low could a person possibly get?

And then, as if to deliver the knockout blow to his scheme, the phone rang.

It was Jack Ashdown, and he'd heard from Lucy again.

She'd been calling him often, at least a couple of times every week. She'd reassure him over and over that she was fine, she was safe, there was nothing for him to worry about, and Ashdown would then ring Joe and pass along anything new or helpful that he'd been able to pick out of the conversation. Which, in almost every case, amounted to nothing. Joe thought he'd seen her once, riding in the back of a big car. He'd run to follow it, missed it at the traffic lights, almost caught up with it at the next. But it had to have been someone else.

'I tried what you suggested,' Ashdown said. 'I think she's going to go for it.'

'Did she mention me, at all?'

'I told her you'd given up and gone home. Said she could check with the hotel if she wanted to be sure. I don't feel very good about this part of it, Joe.'

'Don't get soft. After the last couple of times, she's not going to turn up for anything that has my name attached to it. But if she thinks she's meeting you, that's different. I know what I'm dealing with now, Jack. Should have realised it the first time, but that's what happens when you make assumptions. This time she won't slip away.'

'Tell me straight, Joe. Do you really believe all this is worth it?'

'What do you mean?'

'I mean, what if she really is making out as well as she says? We could be handling it all wrong. Maybe we should be leaving her alone to get it out of her system.'

'In Christine's footsteps? You know where those led, don't you, Jack?'

And for this, as always, Ashdown had no reply.

Joe said, 'Where and when?' and Ashdown fumbled around a little at the other end of the line and then came up with an address.

'Do you think that's where she's staying?' he said.

Joe couldn't be sure without checking, but he thought that the street was somewhere outside of Soho proper and bordering on the fringe of Chinatown. Not too likely to be residential, more probably a row of shops and restaurants and oriental supermarkets. And after such a lengthy period of secrecy, was Lucy going to blow her cover so comprehensively in a single gesture?

'I doubt it,' Joe said. 'But who knows?'

As soon as he'd hung up the phone, he gathered up the toys and slung them, Hamleys bag and all, under the bed. Then he put on his coat to go out.

He had until morning to prepare.

The hire desk made a phonecall on the first credit card that he offered, and then told him that he'd exceeded his limit and they couldn't take the charge. So then he gave them Visa, which he'd hardly been using at all, and twenty minutes later they gave him a car. It was a plain, basic, rock-bottom hatchback, but it would do fine for the distance and had the extra advantage of childproof locks on the rear doors. To let herself out of the back she'd either have to clamber over the seats or squeeze out of a window, and because of the shape of the doors the windows didn't even open all the way. And it didn't much matter because, the way he had it planned, she wasn't going to be in any position to try anything.

At the slow, jerking speed of city traffic at night, he drove toward the address that Ashdown had given him for the rendezvous. Missed the street a couple of times, and had to circle back around to it. What he saw was more or less what he'd expected; lots of business, big crowds full of stupid people who weren't watching the traffic, every other window steamed-up and hung with a brace of Peking duck. He went on around the block, again and again, until a space opened up in a barely-lit alley and he slipped the car in ahead of a Mercedes driver who, to judge from how he leaned on the horn, was well along the way to a heart condition.

He locked the car. This would be fine. He wasn't blocking anything, and at the end of the alley was the street; he'd probably pick up a ticket between now and the time of the meeting, but that would be a small price to pay for the convenience of having less than a couple of hundred yards to drag her.

When he'd managed to count down the numbers and identify the exact address that she'd named, he felt something go cold inside him. He checked again, but there was no mistake. Instead of the café or the restaurant that he'd expected, he found a narrow shop with a few uncontroversial-looking videos in the window display and a more extensive and X-rated stock of tapes and magazines inside. The place was open late and he was able to glance in through one of those cheap glittery curtains that screened the doorway from the street. A couple of browsers, a beefy and balding man behind the raised counter, reading a newspaper. Was this her idea of a joke, or what? It was hardly the kind of place that a girl should arrange to meet her own father, unless she had a cruel streak or a deeply insensitive nature, or both.

Any doubts that he may have had, now vanished. His first impulse had been right.

After two failures, it was time for the gloves to come off.

Ten minutes later, he was standing as a customer in another shop, the kind of shop that he'd only previously ever visited in a raid. The counter assistant was a young man with an ear-ring, artfully unshaven and trailing a whiff of cologne.

'I want a blackjack,' Joe said.

'A blackjack?'

'A blackjack, a sap, I don't know exactly what your crowd would call it. A little leather thing with lead shot sewn up in it.'

'You know they're not legal.'

'The fuck they aren't. Are you going to sell me one, or not?'

He chose the blackjack from a selection on a velvet tray, and then he looked at some handcuffs – real ones, this time, but heavier than regulation and suggestive of overkill. From the same shop he could have picked up enough straps and buckles and ties to restrain King Kong. He could have bought chain mail underwear, or a whole-head rubber mask with nothing interrupting its smoothness but a single, tiny breathing hole.

But he settled for the blackjack, and charged it to Visa.

Then he checked on the car, took the long walk back to his serviced apartment, and spent a restless night staring at the stain patterns on his ceiling.

THIRTY-FIVE

He was out again early; too early even for the car to have been ticketed yet, as he found when he got in and turned the engine over to be sure that the cold and damp of the early hours wouldn't leave him with any last-minute problems. It caught on the second try, and after a minute's revving he switched off the ignition and let it die. No messing around with public transport *this* time. This time, he was going to have everything covered.

The video shop wasn't open yet. He walked around the block a number of times to check all of the approaches, any possible escape route, then he picked up some hot coffee and a sticky croissant and settled in a doorway to watch. It was a cold morning, and a thin jet of steam rose from the pinhole vent on the coffee cup lid. As he waited, he couldn't help thinking about that first night. The tourists, with their Coke and Danish. The lorry drivers in their big, companionable groups, with a much different Lucy Ashdown in amongst them. In his memory, it took on the aura almost of an age of innocence.

The video shop didn't open up until a few minutes after ten.

By then he was thoroughly chilled. He'd shifted position and walked up and down a piece of the street a few times, but this was hardly enough on a day when his own breath hung in the air before him. He shuffled, he stamped, he stayed well back in the shelter of the narrow brick passageway that he'd found as a better lookout point. He'd another half-hour to go before the time of the meeting, but he wanted to see her arrive. It went without saying that he didn't want to be seen, but it was worth the extra discomfort of hanging around for the extra information that he might pick up. How she came, and from which direction. Whether she'd be alone, or would have someone waiting.

But when the time finally arrived, he hadn't seen any sign of her at all.

He gave it a few more minutes. Maybe she was waiting somewhere, and watching as well. Or maybe she was just late.

Or perhaps there was some other, unofficial entrance, and right now she was getting ready to give up and leave by the same way.

He moved out with abrupt decisiveness. He hardly even noticed the complaints of the people that he shouldered aside, or from the cars that were forced to stop as he set out to cross the street.

The beefy man was back on his seat behind the raised counter. His shirt was the same one as the previous night, only his newspaper was different. There was one browser, a sad-looking hawk of a man whom Joe had seen entering a while before.

And that was it.

What now? Flexing his fingers so that they popped with the cold, he looked around tensely. The beefy man looked up at the sound. She might still arrive. He could hop up behind her and pop her one with the blackjack, no discussion, no fuss, just an instant human sack that he could throw over his shoulder and rush to the car. He'd lay it on as gently as he could, and when she came round she wouldn't even remember how it had happened. The browser wouldn't move to interfere, and the man at the counter . . .

The man at the counter said, 'Are you Joe Lucas?'

Joe looked up at him. The man was elevated and screened-in like an auctioneer, to deter attack and to give him an overall view of every part of the shop. Joe would have liked it better if they'd been level.

He said, 'Why?'

'You're expected. Twenty-five quid.'

Joe glanced around uneasily. He'd been thinking that he'd covered every angle, but now he was feeling as if he'd been wrong-footed. 'What if I don't have it?'

'Then you don't get to see her.'

'Well, I don't.'

'We take Visa,' the man said, lifting the card machine from behind the counter and slamming it down on the top.

Feeling slightly unreal, Joe handed up his card.

He didn't bother with the returned slip. Hadn't been bothering with them for a while, now. It wasn't as if they were real money. The beefy man climbed down from behind his counter and led Joe to the back of the shop, where he unlocked a door. Joe looked in and saw a dark stairway, and then he looked at the man.

Who said, 'Top of the stairs. Third door along.'

The stairs creaked as Joe climbed. It was as if he'd moved through a layer of reality and into something older, a prewar world of poor light and brown paint and damp walls. The stairs were barely wider than his shoulders, and there was a smell of old plaster and distemper. When he reached the top, he stopped on the landing for a moment to allow his eyes to adjust; there was illumination of a kind, coming down from a grimy skylight set into the angled ceiling, and it showed nothing much more than three old-fashioned doors and a bare wooden floor. Even the floor wasn't straight.

He moved as quietly as he could. He eased his hand into his trouser pocket, and slipped the blackjack loop over his wrist. The padded teardrop of shot was warm to his touch.

A tap. Just a light tap. Minimal damage, instant compliance.

Without knocking, he opened the door.

THIRTY-SIX

Something wasn't quite right, here.

She was standing at the far end of the room, waiting for him. It was a deep room, like two knocked into one. His end had no carpet, and its walls were panelled with old painted boards like a fisherman's cottage. Hers was draped with dusty red velvet, and there was a worn armchair alongside her in the same material.

When she spoke, even her voice was wrong.

'Surprise, surprise, Joe,' she said.

He looked to the side of the room and saw the plastic speaker from which the sound had come; it was a component from an old car stereo, and it hung from a hook with its wire incompetently stapled to the boards. He advanced to the wall-sized sheet of glass that divided the room down its centre.

'You knew it was going to be me,' he said. And she smiled, faintly.

She said, 'Do you think I'd arrange to meet my own father in a place like this?'

'It wouldn't amaze me. You've got no shame that I can make out.'

It looked like two rooms in one, because that's what it was; Joe had recognised the layout as that of a disused encounter studio, a place whose sole commodity would once have been three or four minutes of stilted conversation with a naked woman in the armchair. The glass would prevent contact, and when the time ran out she'd stand and draw the velvet curtain across to end the encounter. They'd never really taken off, and repeated raids and tougher licensing had killed them completely.

At the glass, Joe stopped.

She was returning his stare without flinching. Her eyes were cool, her gaze level. Her hair had been re-styled and had nothing of the incompetent dye job that had once been her most eyecatching feature. Her clothes were good, and seemed to have been chosen by someone who knew what she was doing. Even her shoes, he noted with a glance down, were expensive, and shoes could be such a giveaway. She seemed older, and she held herself differently. She looked like some rich man's daughter.

Or some rich man's plaything.

'It *was* you I saw in the car,' he said.

'Don't look at me as if I worked here,' she said. 'I just rented some protection.'

'Yeah, some arrangement. You make the booking, I pay the money.'

'I had to set it up this way. I can't trust what you tell me, Joe. Last time I let you make friends, you chained me to a table. I'm not getting fooled again. I can see straight through you by now.'

'You think so?' he said, wondering what it would take to break the glass.

'And I can see through my dad, as well. He couldn't tell a lie to save his life.'

'Or yours.' The answer regarding the glass would probably have to be, nothing that lay immediately to hand. If there had been a chair on this side of the room, she'd had it removed. All that he had was the blackjack, and that wouldn't do it. He said, 'If you're so well-informed and I can't be trusted, what are we doing here?'

'I wanted you to see me, Joe,' she said. 'Do I look as if I'm having a hard time? Do I look as if I'm in danger? Look at me now, and remember what I was, and be sure to tell my father what you saw. Be honest, Joe. I was on the skids, now I'm doing all right. How would you rather see me?'

'This isn't you,' Joe said. 'This is some whore with money.'

The remark went home, hard as a rubber bullet. Her face tightened. Her eyes went from cool to a deep, deep chill.

'All right,' she said, 'that's enough. You don't know anything. I'm closer to my sister now than I ever was when she was alive, and I'm closer to knowing what happened to her. I'm not going to let you mess that up. Go home, Joe. You look as if you need it.'

Joe dived for the door. She seemed to read what he was doing in an instant, but he didn't wait around to see her reaction. He slammed out onto the landing, and kicked open the door to the next room. Given that there was no way through the glass itself, she had to have entered from somewhere. The next room was a garbagey mess of ripped packaging and stacked video cases, and old display material that had been slung in and forgotten. The third and final door opened onto another dark passageway.

The floor was so uneven that it was like running through the Crazy Cottage in a funfair; the building itself seemed to pitch around him like a listing boat. He reached the turning in four long strides, used the wall to speed himself on around the corner. There was another landing here, and more stairs; there was noise of some kind from down below.

A door stood half-open, showing a mirror-image view of the room that he'd just left. Nobody was in sight. He kicked the door all the way back and then, when it bounced against the wall, went in and kicked the armchair around in case she'd curled up and was hiding on that. She wasn't. So the open door wasn't a ruse, and she really had run for it.

'Shit,' he said to the empty room, and then left it to chew on the idea.

He still had a chance to catch her. Those shoes, they hadn't been the running kind. He clattered down the stairs two, three at a time, and almost fell when he reached the bottom.

The noise was that of a restaurant kitchen. Not one of the big places, but one of the little shop-sized Chinese cafés that didn't even display an English menu. There was just the one chef, and he was standing at what looked like a domestic range using a wire scoop in a king-sized wok.

'Did she come through here?' Joe demanded, remembering the last time that she'd dumped him into trouble in a Chinese restaurant, but the chef said something angry and then ignored him and so Joe pushed on past and shouldered his way through into the main part of the premises.

'Did she come through here?' he demanded of the astonished-looking Chinese family at one of the restaurant's six plain tables, and they gave him a look of complete incomprehension.

For a moment when he emerged into the street, he was completely disorientated. Nothing looked familiar, and yet he'd gone around the block again and again in anticipation of something like this. But then a couple of features clicked into place, and the world stopped its spinning. He looked both ways, but saw no running figure. Looked again, more carefully this time, and saw no-one that resembled her at all. There were about thirty shops within sprinting distance. There was an entrance to a shopping complex and another to a four-screen cinema. There was a steady crowd pushing its way along, the usual anonymous array of big-city faces with other things on their minds.

It was hopeless.

For the third time, he'd had her within reach and then lost her. She hadn't simply evaded him; she'd evaded him each time with an ease that had left him looking like a fool.

His anger barely contained, like a storm in a bottle, Joe walked the distance back to where he'd left his rented car. There was no ticket, but there was a big sticker plastered across the windscreen. *Do Not*

Attempt to Move this Vehicle, the sticker read. The offside front wheel had been clamped with a locking shackle.

Well, to hell with it, he thought. Who needs it now? And he took out the keys and threw them onto the bonnet. And then as he turned and walked away he took the blackjack, which had come out of his pocket in the same handful, and tossed it into the first unblocked drain that he saw. The weight of the shot drew it down through the grating and out of his sight like a skittering lizard.

Hold it in, he told himself. Use it. Don't blow it all off like some nobody would.

Stiffly, walking like a machine, he headed across town for his apartment. If anybody had spoken to him, he probably wouldn't have heard. Not that anybody would have been tempted. His face was like something brewed up out of spit and bile.

Back in his room, he carefully laid himself down on the bed.

In the next apartment, someone switched on the TV.

Joe covered his head with his pillow.

The place was jerry-built. The walls were thin.

And the pillow blanked out almost none of the sound at all.

It wasn't even a show that he liked.

Joe came off the bed like a Saturn launcher. He reached the door in a single bounce, and flung it open. The passageway outside was still reverberating from the crash when he started in on the door of the next apartment. There wasn't much to it, just painted ply over a cardboard shell, and its lock went spinning across the room at the second kick.

Joe stood in the doorway, and roared.

A mousy-looking woman sat on the end of the bed, her face a blank-looking *O* of surprise. She was wearing a quilted housecoat, and in her hand was a hairdryer. A man of around the same age was squatting down in front of the TV set, belatedly fumbling to turn down the volume; he was in his underwear, and was as pale as lard.

'Christ almighty,' Joe shouted, 'where do you draw the line? It's the middle of the day!'

'Fuck you, peeping tom,' the woman shrilled. 'Get out of here!'

'I'm turning it down!' the man was gabbling. 'I'm turning it down!'

'Yeah, do that,' Joe suggested, and he walked over and put his hand behind the man's head and pushed him face-first into the screen. The cheap TV rocked on its legs as the man grabbed at it in an over-eager embrace, and Joe turned to the woman on the bed.

The flying hairdryer hit him just above the eye, flex trailing like the tail of a kite, and as he swatted it away the plug whipped around and smacked into his teeth. The fury burst again in his head like an overloaded artery, washing through him in a hot and irresistible wave. He was half-blinded as he reached for her. His hand shot out like a slaughterhouse bolt, and closed on air; she'd ducked out from under, and was already halfway to the door.

'Cheap little slut,' he yelled. 'What would your father say?'

'You tell me,' she said from outside, and then she hit the corridor fire alarm.

The siren noise was terrific. It exploded in Joe's head like a grenade, yet another battering shock to add to the effects that had gone before. He put his fists to his temples. He could feel the blood as it pounded there. He screwed his eyes shut, but it was as if his sight was being destroyed by the light of a thousand flares. He screamed, loud and long, but the pain wouldn't lessen.

So then he sank onto the floor, to make himself as small as possible so that he could wait out the agony. Nothing like this could last for ever. Even the sun had to burn itself out, one day.

As he waited, he rocked.

And as he rocked he said her name, over and over and over again.

THIRTY-SEVEN

She felt bad about what was happening to Joe. Even in the short time since he'd chased the car along the street, she could see that he'd gone further downhill. She felt guilty, she felt responsible. If it hadn't been for her, he wouldn't even be here. He'd be home, doing his job and living whatever life he had that didn't include her. Looking back at his forlorn figure as the car had accelerated away, she'd wondered if there might be some way to set him back on his rails. All right, so she'd used him a little, but this was all way out of proportion.

She couldn't remember where she'd been going at the time. A chauffeur in uniform and the more upmarket end of Bayswater, was all that she could recall. But that side of it was Christine's department anyway.

Should the haziness of her memory be a matter for concern? Their bargain was working, and Lucy didn't care to examine the arrangement any more closely than that. The more immediate problem was with Joe. The next time that she'd spoken to her father, she'd suggested a meeting in the certain knowledge that it would be Joe who would turn up; and he had. Every precaution that she'd taken had proved to have been justified, but she doubted that she'd managed to do any good. Joe had called her some names, and hadn't been reassured at all. He'd become a wreck of a man. He'd lost weight, his eyes were staring and red as if they'd been rolled in grit, and his clothes hung on him like a scarecrow's; it was almost as if, in the course of the past few weeks, he'd been drained of the zest and the energy and the sense of confidence that she'd steadily been picking up. She felt that they'd become bound together, somehow. They were like dancing partners, waltzing away into darkness.

She no longer felt threatened by Joe. She could forgive him the anger, she could forgive him the names. She could forgive him anything if only he'd go home and take away the guilt she was feeling at the idea of dragging him down. He was like a terrier, unable to let go in spite of a beating, and it was hard for her not to feel responsible; because, after all, didn't his persistence show that she'd come to matter to him, at least a little?

On that basis, forgiveness came easily.

But she wondered if, even given time and the success that she was hoping for, he might ever come to feel the same way about her.

Joe was taken in the back of a police van to the Divisional Headquarters on Vine Street. The back of the van held a faint odour of vomit, despite an obvious hosing-out and the liberal use of an industrial disinfectant. He gave no trouble and sat with his head down and his elbows on his knees, hands loose and empty. When the van came to a halt and the loading doors were opened he slowly raised his head and blinked at the light, like some slow-moving reptile whose rock had been taken away.

'Move yourself,' the officer at the van's open end said, and Joe clambered out.

Vine Street itself appeared to be a short cul-de-sac that was hardly more than an alley, and mostly dominated along one side by the towering rear façade of some big hotel. Under the steam vents and the aluminium air shafts and the painted-over windows, kitchen porters were hosing out galvanised bins. The station was opposite, and not nearly as imposing. A police Rover had been parked half-on the pavement, along with a couple of officers' cars. In the rear window of one of these, a handwritten notice read *Murder Investigation – do not ticket or clamp – See Stn Officer CV*. A uniformed man on either side of him, Joe walked past the vehicle to a steel-shuttered garage door which stood just beyond the public entrance, and waited under a camera eye as the door clanked and banged upward to reveal a small covered garage yard. He was taken across the yard, down a narrow passageway lined with stuffed brown paper sacks of confidential waste, and through the door at its end into the Vine Street Charge Room.

Several hours later, after statements and interviews and a considerable number of phonecalls, Owen Nelson went down to take a look at the prisoner in cell number three.

Nelson was thirty-five, although most people thought he was younger. He'd been a uniformed inspector with the Soho Unit for nearly three years, and was probably due for a move; no sign of it yet, but there was most likely a memo waiting deep in the machinery, easing its way out at the speed of a splinter. Rather like God, New Scotland Yard could sometimes work in mysterious ways.

The cell block stood just off the L-shaped charge room, a corridor almost completely without daylight. The corridor and all of the cells had been recently painted, but gaiety wasn't the theme around here.

Two doors down, the gaol sergeant was copying some fresh prisoner details onto one of the name boards from a charge sheet. The sergeant was big and burly, with a rugby player's face and a small trimmed moustache. His name was Rosenthal but everybody, for no reason that Nelson had ever learned, called him Katz. Probably something that had been generally agreed over the remains of the first person that had dared to call him Rosie.

Nelson stopped by *Lucas, Joseph Alan*, and lifted the cover on the spyhole.

The cell had no features other than a low shelf bearing a thin vinyl mattress. Lucas had been relieved of belt, tie, shoelaces, and everything in his pockets, and now he sat in the far corner on the mattress with his knees drawn up and his arms clasped around them, as if to present the smallest possible outer surface to the world. He might have been rocking slightly, it was difficult to tell. He was staring into the space before him. But his mind was clearly somewhere else.

'What's the word?' Rosenthal said, laying down the chalk and moving toward Nelson.

'He checks out. He's a county bobby all right, and they want him back.'

At the door between them Rosenthal stopped, and did a brief visual check of the cell's occupant. 'Thank God somebody does,' he said. Whoever was on the other side of the door, he was singing. In the nick south of the river where Nelson had done his early constable training, such a case would have been referred to as an AFD. He'd always assumed that this was a piece of official terminology until one day he'd asked what it meant, and found out that it stood for Another Fucking Drunk.

He said, 'In fact, they've been looking for him. He was supposed to turn in for a disciplinary hearing over three weeks ago, but he never did. Just took his suspension and vanished down here.'

'What was he up for?'

'He beat up a woman in custody.'

Rosenthal was about to ask something further, but then he stopped himself and said, 'Don't tell me.'

'Yeah,' Nelson said, leaning to look through the spyhole again. 'Can you imagine an uptight bastard like that in the Vice Squad?'

Lucas hadn't moved. Yes, he *was* rocking, but barely. Nelson watched him with no contempt, no outrage, no brotherly feeling. It was as if the sight of the man prodded at a dead spot within him, where no response would come.

'Let's have him out,' he said.

Nelson went out into the charge room. It was deep inside the building and, like the cell corridor, received little daylight through its small, high windows. The main part of the chamber was taken up by a table, long and black and battered, that stood at right angles to the sergeant's desk and had about half a dozen unpadded chairs around it. Nelson went around to the far side of the table, and sat down to wait as Lucas was brought from his cell.

The situation wasn't as clear-cut as he'd have liked. The only complaint to have survived the past few hours was the one relating to the damage of an apartment door; the couple in the next room had wanted Lucas to be prosecuted, crucified even, but had somehow formed the impression that the police would be able to proceed without any further input from them. Nelson didn't know their background story, and didn't want to. But at the first mention of statements and the prospect of court appearances, they'd suddenly become tight-lipped and forgetful. They wouldn't say anything, sign anything, or even give their addresses. Then they left the building muttering something about justice.

Sometimes you just couldn't win. When people were in trouble, the police were more welcome than the Lone Ranger and Tonto. Any other time, they'd believe anything they heard as long as it was bad. Nelson's experience was of an organisation that had its regular human share of good soldiers, time-servers, wasters, whiners, climbers, saints, piss-heads and heroes; and when the pressure was on, probably more of the latter than it was fair to expect. Things happened, one heard stories, but overall you got on with the job.

But then along came someone like Lucas, and put the mark of Cain on everybody. Handling him was going to be a delicate business, and Nelson was more than relieved that the job wouldn't fall to him.

Lucas came to the table, his shoes in his hand. Apart from being tousled and run-down, he seemed normally competent. He pulled out the chair across from Nelson and sat down, placing his shoes on the floor beside him.

Then he folded his hands on the tabletop, and waited.

Normally, any ordinary citizen subject to dropped charges would receive a stony-faced apology and the opportunity to leave via the public foyer. But Lucas was no citizen, and the situation was anything but normal.

'I don't know who you think you are,' Nelson said, 'or what you think you're doing. But this is the last time you do it around here.'

'Is there a charge?' Lucas said patiently.

'I'll tell you what's going to happen. Two of the lads are going to go back to the apartment hotel with you. You pick up your gear and you settle your bill. There'll be no more trouble. Then they'll take you to the station, they'll watch you buy your ticket, and then you'll get on the train and you'll bloody well stay on it until you're back where you belong. Am I making myself clear?'

'What happens at the other end?'

'Being perfectly honest, I couldn't give a stuff.'

And Lucas shrugged.

After all, it wasn't exactly as if he was being given a choice.

THIRTY-EIGHT

Lucy sat, her hand over her eyes, and thought about the way her life was heading. She thought about how it usually went.

Mornings, she'd sleep late. She'd a sense that she dreamed, but then could never remember what. She'd remember odd images, odd words, the way a place looked. Often it was that same suite, in the same hotel. And that was about as much as she cared to recall.

The afternoons were mostly her own. She'd go shopping, now that she had some money, or go to see places that she'd heard of. She went to the Wax Museum, she visited the Tower. She went to Trafalgar Square and dodged pigeon shit. The afternoons were also good for going to the cinema; they had all of the stuff that would take about six months to make a brief appearance in her home town, and she could see it on decent-sized screens instead of one like the end of a shoebox.

In many ways, the movies were best of all. They helped her not to think too much.

It was early one evening, coming out of the Empire in Leicester Square with a head full of Harrison Ford, that she'd seen Gary again. Gary, the hospital porter who'd helped her out and whose friends had treated her so strangely. She hadn't forgotten that she owed him taxi money. There was a line already forming outside the cinema for the next performance; Gary wasn't in it, but he was waiting to one side where a number of cutoff cast-iron pillars made an ideal site for leaning and lounging. He was in his good clothes. It was already dark but the square glowed with marquee brilliance, and none more brilliant than the Empire's. The electronic billboard with its tacky Stardust effect was the ultimate nothing, an entity written entirely in light.

There he was, an island of stillness in the flow of pre-Christmas shoppers and tourists, and Londoners heading into the glittering heart of the capital for the best of all possible times. He was looking around, and hadn't seen her.

She called his name.

At first, he didn't hear. Then she saw him look around quickly, but in all the wrong directions.

182

So she called him again.

This time, he saw her. She was walking toward him now, and she saw him rise as if stung and then start to back away. 'Hey, Gary,' she said, but it made no difference. This was all wrong. There was something in his face that had no right to be there, and the fact that it was so unexpected made it hard for her to recognise; but recognise it she did, and its presence bewildered her.

Fear.

Gary bumped someone, didn't seem to notice. He continued to back off.

'I don't know you,' he warned her. 'Leave me alone.'

'Gary?' she said. 'I only wanted to tell you thanks.'

'I don't want thanks. I don't want anything from you.'

'And I owe you for the taxi.'

'You don't owe me for anything. Just stay away from me. I don't want any more trouble.'

She couldn't get near. But then, by a makeshift badge stall surrounded by litter and empty cider bottles, they got into a group of people before a West African busker. His long hair was tied back in a scarf and he was playing guitar to a whistling song. The crowd that he'd pulled wasn't much, but it slowed Gary down a little.

'Gary,' she began, and with disbelief saw his fear become actual terror.

'Fuck off, will you?' he almost screamed, and he thrust a chicken's claw up in the air before her face. The chicken's claw was his hand. It was twisted and thin, and lined with two long, fresh-looking operation scars like zips. The scar tissue was pink and shiny against the natural brown.

She stopped, staring, understanding nothing.

'Haven't you done enough?' he demanded.

And then he turned and stalked away.

He almost ran.

That had been . . . what? Four, five days ago? It was impossible to be sure. Sometimes the days and the nights ran together. The days she mostly piddled away, while so many of the nights belonged to Christine. Progress seemed to have halted; two more furtive searches of Charlie's office had turned up nothing other than his hidden Scotch bottle but then, every evening of the day after a job, she'd see him go in there empty-handed and the book would be on his desk when he summoned her. She was getting pretty good at inventing details for him to note down. Maybe Christine was feeding them across without her knowing, it was impossible to say.

Now Lucy sat, her eyes covered. With her spread hand she could pinch both of her temples and she'd been sitting like this for a some time, holding out the light. For a while, there, she'd been convinced that everything was coming together. But it hadn't, not completely, and now she was beginning to have the feeling that all of the best chances had been narrowly missed and the whole thing was now starting to come apart again.

Someone moved, close by, someone whose approach so far had been in silence, and she quickly took her hand away.

He stood before her. A dark figure, tall.

He said, 'Is everything all right?'

'I think so,' she said, straightening in her seat and looking around like someone who'd fallen asleep on a long journey and awoken in an unfamiliar place. 'How long have I been here?'

'Half an hour, more or less. I don't always like to disturb you.'

'I'm sorry if I'm doing anything wrong. This is strange for me. I'm not used to being in a church.'

He gestured around, as if commending the place for her use. She was in the third of its twenty-odd rows of wooden seating. One city centre chapel, probably a listed building, Georgian stonework, Victorian plumbing, congregation almost nothing. Lavender wax on old timber, bad light through yellowed glass, air like the inside of a grave.

'Whatever you want from it,' he said, 'that's what it's here for. Have you been away?'

'Since when?'

The cleric raised his eyebrows, half-amused. Not as if they were old friends, but as if there was no reason on earth why, given time, they couldn't be.

'Don't you remember?' he said.

'I've been through some interesting times of late,' Lucy told him, and smiled along with him when she saw that he understood the reference she was making.

But her smile died as the cleric went on.

He said, 'Perhaps you've forgotten. It was a while ago, now, more than a year. You sat in that same spot and I stood right here. You said that you weren't a Catholic, but there was something that you wanted to confess. I said that it was all right, because I'm not a Catholic either but if you wanted to talk, I was willing to listen. But then you left. When I saw you again last week, I wondered if you'd changed your mind.'

'I was never here last week,' Lucy said.

'Well if it wasn't you, then you must have a twin sister.'

Abruptly, she stood.

She wanted to make some lightweight remark that would let her out gracefully, but nothing came.

'Wait,' he said with some concern. 'Whatever it is, don't run from it.'

But she waved him back and scrambled awkwardly out of the pew.

She didn't run.

But she made it to daylight in one hell of a hurry.

THIRTY-NINE

Josie found her when she turned in for work at the club that evening. Lucy had curled up on a pile of old throwouts in the corner of the Wardrobe department, and had pulled some of them over herself like a burrowing animal.

'Hey,' Josie said. 'Hey, come on, what's all this?' And she teased her out and straightened her up a little, and then she went over to the makeup table and tore off a length of the soft toilet roll that she used instead of Kleenex, and then she sat on the floor beside Lucy and put her arm around her shoulders.

'What's happened?' she said, but for a while Lucy could only shake her head.

'I don't know, Josie,' she managed at last. 'I think I'm losing my grip. I was okay at first, I thought I was going somewhere. But it's been weeks now, and no progress. I'm sliding too far in. The most terrible things are starting to seem normal.'

'I *did* warn you,' Josie said gently.

'I know. What am I going to do?'

'You could just walk away.'

'Could I?' Lucy said, looking up at her, and right at that moment Josie would have sworn that some kind of a façade had dropped and that she was returning the gaze of a six year-old.

'Anybody can do anything,' Josie said, which she knew was only so much bullshit but which she also believed was a reasonable dictum for getting a person through life. After all, it didn't need to be true. It only needed to be true enough of the time.

Lucy seemed to take it in, and to give it her consideration.

'If anybody can do anything,' she said, straightening a little amidst the old clothes and the discards, 'then I can carry on.'

Oops. That hadn't been the intention. Josie squeezed Lucy's shoulders and said, 'What about this Joe person you've talked about? Can't he be of any help at all?'

'No,' Lucy said, shaking her head and looking down. 'He means well, but all he ever does is try to grab me and take me home.'

Someone went by outside the door, but didn't look in. Josie said, seriously, 'Perhaps he's not wrong. I've been watching you, and the

186

price you're paying is too high. This whole thing's destroying you. You're in a dead end as far as Charlie's records are concerned, and even if you get your hands on them you've no guarantee they'll be of any use. And even if they were . . . well, they won't bring Chrissie back, will they?'

But she could see that it was too late.

Perhaps there had been a moment where Lucy's guard had been down and she might have been diverted, but the moment had now passed. *It was worth a try*, Josie thought sadly. Anything was worth trying once, except for Yugoslavian chocolate.

Lucy got to her feet. Josie's hand slid from around her as if she'd been holding nothing more substantial than a wisp of smoke.

Lucy blew her nose.

'I'd better get to work,' she said.

A short time later, a car pulled into the underground drive-through that had been set aside for taxis and pick-ups at the mainline rail terminus. This was where Joe had brought Lucy, what seemed like an age before, and this was where he'd lost her.

This time Joe was the prisoner, and two strangers his escorts. Neither of them knew him, the assignment wasn't exactly official, and the one who owned the car was itching to get Joe dumped so that he could turn around and make the slow, crawling drive across town to his home. It had been a long day for him already, and if he made it back before nine he was going to be lucky. The other man was in no particular rush to be anywhere, being newly-divorced and having been thrust back into bedsit-land alone and at the age of forty-two, but out of a range of possibilities the prospect of hanging around on a station platform with Joe Lucas had to rank among the lowest.

So they pulled in ahead of the taxi rank in the underpass, and the one next to Joe leaned across him and opened the door, and almost in unison they told him to bugger off home. Joe got out slowly, stiffly, and he straightened up and took a deep breath of the exhaust-tainted air. The lighting down here was bright, the surroundings that depressing blend of streaked concrete walls and painted metal fittings that had become the principal feature of late twentieth-century gothic. An observer would have seen a raggedy man with his possessions gathered into a couple of carrier bags, his hair uncombed, and no life in his eyes at all. They'd have seen him walk toward the escalators as the car drew away, moving as if on some rudimentary automatic pilot.

And then, as the escalator carried him up into the main concourse of the station, they'd have seen the spark returning almost like the glow of a neon tube being borne up into a powerful field of energy.

FORTY

He dropped what luggage he had into the nearest garbage receptacle and then, ignoring the ticket windows completely, headed over toward the phones. Most of them seemed to be the kind that took the prepaid cards that he never had, but there were a couple of pay booths at the end of the row and he made for those. One was coming free as he approached. A few people were waiting and one of them called out angrily as Joe stepped in ahead of them all, but he gave him a one-second blast of his sub-zero gaze and said, 'Police business,' and then he turned his back and forgot the man completely.

His small change had been returned to him, along with his belt and laces. He fed the slot, dialled Jack Ashdown's number, and then fed it some more.

'Oh. Hello, Joe.' Always that first momentary disappointment, with Jack Ashdown's realisation that it wasn't the voice that he was most hoping to hear. 'How's everything?'

'Hunky fucking dory,' Joe said. 'I've had a change of air and the chance to do some thinking. Lucy's been phoning you regularly, right?'

'Not regularly. Just whenever she can.'

'What time?'

'It could be any time. Mostly evenings, but not always.'

'And she'd never say where from.'

'She made me promise not to ask.'

'But you know where, don't you, Jack?'

A fatal hesitation. It told Joe most of what he wanted to know.

But it hadn't yet told him everything.

He said, 'When she first started making the calls, how did she pay for them?'

'I don't understand.'

'Like hell you don't. She was living hand to mouth and she wouldn't spare the cash if she could help it. I reckon she was calling collect and that you were accepting the charge.'

'Maybe once or twice. I don't know. It's something I don't remember.'

'Had your phone bill yet, Jack?'

Another silence at the other end of the line. Ashdown could have hung up on him now, and messed him up completely. But Joe knew that Ashdown would do nothing of the kind.

Joe said, 'If you've been billed, then you've also had a statement giving the number that she called you from.'

The silence continued.

Then Jack Ashdown said, 'I wasn't going to say anything. Not unless there was an emergency.'

'You think this has turned into a game, or what? This entire business is an emergency, Jack, or had you forgotten that? You're letting me run around like a headless fucking chicken while you've got the one piece of information that could lead me straight to her!'

'I'm not letting you do anything, Joe. You're doing it because I can't stop you.'

'Well, pardon me. Who asked who, Jack? You think I'd have screwed up my own life like this if you hadn't come along with your cap-twisting routine and your sob story all about how you were losing your little baby girl?'

'That was then. But you've changed. You started to scare her. Now you've started to scare me.'

'So instead of letting me finish it, you let her carry on giving me the runaround.'

'She says she's doing fine. I'm starting to believe her.'

'Shall I tell you what it *is* she's doing, Jack?'

'I don't want to know.'

'Say that again?'

'She's told me that it's nothing she regrets. That's good enough for me.'

'She's screwing for money, Jack. Just like Christine before her. She's riding in big cars and she's dressing like a tart. Somebody's running her, somebody's using her. I might have stopped it already if it wasn't for you. What kind of a father do you call yourself?'

'I'm going to hang up.'

'Want to bet?'

And Joe waited, cruelly, and nothing happened at the other end of the line.

And then he said, 'Give me the number, Jack.'

It seemed to ring out for a long time. Then someone picked up and he heard a woman say a curt and cautious, 'Yes?'

'Is Lucy Ashdown there?' Joe said.

'I'll check. Who wants her?'

'Just tell her it's a friend.'

There was a moment's hesitation and then the woman said, 'This wouldn't be Joe, would it?'

Joe's mind raced. Blow it now, and he'd be stuck. The number was useless to him as long as he had no address to go with it. But if Lucy had talked about him and given out some kind of general warning, this could be as far as he'd ever get.

So he simply said, cautiously, 'It might be.'

'Don't be cagey, Joe,' the woman said. She seemed to have dropped her voice and moved in closer to the phone, as if to avoid the chance of being overheard. 'She's told me all about you, but don't count me as an enemy. My name's Josie. I work with her, and I'm about as close to her as anyone around here.'

'Go on,' Joe said.

'She's as tough as they come, but I think she's at her limit. I don't believe she ought to go on, Joe. I think she's all set to do herself some permanent harm if she pushes it any harder.'

'Where is she now?'

'Out getting the coffee. She's really low. I know you've had problems with her before, but I don't think it'll take much persuasion to get her to give up. But I do mean persuasion, not strongarm stuff.'

'I'll do whatever's necessary,' Joe said.

'Can you be at the stage door in an hour?'

'The stage door of where?'

She told him where to go, and how to find it.

'I'll be there,' he said.

FORTY-ONE

It had only taken a few weeks for Lucy Ashdown to become one of the more useful ringers on Charlie's list of reserves. She could be matched to any of four performers in the floorshow; Josie wasn't sure why, but it was as if her teenager's skin and certain odd, somehow held-back elements of her personality made her into a blank sheet onto which anything could be drawn. Josie reflected on how easily, with just a change of clothes and a few amateur touches, Lucy had managed to transform herself into a resurrected image of her own sister. Nothing that would stand looking at too closely, of course, but it was like all the best illusions that she'd ever seen, onstage or off – because for all its contrivance, in the moment of perception it somehow transcended reality.

And it was destroying her. Of this much, Josie was sure.

Josie's job was to suggest the changes with the most minimal effects, but the truth of the matter was that she could probably have slapped on the makeup with a billposter's brush and the trash would be equally fooled. This was the case with Lucy, and it was the case with just about all of the recruits that Charlie had gathered together in his long and shady backstage career. Perception was a weird thing. Nobody really knew what they saw. Mostly, they saw what they expected – and because the trash with whom Charlie had his dealings were rarely the deepest or most sober of men, their expectations tended to be predictable and few.

She had no pride in what she was doing. Her cut of the money wasn't even so great. But then, neither was her regular income from the Cage. With Pamela it was always the same – don't worry, we don't need it, the bills are all covered, I can take care of everything – but Josie would rather have packed her bags and moved out than go along with such a line. Without self-respect, everything else was a sham. Strange, she'd think, the way life could sometimes go – how you'd take on one humiliation simply in order to avoid another, and reckon yourself ahead.

After she'd completed her delivery round of the dressing rooms, Lucy came back into the department, took off her coat and threw it in the corner, and then threw herself onto one of the available chairs with an equal lack of ceremony. She was slumped, dejected. For once, her mileage was beginning to show.

Josie said, 'You shouldn't be working tonight.'

There was no need to specify the kind of work that she meant, because both of them knew. Charlie had already been by, and needed to do no more. Lucy said, 'It doesn't matter.'

'Don't kid yourself.'

'It doesn't. I just tune out and let Chrissie take over. She handles it all. I'm not even involved.'

Out of all the women that she'd processed for Charlie, the hard cases and the desperate and the downright kinky, she'd felt affection for none until Lucy had come along. Not even for Christine, whom she'd found distant and uninterested, as if in her mind she'd created a better place and preferred to wander there. When Lucy had first talked about Christine taking her over, Josie had assumed that she was merely finding words to describe some devised means of survival. God knows, she needed it, considering her obvious distress after that first night. But now Josie was gradually coming to realise that Lucy was treating it not as a metaphor for anything, but as the literal truth.

She went over and crouched down before her chair, so that their faces were level.

'You scare me when you talk like this,' she said.

Lucy was uncomfortable, but could hardly look away. 'Why?' she said. 'It works out pretty well.'

'I didn't like it when you started, and I like it even less now. At least you had a good reason in the beginning.'

'I still do.'

'No, you don't. You got nowhere and the reason leaked away and now you're just doing it. You got nowhere, you're going to get nowhere. So what's the difference now between you and the rest of them?'

'Don't do this to me,' Lucy said quietly.

'Admit it. You're at the end of the road.'

'No. There's more. I came here to do something. Not to get screwed and make money.'

'But in the end that's all there is to it, isn't there?'

'I'll think of something else.'

Well, you had to give it to the kid for determination. The problem was that determination seemed to be all that she now had left, and it wasn't a currency that was likely to get her any further. Josie glanced at the old folding travel alarm that she kept open on the makeup table, and said, 'I have to go somewhere for a minute. What are you going to do now?'

'I'll be around for a while,' Lucy said.

And so Josie left her there, intending to be as quick as she could on her errand and to return before Lucy could wander away to think her thoughts of darkness somewhere else.

There were no goodbyes, no final glances around to fix the details of this tacky, tawdry workplace in her memory. There was no particular sense of occasion, no fear, no sudden awareness of unrealised longings. No hint that she was about to walk into the last surprise party that she could ever expect to see.

As she headed through the basement corridors that would lead her to the stairs and the stage door and thence to the waiting Joe Lucas, Josie's thoughts barely touched on the subject of dying at all.

FORTY-TWO

Joe had been in the alley for a while already, enough to scout the area and to be sure of his ground. An hour hadn't been much in the way of preparation time, and he'd been forced to improvise. Fortunately, the alley's rubbish skips were like twin goldmines. They were huge wheeled galvanised cylinders, each taller than a man and of the kind that could be chained to a garbage wagon and then hoisted and inverted in one great burst of hydraulic power. Joe had climbed up over the side of the nearest and lowered himself in, rubbish sliding unsteadily beneath him, and then he'd found his balance and hunkered down and started to sift. He had only a weak light to work by, from a solitary streetlamp near the end of the alley, but it was enough.

Someone else had been here before him, tearing open the bags of perishables in search of anything worthy of rescue. The stink was terrible. But one of the offices in the area must have been undergoing a thorough make-over, because along with the garbage and a tangled mess of strip aluminium and ceiling tiles he found a number of office throwouts that included a desk lamp with about five yards of trailing flex. Bracing the lamp with his foot, he jerked the flex out and then had to steady himself as the unstable ground beneath him shifted. There was no plug. It was thin stuff, almost bellwire, but when he wrapped a length around either hand and then pulled, it didn't seem to stretch.

He clambered down, dusted himself off.

And then, in the shadow between the skips, he settled down to wait.

He couldn't see his watch, but that didn't matter. For this, his patience would be infinite. Traffic passed the end of the alley, but no-one came in.

He wouldn't have expected them to. With the one exception, all of the doorways in the alley seemed to be back entrances and delivery doors for daytime businesses. At this hour they were all barricaded and fortified, protected by wire and armed with heavy padlocks. And being a dead end, the alley led to nowhere else.

Joe crouched, and waited, and tapped out a slow and silent rhythm on the ground before him with a loop of the wire.

He heard a *thunk* as someone hit the crush bar on the inside of the stage door. A yellow slice of light appeared around its edge.

He moved like flowing mercury, out from his shelter and sliding along the wall toward the door . . .

Which opened wider, throwing a long and somehow bizarre shape of light across the alley, everything exaggerated and distorted including the elongated and backlit shadow moving out within its frame . . .

And he heard the shadow speak as it moved, and tentatively, questioningly, he heard it speak his name . . .

And as the all-too-solid original took a single step out from the doorway he dropped the loop of wire over its head and, like a man straining to start an outboard motor, suddenly hauled it tight for all he was worth. Then, as he felt the wire disappear into the flesh, he held it there.

She started to fight, but he was ready for that. He dragged her backwards and off-balance, and then kept her moving so that she couldn't recover. Joe had no illusions about how it was to kill someone. It always went one of two ways. Either like a snap of the fingers, leaving a sense of bewilderment at the ease with which the line between existence and history could be crossed, or else it was damned hard labour which could seem to take forever, like attempting to snuff out one of those trick candles where the flame dodged and dipped but wouldn't disappear.

When they were underneath one of the fire escapes, he stopped. It was an old strapiron stairway with a counterbalanced ladder which, assuming that somebody kept it oiled and tested, would drop to give one-way access to ground level. He had to hold her one-handed for a moment, and to hold her steady even though she was fighting him hard. There was fury but not much strength in it, like the tantrum of a very small child.

'Not much longer,' he promised, and threw the loose end of the wire over the lowest part of the ironwork. Because he'd wound so much of it around his hand, the bundle went with some weight and accuracy and then tumbled, unravelling like a falling spider, on the other side.

He let her go, and caught the free end of the wire with both hands. She dropped to her knees, clutching at her throat, but the wire was probably in too deep already. Her lungs would be full of stale air that she couldn't release, while her brain was already filling with static from lack of the same.

Taking it slowly, watching the wire for any tendency to break, he

196

hoisted her body into the air. As her feet cleared the floor, one of her shoes fell off. She jerked around and the wire stretched a little, but that was all.

There had been no sound since the sound of his name.

She hung and twisted, and if she felt anything when she dropped a little as he tied off the line to a handy window bar, she didn't show it. *Good piece of work, Joe*, he thought with some satisfaction, as she turned slowly on the wire.

The wire creaked. Her face came around and into the light.

And Joe frowned.

'Oh, fuck,' he said. 'Who're you?'

FORTY-THREE

Charlie looked in, wanting Josie, but Lucy couldn't tell him where she'd gone. She'd moved over into the makeup chair and had been studying her own face in the mirror. It wasn't an act of vanity, or even a professional kind of analysis; it was more with the unease of a person who picks up something familiar and finds that, at some unrealised point in the recent past, it has somehow been exchanged for the property of a stranger.

'I don't know where she went,' Lucy told Charlie. 'But don't worry. I know what to do. I can get ready on my own.'

Watching her in the mirror, Charlie moved into the room and half-closed the door behind him. He lowered his voice, just enough.

'You've really taken to this, haven't you?' he said.

Lucy turned from the mirror. 'Is that how it looks?'

'Don't misunderstand what I'm saying,' he said. 'There's a way to go yet, but you've got the makings of a real professional. How would you feel about that?'

He almost made it sound as if this was something that he'd expect her to be proud of. She said, neutrally, 'It's nothing I can't live with.'

He nodded, watching her with the narrow, approving eyes of an experienced horse thief. 'Talk to some of the others if it gets to be a problem,' he said. 'Anything else, you talk to me.'

'The only thing I get scared about is the chance of someone turning rough.'

'If ever I think that's a possibility, I don't make the deal.'

Oh, sure, Lucy thought cynically, and she said, 'Has it ever happened?'

'Once or twice,' Charlie conceded. 'But never anything that couldn't be handled.'

'Ever happen to Christine?'

'Off the top of my head, I couldn't say.'

'And I don't suppose you could check.'

He'd already seemed to sense that she was steering him somewhere. Lucy didn't for one moment think that she could trick him or trip him, but knew that he'd see her as young and naïve and so might just let her get away with a little more.

198

He said, 'Check where?'

'In the record book.'

'What record book?'

His gaze was steady, his face didn't change. She'd seen the book a dozen times and he knew this perfectly well; he was challenging her to go further, but Lucy now knew better. She shrugged and looked away, to indicate that she was backing off.

Charlie came over, hitched himself half-onto the edge of the makeup table, and looked down on her. She felt uncomfortable. He was too close, and she didn't know where to look. She had a sense that Charlie was about to get paternal with her, and the prospect was an embarrassing one; but at least this would be better than his anger.

He said, 'Now, listen. All that stuff's strictly off-limits. As far as you're concerned there's no book, never was. It's my security and it's your security, but the information works both ways. Let that stuff get into the wrong hands, and it could hang us all.'

Lucy nodded slowly, trying to look thoughtful and responsible.

'I couldn't have a quick look through it, then?' she said hopefully.

But Charlie gave her a pained look as if to say, *You've got to be joking*, and Lucy tried to cover her tracks by pretending that, yes, of course, that's exactly what she had been doing.

And Charlie, believing none of it and letting her see as much, slid down from the makeup table and went over to the door.

Before withdrawing, he glanced around the department.

'Looks like you're in charge for now,' he said, and let himself out.

He'd been more on-target than either of them had known. Josie didn't reappear for the rest of the evening, which pissed Lucy off mightily. She'd never been left completely alone before; for the space of a phonecall or an errand, perhaps, but never to the extent that the final responsibility for any of the work had been hers. As she scrambled around and tried to stay level, she watched for Josie's return with the thought that, when she finally arrived, she'd damn well see what a tough time Lucy had been having. But the fluster and the harassment were largely wasted, because Josie didn't return at all. Her coat hung on the back of the door, her handbag stood open on the side. As the second show was coming to an end, Lucy sat herself in the makeup chair and made a sullen face and checked her watch frequently, with the idea that Josie should catch her doing it as she finally came in through the door.

But it didn't happen.

So then, with no better grace and without even a passing thought for Josie's safety, Lucy pinned back her own hair and began to carry out the makeup job that she'd undergone so many times before.

A while later, when she was finished and dressed and sitting alone, Charlie came to take her out to the taxi.

'It's repeat business tonight,' he said as they climbed the rough-cast stairway to the alley exit. 'Or did I already tell you?'

'No,' Lucy said as Charlie banged on the crush bar to open the door. It really wouldn't matter to her, one way or the other. As usual she planned to shut it all out, and let Christine take over.

'It's not the usual setup. He isn't here, so I have to take you to the hotel myself. You're not going to believe this. He's waiting to buy you supper after the show.'

They went out into the alley. Her taxi was already there, having reversed all the way back from the street. The alley's dead end glowed red in the wash of its brake lights, long shadows being thrown by the garbage hoppers over on the far side, and the sound of the cab's turning engine had a hard edge in the chill night air.

'So,' Charlie was saying as he moved ahead to open the cab door for her, but then he stumbled slightly and muttered a curse. He gave a kick, and something skittered across the alley and bounced against the wall opposite.

A woman's shoe, Lucy noted. You got all kinds of crap being dumped in a place like this.

'So since he asked for you again,' Charlie went on as she climbed past him into the back of the cab, 'make sure that whatever you did for him, you just keep on doing it.'

He got in alongside her, slammed the door, and moved forward to speak to the driver. The side window was open a couple of inches, and Lucy closed it.

Outside, something moved in the shadows.

Lucy sank back into the darkness at the rear of the cab, and waited. *Okay, Christine*, she thought. *This is as far as I can go.* She closed her eyes, tried to clear her mind, tried to let the world fall away with the rhythms of the journey.

But this time, nothing happened.

FORTY-FOUR

They pulled in before the big hotel that overlooked the park. Even though it was late, the broad carpeted entranceway was brightly lit and all of the available off-road parking space was crammed with a mixture of upmarket image cars and stupefyingly dull, staggeringly expensive saloons. No chauffeurs waited. People who employed chauffeurs went to better places than this; like many of the cars it was an image hotel, all bright expensive surfaces with no detectable trace of a soul underneath. From the basement casino through the ground-floor restaurant to the top-floor penthouse, it was little more than a money pit for any out-of-towner with an expense account.

Charlie leaned forward and said to the driver, 'Keep the meter running. I won't be staying.' And then he turned to Lucy. 'Well, kid?'

Lucy didn't move.

Frowning, Charlie said, 'Something wrong?'

She looked at him with a rising sense of panic that she tried to conceal. She'd been waiting for Christine, but Christine hadn't come. It was as if she'd been calling on a dead line to an empty building.

She tried to speak. Her throat was dry.

She cleared it.

'I was just trying to get a couple of thoughts together,' she said.

'Think on your own time,' Charlie said impatiently. 'This is business.'

He stood by the cab with the door held open, and Lucy climbed out in a daze. She didn't know what she was going to do, how she was going to handle this. It was worse than the first time. At least the first time, she'd only a vague notion of what might lie ahead.

They went into the foyer.

Instead of going straight to the front desk as usual, Charlie guided her towards the restaurant. She couldn't help wondering how the two of them looked. Charlie was in a dinner jacket and black tie, but it was the outfit that he wore every night of his working life and its shape was starting to go. And she was feeling overdressed and underconfident . . . Christine might have carried it off, but Lucy was feeling cheap and obvious.

They waited by the desk of the Maître d'Hôtel, and the Maître d'Hôtel took his time in appearing.

He looked at her, then he looked at Charlie. She could see his disdain, and it wasn't so much for her – she hardly seemed to count for anything at all in his eyes. Charlie was the one who seemed to be inspiring his contempt. It wasn't simply a matter of class, it was the feeling of the big-league operator for the non-contender. Black tie and a waistcoat would never make Charlie look like a playboy, only like a bartender.

And, totally unexpectedly, Lucy found herself moved by a brief surge of affection and pity.

'Table for Mister Wingate,' Charlie said.

'One moment,' the Maître d'Hôtel said, 'while I check,' and Lucy was pretty sure that whatever it might say on the reservations list, no booking in the name of Wingate was about to be found. Terribly sorry, sir, now sod off.

But Charlie said, 'You don't need to check, he should already be here. I've brought along his guest.'

'Oh.' The Maître d's expression was chilly enough to freeze a slug of flying spit. 'Will you be staying?'

'No thanks,' Charlie said, totally unfazed. 'I've seen the kitchens.'

Charlie walked away and the Maître d'Hôtel watched him with the eyes of a deep-sea predator, all dull surface and no depth. Lucy wanted to call after Charlie, to beg him to come back and to take her away; this was all wrong, it wasn't the way things were supposed to go at all. But she didn't move and she said nothing, and the Maître d'Hôtel didn't so much turn his attention to her as give her the briefest of glances.

'Stay here,' he said. 'I'll send a waiter to take you over.'

'Can't you do it?' Lucy said, but he was already moving away.

She watched his back for a moment.

And then, loudly enough to be heard from some of the nearer tables, she said, 'Wait a minute.'

He stopped, and looked back.

She said, 'What makes you think you can look down on me?'

But he didn't even reply. He simply shrugged, almost imperceptibly, and walked on.

Lucy was left to kick around by the unmanned Reservations desk for a couple of minutes, and then a waiter appeared to lead her over to the table. She felt as if every pair of eyes in the place was turning toward her. The fact was that almost nobody even as much as looked her way as she passed, but the tight knot of embarrassment stayed deep within her all the same. The decor in the low-ceilinged room was mostly of wicker and bamboo, with plenty of foliage washed by a green light so vivid that its effect was one of utter unreality. Some of the casino crowd were here, an assortment of dinner jackets and plunging cocktail dresses. Many of the tables were screened from one another, and staggered over different levels. The effect was that of an attempt at Mediterranean good taste, contrived by and for people who had no taste at all.

The table stood somewhere in the middle of the room, but was partly screened from Lucy's approach by a trellised partition topped by some overspilling broad-leafed plant life. As Lucy came around and into sight, a seated man began to rise.

He hovered with a nervous half-smile as the waiter drew out Lucy's chair and seated her. Only then did he drop back onto his own chair. She hadn't expected to recognise him, but she did.

She even remembered his name. Russell. The young, nervous and over-eager man who'd been the first of her assignments for Charlie. He seemed almost overcome by her arrival, as if she'd breezed through his mind and driven out whatever it was he'd been planning to say. He looked around the table, fidgeted for a moment, then spied the single long-stemmed rose in a box that was lying directly in front of him.

'This is for you,' he said, picking it up and offering it to her.

She looked at it. 'Really?'

'It was an impulse. Just a token thing.'

She took the boxed flower and then, after holding it for a moment and wondering what to do with it, laid it down alongside her place setting. She'd never seen so much silverware, and all laid out for one person. Her napkin had been folded to resemble a half-shell and it stood upright, unsupported. They had two wineglasses each. There was a lit candle between them.

'There was no need to go to all this trouble,' she said.

'But I wanted to. And I read about how dancers burn up the calories, so you're to order whatever you like.'

She peeked over at the ice bucket which stood, almost out of sight, at his elbow. 'Champagne as well,' she said. 'I don't know what to say.'

'No need to say anything,' he said, and he smiled sheepishly. 'I'm getting to be able to read you better and better. You see, I've been watching you.'

'When?' Lucy said, with a sharpness that seemed to surprise both of them, and he quickly stumbled on in an attempt to limit the damage.

'I've been coming to the show every week,' he explained. 'Twice, in some weeks. I've got it timed so that I arrive just before your French maid number, so I don't have to sit through all the rest of it. You're very good.'

'Thank you,' Lucy said hollowly. This was even more unreal than the decor.

'Is that you singing, or someone else?'

'It's all on tape.'

'But is it you?'

'No.'

Maybe she could handle this, after all. The waiter came with the menus and then disappeared again. Her host repeated that she was to order anything that she wanted and she stared at the words on the card, taking none of them in. He seemed disappointed that she hadn't been the one on the music track, but not too much.

'Well,' he said, 'I think you're the best thing in the entire show,' and she thought, *If only you knew.* And then he added, 'What did you do before this?'

'I was on a cruise liner,' Lucy said absently, continuing to study the menu while her mind raced through all the angles. Somehow, she'd have to end it before they moved up to the room, or the suite, or whatever Charlie's contact had lined up for them.

Russell was nodding. 'The programme notes said you'd been in *Cats.*'

Programme notes? This was the first she'd heard about any programme notes. She hadn't even been aware that the show *had* a programme, other than the stuff they put on the show board in the foyer. 'They make all that up,' she said, dealing with the problem as roundly as she could.

'You mean, none of it's true?'

'No.'

He seemed disappointed, but he'd survive it. 'Just goes to show,' he said wistfully. 'You can't believe everything.'

'That's the way to be,' Lucy said. 'Look, the Cage is a clip joint and this one's the same only more respectable. How much is all this costing you?'

'Don't worry about that.'

'How much, Russell?'

He balked for a moment.

'More than I can afford,' he admitted.

She looked at him hard, trying to read him, and he shifted uncomfortably. 'You don't need this,' she said. 'You're not hopeless or past it or just passing through. So why are you doing it?'

'For you,' he said.

'I don't need it.'

'But I'm in love with you.'

Alarms. Danger. Damn it, she should have recognised that puppy-dog sickness look in his eyes from the beginning. She'd assumed that he was probably a touch simple. But actually, he was simply smitten.

'Now, Russell,' she said. 'Wait a minute. That just isn't true.'

'But it is,' he insisted, as if this somehow ought to be the best news she'd ever heard in her life. To Lucy, it was less than welcome.

'You don't even know me,' she warned him. 'What you're all fired-up about is a fantasy. I'm not who you think I am. I'm not even a dancer. And when I go upstairs with somebody, that isn't me either. It's all a cheat, Russell.'

'I don't care,' he insisted, loudly enough to turn a few heads. But only a few, and just for a moment.

'You're not listening to me. You've been had. Now you're trying to walk through the mirror, and it isn't going to work.'

'I want to know everything about you. And I want you to know me.'

'Forget it, Russell,' she said, starting to rise. 'That isn't going to happen.'

Suddenly he was on his feet, grabbing at her sleeve.

'But I've *paid* for you!' he said, and this time it was loud enough to stop every conversation within a radius of twenty-five yards. Jaws dropped, spectacle lenses glinted as heads turned . . .

And Russell found himself looking in dismay down the point of Christine Ashdown's switchblade.

Somebody gasped.

'Back off,' Lucy said, keeping her voice low. 'I don't care what you paid for. This is the line, and you don't cross it.'

Jerkily, with less than perfect co-ordination, Russell managed to release his grip on her. Then his legs gave way, and he dropped back heavily into his seat.

'Out,' the Maître d'Hôtel growled from by her ear. 'Now.'

'Don't worry,' Lucy said, and glanced around. Past the shocked faces on the next table, she saw an expensive-looking bottle of red wine and some half-filled glasses. She reached over and took one, and nobody moved to stop her. And then, before anybody could realise what she was doing, she turned her wrist and tipped the entire contents of the glass down the Maître d's shirtfront.

'That's for being a prick,' she said, and walked out.

FORTY-FIVE

Surely the news couldn't travel so fast; but even as she emerged from the restaurant, the night manager was hovering in the foyer with a vague, Oh-shit-don't-tell-me look on his face.

'What's gone wrong?' he said, looking from Lucy to the rising commotion that was beginning to emerge from the restaurant behind her.

'We can talk in your office or we can talk out here. I don't care either way.'

There were night staff all around them now; porters, one of the late receptionists, even a couple of the busboys from the restaurant. They came so far and then they stopped, looking confused and wary. Lucy looked down and realised that she was still carrying the switchblade.

Quickly, she put it away. The night manager told the assembling crowd, 'Thanks, everyone, you can go on back to your work. I'll handle this.' And then, hustling her along without actually touching her, he got Lucy away from being the unwelcome centre of the foyer's attention and ushered her into an office behind the reception desk.

It was a dismal little room. None of the design budget of the public areas had been wasted back here. It had a vague familiarity to it, and she wondered if she might have been in here before.

Maybe she hadn't quite been herself at the time.

The night manager didn't meet her eyes. He paced around behind his desk, running his hand through his hair, uncertain of exactly what he was going to do. In here, he seemed younger than she'd first assumed. Like the rest of the staff, he wore a burgundy-coloured uniform although, apart from his name tag, it could have been taken for a regular formal suit. His shirt was so white that it must have been starched. There was a cold sheen of sweat on his forehead.

'What the hell are you doing?' he said. 'Are you trying to get us all strung up?'

'I could care less,' Lucy said.

'Oh, thanks,' the night manager said, looking heavenward. 'Thanks, Charlie. Just what I needed, a psychotic fucking harpy. You were never like this before.'

206

'Maybe not. That's because I needed to get somewhere. Now I need to go further, so I'm changing the rules.'

Now he looked at her, and he pointed a finger. 'Listen, you,' he said. 'You don't make the running around here. What you just did was right out of order. I'll be lucky if I come through this with my balls still attached.'

'Look at me,' Lucy said, 'I'm in tears. You think it's bad now, stick around. I've got a police contact who'd just love to know what kind of racket you're into, here. And if I don't find out what happened to Christine Ashdown, I'll make sure that he does.'

He blinked, as if she'd hit him from some unexpected direction.

'Who?' he said.

'Christine Ashdown. I'm her sister.'

He groped around behind him until he found a chair, and then he slowly sat.

'Damn it,' he said, 'Charlie never told me. I assumed he'd just picked you for the resemblance.' And he shook his head in wonder, his earlier agitation all but undercut by this new discovery.

'Did she ever come here?'

'A few times,' he admitted.

'What about the last time of all?'

'Maybe.'

'Maybe doesn't tell me anything.'

'And threats from kids don't exactly make me inclined to co-operate. Why don't you just ask her?'

'She's kind of hard to reach. How well did you know her?'

He shrugged. 'I didn't see her so often.'

'But you've got a reason to remember her.'

He sat back in his chair, calculating now. 'What's the comeback for me if I tell you?'

'Nothing,' Lucy said, taking another chair from by the wall and bringing it over so that she could sit facing him across the desk. 'I'm not sorry for anything I've done, but I'm not proud either. I did what I had to. That doesn't mean I'd want my dad to read about it in a newspaper.'

He thought it over. But by then she already knew that he was going to tell her. She could read the signs. What she saw amounted almost to an urge to confess; not to any offence, but to something that was old and troubling and somehow unresolved. She knew that it was time to ease off, don't push too hard, just wait and let it come out.

'We had an accident here,' he said quietly. 'I think that's what decided her to quit. In fact, I know it was.'

FORTY-SIX

He said, 'I don't remember the date. It was near Christmas, that's all I know. Bitch of a night. It was raining. There were three of them, all in their twenties, and they were as pissed as farts. Two of them could handle it but the other one . . . I'd have called him a mother's boy.

'Charlie phoned to say they were coming over. They wanted champagne. This time of night, the reservations are pretty well settled; all I have to do is pick out a room in one of the quieter areas and then take them up on a passkey. Charlie gives me a cut, I slip something to the maid in the morning, she makes the room over and nobody ever asks anything.

'Anyway, one o'clock in the morning, and the three of them come rolling up with your sister in tow. At first I thought trouble, but then I started to get the picture. The mother's boy had never been laid in his life, and your sister was his graduation present from the other two. I kind of caught her eye when the others weren't looking. She didn't exactly like the situation, but it was no big deal for her. Let's face it, all she'd have to do would be to sit and let him sleep it off for a while, it was probably what the kid needed most, and he'd never remember anything different. Just pull his shirt out and mess up his hair a little, and his friends would be happy. He was too far gone to give a damn about *anything*.

'So we all go up in the lift, and the two bucks as good as carry the mother's boy into the room; he's almost completely gone, and they sit him on the bed and they pour some of the champagne down him and then they come out. They wanted to stay and listen at the door, but I wasn't having that. I virtually had to drag them away.

'I've got them halfway down the corridor, and the door opens behind us. It's Chrissie and she says, I don't like the way he's looking. So I go back and I'm standing in the doorway, and there's this kid on the bed and he's thrown up all over the cover and now he's starting to shake. I've seen just about every kind of drunk, but I've never seen one shake like he did. It was more like a fit and I'm thinking Oh, shit, how do I handle this? And while I'm doing that, the two bucks are pushing past me into the room and they've got his shirt open and they're really doing a number on him. They'd gone from legless to stone cold sober in nothing flat. One's doing his pulse and the other's doing heart massage but nothing seems to be making any difference. And all I'm thinking is, for God's sake let's get him off the premises. If he's going to die on us, let it happen somewhere else.

'So then I grab hold of Christine and drag her out. She's white. She says that's it, forget it, nothing's worth this, I'm going home.'

Lucy had been saying nothing, letting him speak without interruption; he'd seemed almost to forget that she was there, but now he fell silent as if the vividness of the memories inside his head had made the words somehow redundant.

Which was of no damned use to Lucy at all, and so she prompted, 'She actually said she was going home? I mean, right away?'

He seemed to stir, and became aware of her again. 'More or less,' he said. 'I told her that she could do what she liked as long as she got her arse out of the building, and quick. I got her all the way along to the lift and put her in it. I can remember what she said then. She said, I've had enough. It doesn't get any lower than this. Tell Charlie I'm out of it, I'm leaving town and making a new start.' The words seemed to make him smile, but there was no cruelty in it. Nor tenderness either, but more a wistful thought of a better world where such things as new beginnings could actually take place, and which he could never realistically expect to see.

He went on, 'When I got back to the room, it was empty. I hadn't been gone more than a minute. They must have used the service lift. This was one that I didn't want the maid to know about, so I cleaned it up myself. None of us ever saw your sister again after that.'

'Do you know the names of the boys?'

'Only Charlie could tell you that.'

'If I can get it out of him.'

'Yeah,' the night manager said with the dry kind of irony usually reserved for flying pigs and hell freezing over. 'Good luck.' And then, as Lucy was rising, he said, 'Did it ever work out for her?'

She stopped. 'What do you mean?'

'The new start she was going to make.'

She watched him for a moment. She saw no attempt at deception, no trace of an attempt to manipulate. It was a straight question, and he genuinely didn't already know the answer.

And so Lucy said, 'Well . . . she got away from all this.'

He nodded slowly, as if this was good to hear. 'She was okay,' he said.

And Lucy, who could spot the point at which casual sentiment tipped over into bullshit, said, 'Yeah. I can see what fond memories you have of her.'

At which the night manager shrugged.

And Lucy walked out of his office, and out of the hotel, and into the night where a soft winter rain had just begun to fall.

FORTY-SEVEN

There was a song that kept running through her mind, for no other reason than that of the atmosphere conjured up by its opening line, which was *Midnight at the Oasis*. It was well after midnight and the cold surface of the Thames had only its elemental nature in common with a desert pool, and although she was once again sitting in the shadow of the Sphinx it was on cold, wet stone and not on sunbaked sand.

But what did it matter? It was just a feel-good song, a piece of ephemera, and Lucy was feeling surprisingly good. They'd always taught her that the only truly good things were those of permanent value; her first school had been a church school, and twice a week they'd had to set their chairs in a raggedy half-circle and fidget their way through one of the vicar's haranguing lectures on Life. He was a small man, bald and beady-eyed and turkey-necked, and only in retrospect could she see that he'd probably been something of a mental case as well. She could only now assume that Life had served him badly in some way, at least in his own opinion. Most of the time he probably kept the fact well-concealed, but give him an audience of five-year-olds behind closed doors, and the brakes would come off. His regular message was, in essence, that everything they thought of value was actually worthless. Their toys would fade or break, their pets would die, and they themselves would grow up and get old and surely follow if they didn't knuckle under and live their lives in dread and apprehension of the Holy Spirit. Unfortunately, he never seemed to be able to give them an explanation of what this Holy Spirit was supposed to be. It was something that you had to swallow whole, like a stone of uncomfortable size, and the act of swallowing was called Faith. And then he'd maybe see two small boys holding hands, and the Holy Spirit would be forgotten while he hauled the bewildered pair out in front of the rest of the class and subjected them to a blistering rain of sarcasm.

Lucy wasn't sure if she believed in God or not. On the whole she reckoned that she probably did. But from those earliest days, she hadn't believed in the Church at all; not one scrap, not one iota, and this was why she'd been so surprised to discover herself in such a place only the previous morning. God was something that you glimpsed in only your rarest moments, and couldn't put a name to. Church was a place where there was a name for everything.

But then, it hadn't really been her choice to go there at all. It had almost certainly been Christine's.

Before her, the river slowly heaved and the riverside lights danced in its swell. Only one train crossed the near-distant bridge at this hour and that had been a night train going nowhere, its carriages empty and its windows dark. She wasn't really dressed for this. Her gown was thin and her jacket, a stage-prop fur, was too short. The cold of the riverside steps was rising up her spine like mercury in a glass.

But Lucy didn't care.

This was one of those moments; not of ecstasy, exactly, but of utter calm. They didn't happen often, and could come at the unlikeliest times and places. They had one big enemy, and the enemy's name was Routine. Something that she hadn't known much of, in this past year.

In fact, she'd known little peace at all. But had she come on a journey, or what?

'Tell me how you're holding up, kid,' Christine said from beside her.

'I'm doing fine,' Lucy said.

'I was worried about you for a while.'

'So was I. But it's like one of those arcade video machines, sometimes you hit things you have to get through. Next time you open your eyes, you're in a whole new phase of the game.'

'So you reckon you're getting somewhere.'

'Watch me.'

'Don't worry, I am.'

They sat in silence for a while. Two wraiths, and a river full of shadows and stars. And then Lucy said, 'Why did you leave me like that?'

'I never left you,' Christine said.

'And what about our deal?'

'I can't do anything that you can't do. I can't tell you anything that you don't already know. Because I'm Christine, but I'm also a part of you. Once I was alone, and it was the most terrible thing in the world. But then you picked me up, and you made me your mission – and in spite of everything that I'd lost, I gained something that I'd never had before. As long as you remember, I'll always be with you. But as soon as you forget me, I'm gone.'

'I'll never forget you,' Lucy said.

And then she looked at the empty stairway beside her. The wet stone glinted yellow with a reflection of the embankment lights above. There was traffic along it even at this hour, while across the river an abandoned generation slept on like larvae in their paper cocoons.

She took a breath of the cool night air.

And then, a little stiffly, she began to get to her feet.

FORTY-EIGHT

The first light of dawn found Joe in Lucy's basement room at the mews cottage. He was crouching amidst the emptied-out debris of her possessions, sorting through them with a patience that was deceptively gentle. Two floors up, the red-headed woman lay face-down dead on her own bedroom carpet. She'd been easy to surprise; she'd been expecting someone else. Probably her dyke friend who was now feeding the rats in one of the alley's big trash hoppers.

He'd waited for Lucy but then, when she hadn't come out alone, he'd stayed well back in the shadows. By this time he'd let Josie's body down and was checking through her pockets, which was a no-hope situation if ever there was one – women almost always carried their stuff around in handbags, and hers had to be back inside the building somewhere. After the cab had departed he'd returned to the body search; a couple of rough-looking kids came sneaking up the alley for purposes unknown, but a long, low growl from the shadows sent them running. He found nothing on Josie but a couple of folded Kleenex and a Tube ticket, but then when he rolled her over he heard a faint clink of metal on stone. It was from something on a thin silver chain around her neck, and after snapping it free he stood up to inspect his find in the available light. At first he thought it was some kind of a St Christopher medal, but it seemed too thick. When he put his nail to the edge, it sprang open like a locket and he drew out a concertina-folded strip of paper.

The first thing he saw was her blood group. Then something about blood sugar. It was some kind of a medical thing; he'd seen the bracelets before, and this was just another variation. He spread the strip out to full length. It gave her address, her phone number, her next of kin . . . he tore off this last part and put it back into the locket, which he returned to her body. It was the only piece that she'd be needing from now on.

And then, when he'd hidden her and covered her over, he set out to find where she'd lived.

After the minor unpleasantness with the redhead, he'd felt able to shake the place down without much fear of interruption. He'd known Lucy's room as soon as he'd seen it. That temporary-looking, fold-out bed, her clothes on hangers, the unzipped valise that had once belonged to her sister Christine. He turned the bag upside down and dumped everything onto the floor, and then he did the same for the drawers and for the wardrobe. A few things got torn along the way. Nothing he could help.

And shortly after the daylight found him, he was pensively studying a box of a dozen contraceptives that he'd turned out of her soapcase.

It was almost as if he'd hit some kind of a block. He couldn't go back, he couldn't go on, and yet he wasn't entirely sure why he'd stopped. He felt like some programmed thing with a piece of its instructions missing, battering itself repeatedly against the same piece of wall while a door stood open only a few feet away. He felt dulled and stupid. He kept rereading the Kitemark, the safety standard on the side of the pack.

And then he saw her pass by outside the window, and heard her climbing the steps toward the front door.

It had only been a glimpse, but it had been enough. He was back on the rails, and moving again. There was a thin leather belt in amongst the mess on the floor, and he grabbed it on his way to the door. He took the stairs up to the hallway two at a time, the carpet absorbing almost all of the sound. Then he snaked back through the house in silence, arriving at the front door just a couple of seconds ahead of her.

He could see her shape through the frosted half-glass; he didn't think that she'd be able to see him but he stayed close to the wall, just in case. When she came through the door, he'd be behind it. She'd hardly know a thing. Joe sincerely believed that it wasn't in his nature to be cruel. He got the ends of the belt around his hands and wound them into a good, tight grip.

The shape outside had stopped, and seemed to be looking for something. He could see masses of blurred colour, not much more. The hair gave her away. He supposed that she'd be looking for her key. He held his breath, not wanting to make the slightest sound that might betray his presence.

After a moment, she seemed to find what she was looking for and stepped up to the door.

He'd only a vague notion of what was going to happen after this. It had occurred to him that maybe, just maybe, they'd be able to link him in with what he'd done. Perhaps, when he'd dropped her, he'd better give a little thought to damage limitation and the covering of his tracks. Rearrange the scene a little, write himself out of it. The problem was that the whole thing had become so complex – it wasn't only what he was going to do now but there was the stuff

back at the club, there was Ashdown and what he knew, there was
the whole sorry business of his suspension and the charges against
him . . . taken one piece at a time it seemed bad enough, but taken
all together it was far too much for his mind to handle. His thoughts
tended to be deflected away, as if from a fast-running flywheel.

Far better to take it in stages, to concentrate purely on the shortest
of short-term problems. The most immediate of these was the demise
of Lucy Ashdown. It wouldn't be hard to achieve. She was already
within arm's length, only the door standing between them to prevent
him from reaching her, and she clearly suspected nothing because
she was moving in and as her hand passed close to the glass, he
could see it in vivid pastel detail.

But then he frowned, because the key that he'd been expecting
didn't appear anywhere in the picture –

And the lock didn't turn as he'd been expecting it to –

And instead the folded slab of a newspaper slithered through the
mail slot and dropped at his feet, and the figure on the other side of
the glass turned and moved away, and seconds later he could hear
the sounds of its descent down the outside stairway.

The newspaper slowly unfolded itself on the mat, flopping open
to reveal some glossy law magazine that had been placed inside.

Joe lowered his hands, with the belt still around them.

And then he lowered his head, and breathed out.

And as Joe Lucas was unwinding from the pitch to which he'd
momentarily raised himself, Lucy was seated at a side-table in a
Wardour Street coffee shop. The tables were high in a breakfast-bar
style and so were the stools, and on the walls were movie posters
and signed eight-by-tens. Two of these featured stars that she'd
heard of, the others had an inescapable bit-playerish look about
them. Takeaway business was brisk and the expresso machine
howled and hissed almost constantly for a steady traffic of hard-
looking, fast-talking men with tattoos and torn jeans. They took out
large orders of tea and coffee on cardboard trays, and after wondering
for a while if they were anything to do with the film business Lucy
finally decided that every last one of them was probably either a
builder or a shopfitter. Apart from the bike messengers, that was,
and these were easy to distinguish because they were young and wiry
and bizarrely dressed, and their eyes seemed to have a certain glaze
on them from being on a permanent adrenaline high.

The girl behind the counter was Mediterranean in her appearance,
with a big shock of dark curly hair out of which she peeped as if

from hiding. She seemed uncertain of her English, and asked for everything to be repeated. People came and went, but almost nobody stayed to eat; Lucy had the dining area beside the counter more or less to herself, apart from a business type in an Aquascutum raincoat who sat two tables away reading a caravan magazine.

Which was fine, because it meant that there was no pressure for her to move on. Her sole purpose in being here was to kill some time. She'd thought about going back to her room for a while, maybe find out from Josie what she'd been caught up in the night before, but it would take her more than half an hour to walk. Any other day, but not today. She probably had enough cash for a taxi, but the taxi habit still came hard to a girl from the sticks who wasn't even used to being able to afford bus fare. She couldn't help how she was, and she certainly didn't want to change.

Her tea grew cold, which was no great loss. It was buying her some time and some space, nothing more. When the cold engine that was the city had coughed and kicked and finally started up for the day, then she'd set out about her business.

She reckoned that she'd considered just about every possible course. She couldn't simply go on as before, not after what had happened in the hotel's restaurant. If anything, she was relieved at the outcome of that particular incident – Josie had been right when she'd said that after going so far Lucy was now marking time and getting no further. The more she thought about it, the more certain she became that there was really only one avenue open to her.

So when the expresso machine was quiet for a moment, she leaned over to catch the attention of the man in the Aquascutum raincoat.

He seemed startled.

'Excuse me,' she said, 'but would you know which is the nearest big police station in this area?'

FORTY-NINE

Charlie wasn't in the greatest of moods today. His old worries about his heart had come back, and he thought he was maybe starting an ulcer. He knew that he looked like an ox, but that counted for nothing; an ox could drop in its tracks just as easily as anything else. All that it would take would be a couple more calls like the one that he'd received at home, at three o'clock that same morning, from the night manager of a certain parkside hotel.

He came in on the Tube as usual, and walked the last quarter-mile. When he came down the alley toward the club's stage door he could see that there were three rough-looking teenagers who'd clambered up the side of one of the big waste bins and were lifting stuff around inside.

'Oi,' he shouted up to them. 'What are you poking around at?'

'We're not doing any harm,' one of them said.

'I don't want to hear about that,' he said. 'Look, you're throwing shit everywhere. Just clear off.' And then, as they mumbled and made half-hearted climbing-down gestures that he knew would probably stop as soon as he was out of sight, he opened up the door to the club and let himself in. The crush bolt made a dragging, trailing sound across the floor, once to open and again as it closed. The rough-cast stairway was dark, but there were lights further on down and he could hear the faint strains of the show tape playing over the speakers in the club proper. Rehearsals, if you could distinguish them with the name. They'd had a choreographer in when the show had first been set up, but no-one had been near it since; replacement dancers had to pick up the routines from the others, and some of the results could be kind of interesting. Charlie knew that it was no way to run a cabaret, but it wasn't his department. Choreography cost money, and no-one out front really gave a toss anyway; but all the same it rankled, because it seemed to say something unignorable about the station he'd reached in life. He tried to tell himself that it didn't matter, that you could find the same situation all over the West End; back in the long-lost days of sweetness and light he could remember taking his wife to a performance of *Jesus Christ, Superstar* when it had gone through so many cast changes that no-one was even bothering to count, and what a bunch of wankers *they'd* been. The band was tight, but everyone else had seemed to be making it up as they went along.

Nineteen seventy-five, or thereabouts. A heartbeat away, and yet another life entirely.

Where did the time go?

Almost as soon as he walked through the door of his office, his phone started to ring.

It was Lucy Ashdown.

'You've got a nerve, after last night,' he told her.

'No time to talk, Charlie. I'm phoning from Vine Street police station.'

He felt his heart leap, dangerously. His doctor had checked him out, told him that he had nothing to worry about. But what did *they* know?

He said, 'Why?'

'I've turned myself in.'

Suddenly, he had to sit. He reached for his chair, missed the first time, and then drew it over. Once in it, he closed his eyes. 'You stupid little cow,' he said.

'It's not only because of last night. I wasn't going to tell them anything about you, but you know what I found out? They already know about the racket. Everything, even the records you keep. They're on their way with a warrant right now. I'm supposed to be calling a solicitor but I thought it was only fair I should warn you instead.'

She was saying something else, but he'd already dropped the phone.

He jumped up, turned the chair around, and stepped up onto it. This brought him within reach of the ceiling. The ceiling was of the suspended kind, a lightweight grid of porous tiles with an airflow space above. The pores were choked with dust, and the tiles were yellow with age. One of them was loose, and easy to lift. He knocked it out of the way, reached into the dark space above, and drew out his record book. He almost lost his balance and tipped the chair over as he scrambled back down to floor level with it.

Fumbling, panicking, he got the grey metal wastebin from under the desk and set it on top. The book didn't quite fit, even at an angle. How long would it take them to get from Vine Street to here? Five minutes, no more. He dragged open a desk drawer, looking for matches. There had to be some around somewhere, from before he'd quit smoking when he'd first started to worry about his health. No good. He tried another.

His health. His heart was pounding like a steamhammer. They could be banging on the outside doors right now, and he wouldn't hear a thing.

He found the matches, shakily opened the box, and spilled them everywhere. He had to get on his knees to find one. When he tried to strike it, it broke. So did the next. He had to put three together to get a successful flame.

And then the fucking book wouldn't burn.

Charlie was almost in tears. The book stood in the wastebin on the desk like a monument to his misdemeanours. Even now, he couldn't think of them as crimes. He'd been making a living, that was all, and now he was going to swing for it because *the fucking book wouldn't fucking burn*!

Maybe he could eat the pages. He tried to get the book out of the wastebin.

It was wedged fast, and wouldn't come.

He'd have to hide the whole arrangement, wastebin and all. Not here – they'd probably be taking the office apart – but somewhere, anywhere else in the club. Under the stage, maybe, or up on the grid. He stuck the wastebin under his arm and scrambled to the door. Later, he could come back and do the job properly. Right now there simply wasn't time.

The door swung open.

Lucy Ashdown was waiting right outside.

'April fool,' she said.

FIFTY

Although he'd never been blessed with a particularly vivid imagination, Charlie saw it all in an instant. When she'd called him, she'd been no closer to Vine Street than the corridor pay phone just around the corner.

She'd tossed him some bait, and he'd swallowed the rod.

'Oh, God,' he said weakly.

Lucy took his arm, and guided him back to his chair. She dusted his footprints off the seat and then helped him to settle. She took the wastebin and the book from his hands, and he could offer her no resistance. She glanced up at the ceiling once, as if in appreciation of the solution to a tough puzzle that she'd been unable to crack without help; the tile was still stuck in the open position, and Charlie was in no state to clamber up there and fix it.

'Need a drink, Charlie?' she said with what sounded like genuine concern. 'I know where you keep it.'

He managed to nod, and she went straight to his other hiding-place and brought out his half-bottle of Johnnie Walker.

'Better?' she said when he'd taken a couple of swallows, and he managed to nod again.

She moved around to the other side of the desk. For her, the book came out of the wastebin with almost no trouble at all. She looked at the insignificant scorch marks on its cover and said, 'This wouldn't have been necessary if you hadn't been so cagey with me. How else was I going to get what I needed?'

He made an ineffectual grab for the book, but his heart wasn't really in it. She moved easily beyond his reach, and he dropped back.

'No need to help me,' she said, 'I know exactly what I'm looking for.' She laid the book on the desk, and opened it up. This was the first time she'd ever had a close look at the entries, and she seemed to approve. 'This is really well laid-out. I was never much good at dates and figures. Bit of a washout all round at school, really. But there's one date I don't think I'll ever forget.' She flicked back through a number of the loose-leaf pages, quickly at first and then slowing as the date that she was seeking came closer. Even though she was making light of it, Charlie couldn't mistake the fire that animated her when she reached his entries for the final night of Christine Ashdown's brief career.

These were obviously the pages that she wanted. She unclipped the binder rings and removed them.

'Thanks,' she said. 'This'll be really useful. Now go home and rest for a while, Charlie. You seem to have had a nasty shock.'

Then she reclosed the book, stuck it back into the wastebin, stood the wastebin on his desk, and withdrew.

Leaving Charlie to take his own pulse, to practise his deep breathing, and to wonder if he'd ever be able to untighten his sphincter without medical intervention.

On balance, he reckoned probably not.

FIFTY-ONE

Lucy's use for the place now over, she cut down by the stage and went out through the main part of the club. House lights on, clear of customers, tables unlaid, it looked like a barn and felt about as well-heated. The stage was empty but four of the dancers – two old hands, two new – sat in a huddle in the corner by the bar, dressed in their practice motley and trading stories about bad managements and past physiotherapy. She crossed the floor, climbed the carpeted steps by the cloakroom, and pushed through the double-doors into the main entrance corridor. The padlocks would be off at the main entrance by now, for the late-morning mail and for bar deliveries. Technically, it was against house rules for an employee to enter or leave the building via the foyer. Technically, the offence merited a written warning that could lead to a sacking.

But since, technically, she'd never even been employed in any official capacity, she could hardly have cared less.

And besides, she had no plans to return.

(And in the alleyway behind The Gilded Cage, the three teenagers crouched high amidst the rubbish and looked down on the body of the middle-aged woman that they'd just uncovered.

'*I'm gonna be sick,*' said one.

'*No you're fucking not,*' said another.

'*Shurrup,*' said the third. '*I'm tryna think.*'

'*I'm really gonna be sick,*' said the first. But none of them moved, and one of them looked away.

Then the second one said, '*We'll have to tell someone.*'

'*Like fuck,*' said the third. '*They'll lock us up.*'

'*Just a phonecall then,*' said the second. '*We don't have to give 'em any names.*'

'*You can, if you're daft enough,*' said the third. '*But check her for money before we do anything else.*'

There was a silence for a while, and still nobody moved.

And then the second one said, '*I never saw anyone make a face like that. You wouldn't think it was possible.*'

The third teenager nodded, with nothing to add to this statement of self-evident wisdom.

And the first one said, '*Who's gonna look for the money?*')

'We'll have it for you in a couple of days,' the woman told Lucy.

'I need it now,' Lucy said.

'It's not as simple as that.'

'I'll pay double what I paid last time. Cash. I really don't want to hang around.'

She was back in the offices of the business services agency. On the desk before her lay a slip of paper, onto which she'd copied the basic details of a single credit card entry noted in Charlie's records. Out of all of them, this was almost certainly the one. The name was Wilson – too common to be worth checking against the phone book and, besides, what could she say? She could alienate a whole list of people, and still come away without knowing which one of them she actually wanted.

No, there was only one route that she could follow. Identify, isolate, and then confront. It had worked with Billy, truck driver and reluctant witness – but Billy had only been a rehearsal for this, the main event.

She waited as the woman disappeared into one of the inner offices, moving to the window and taking a look down into the street. The window didn't look as if it had been cleaned on the outside in years, and there were splashes of pigeon droppings on the sill. From somewhere far away, she could make out the screaming whine of an emergency vehicle in a hurry. Back home, it was a sound that meant something. Here, it was just a regular part of the background.

She lowered her head, leaning her forehead on the glass. It was cool against her skin. Suddenly, almost overwhelmingly, she wanted it all to be over.

And soon it will be, she thought, straightening as the woman came back.

'You can have it in an hour,' she told Lucy. 'Or isn't that soon enough?'

'I'll try to hold out. Can I use the phone?'

'You'll find one on the next landing.'

'Dad?' she said. 'It's me.'

As always, he seemed pleased to hear from her. She could almost hear him making the effort to be cheerful, as if he was afraid to disappoint her in case she decided not to ring him again.

He said, 'How are you? Still all right?'

'I'm fine. Listen, tell me something. Does Joe still call you?'

'Yes, the same as you do. But while you're calling to say don't worry, he's calling to say no luck. I've tried to tell him to come home, but he won't let it go.'

There was a slightly false note in there, somewhere. He definitely wasn't as happy as he was trying to sound.

She said, 'Well, it won't be going on for much longer. I think I'm nearly there. In fact, I'm going to need him. In a professional capacity, I mean. You can tell him that if he wants to meet me, I'll be able to prove that I was right all along.'

'Meet you where?'

'I'll know for certain in about an hour. Soon as I do, I'll call again and you can pass it along to Joe. I'm near the end of the trail, Dad. I'm sure of it.'

'And then what?'

'Then I'll come home.'

After she'd hung up, she went back to the stairwell and sat down to wait. The stairs were cold and draughty and the light wasn't good, but she'd placed herself so that the agency's receptionist would be able to see her through the glass-panelled door if she should happen to glance up.

There were almost certainly better places to hang around.

But none of them would do for today.

FIFTY-TWO

Once it had been his hand. But Gary had come to think of it as The Hook.

His fingers would bend and there was still some strength in them, but his palm wouldn't uncurl and the tendons to his thumb had become shortened, giving him problems whenever he tried to pick anything up. Sometimes he'd sit and look at it, and his eyes would sting with the tears of despair. He'd never had a serious illness since a bout of pneumonia in childhood, and he'd never been less than whole. At first it had seemed that the damage was slight, just a lot of pain and some bruising, and even after X-rays had shown a number of broken bones there had still been no reason to suppose that he wouldn't heal. They'd set his hand and cast it, and then after a second set of plates a week later they'd broken off the cast and operated. From that point onward, it had been downhill all the way. It was as if his hand had begun to die on him, turning in on itself like a leaf, drying out and getting thin. If he could ever be granted one wish in his life, he knew exactly what it would be.

He'd wish that he'd never set eyes on the Ashdown girl.

Now they were talking about giving him some kind of a disablement classification, which stung. He'd had a couple of sessions with his union rep and had been told not to worry, it was just a way of filling some quota; if anything, his job was probably more secure now than it had been before. Unless he dropped somebody, of course, at which point they'd have to consider transferring him to light duties. Light duties. He was twenty-seven years old, for Christ's sake.

As far as anybody knew, he'd mangled himself while helping a friend with some car repairs. He'd been working one of the axle springs free on an old Cortina when the jack had given way. This had been the story that he'd used when it hadn't seemed so serious, and it was the story that he was sticking with now. To backpedal and tell any part of the truth would be to admit his complicity with the Ashdown girl, which was something that he didn't want to be drawn into ever again. He'd seen her once, on the street, and been terrified; not so much of her, but of the bastard who'd maimed him and who stalked along behind her like a shadow.

226

He was beginning to wonder if they weren't already softening him up for some kind of a change. They'd altered his shift pattern twice in the past fortnight, and each time he'd been taken away from working with patients and given something fiddling to do. He'd shifted a lot of linen, some bags of which weighed in like a circus fat lady. So much for so-called light duties. Tonight he'd been running swabs from the theatres down to the furnace room, in sealed bags and boxes that had been taped and marked with every imaginable hazard warning. And it wasn't only swabs; one tightly-wrapped package had the general shape and the unmistakable weight of a human arm. To put it on the slide and send it into the flames had seemed like a bitter, bitter joke. He'd slammed the door, thrown the lever, and as the deep belly-roar of the gas jets had begun to thunder like a train beneath the room he'd thought, *What a way to spend Christmas.*

And then he turned away, leaving the cotton waste and the human tissue to render down to a common, indistinguishable ash. Somebody would run the ash through the crusher to become an even finer powder, but it wouldn't be him. He was finished, he was going home.

More than a week yet to the big day itself, but already the atmosphere had begun to warm up. The pathology lab had kicked off with the first of the parties, and everything had gone pretty well although nobody had wanted to touch the sandwiches. There was something unique about a hospital over the Christmas period, and most years he'd made a point of working for as much of it as he could. This year seemed different, as if his heart wasn't in it. His heart didn't seem to be in much of anything, right now. He wondered if his outlook would change, or if this was going to be the pattern of it for the future.

Tonight, over in the nurses' home on Huntley Street, a bunch of junior doctors would be putting on the usual end-of-year revue. The room would be packed shoulder-to-shoulder and the show, if previous years were anything to go by, would probably be okay. A lot of the jokes tended to go straight over his head, but there was always some good stuff about the management and more than once he'd noticed senior people leaving with red faces before it ended. And then afterwards came the disco, where it was about as difficult to score as it was to hunt chickens with a machete. Okay, so he was a porter, low man in the hierarchy, but this was the kind of time when the barriers went down and he didn't have to wear a label. Usually, he'd make the most of it.

But this time, he didn't feel the same.

The Hook was a part of it, but it wasn't only that. It was as if he'd crossed one of life's bridges; there was no going back, and the view wasn't the same any more. Things went in phases. Like with your

227

first car, before you came to realise that every damn one of them ran down and rusted no matter what. Or your first dog, where much the same applied. There were things that you knew, and there were things that you only *thought* you knew; and when something happened to shock you out of your ignorance, then the change in your perceptions could never be reversed. Gary could remember with utter clarity the first time that some other kids had called him a Spade. He'd thought that it was a nickname, that it meant nothing special, and they'd let him go on thinking that way until he'd found out different. It was as if. . . well, there was no describing the feeling. Betrayal was about as close as he could get.

He'd never exactly believed that his life was charmed – youngest in a family of seven in Stoke Newington would have been a damned strange place to start out from if that had been the case – but he'd never believed himself to be one of life's victims either. All of that had changed in the course of five minutes in the ancillary staff's locker room, and the sense of betrayal had been exactly the same. No movie that ran in his head had ever worked out as this one did. It was as if his confidence, like a target decoy, had been blown clean out of the water.

Put on the glad rags and go out and party, after that? He could as easily spread his arms and fart and fly.

He ran the trolley down to the corridor's end and left it there for someone else to pick up and use, and then he doubled back and started to walk the distance to the locker room. From somewhere far-off in the building, he could hear a faint echo of the nurses' choir. They were rehearsing carols for Christmas Eve when they'd move singing from ward to darkened ward and make the children's eyes shine with awe, and the old people's with tears. The sound was unreal, ethereal; the music of heaven as it must echo in the airshafts of hell.

He went into the locker room, and someone was waiting.

'Gary,' she said.

FIFTY-THREE

He stopped in the doorway, and would go no further.

'Oh, shit,' he said. 'Don't do this to me.'

She looked good. Even though she scared him, a part of him had to admit it. She carried herself differently and in her attitude, if not in her appearance, she seemed about ten years older. A kid had led him into trouble. Now a woman had returned and was probably going to lead trouble back to him, and he wanted no part of it. His first impulse was to turn around and walk away, blank her out, pretend he hadn't even seen.

The problem was, it was raining sleet outside. And his jacket was in the locker behind her.

'What's the matter with you?' she said. 'I barely said hello.'

'It's enough.'

'I need your help again.'

'Helping you was the most stupid thing I ever did in my life. I don't intend to make the same mistake twice. How did you get down here?'

She ignored the question, and didn't seem to be able to understand his agitation. She said, 'All I want is to speak to one of the doctors.'

'So, make an appointment. You don't need me for that.' He was thinking maybe, just maybe, he could dive over to the locker and grab his coat and get out. It felt almost like being in the presence of nuclear waste; the longer he stayed around her, the more danger he'd absorb. All that it would take would be a little nerve. Surely he had some left, just a little?

'Gary,' she said, with a bewilderment that surely had to be faked, 'what *is* this?'

So after a quick glance behind him to check that there was nobody coming in on his blind side from the corridor, he crossed to his locker and pointed to the bulge in its door. He'd had to pound it flat with his shoe before he'd been able to get it to close again. 'See that?' he said, and then he held up The Hook. 'Now see this? It's what it cost me to help you out. Not that you care, after you got what you needed.'

She looked from his hand to the door, hardly able to bring herself to make the connection. 'How?' she said.

'Your friend with the temper who follows you around. He's sick. He shouldn't be walking the streets.'

'You mean *Joe*?'

Okay, so she hadn't known. He could see in her face that he'd surprised her, but that made no damned difference to Gary at all.

'I don't know his name,' he said. 'I don't *want* to know his name. I don't want anything more to do with you. So, watch my lips; goodbye.'

She had to step back as he grabbed his coat. She was trying hard to catch up with this new revelation, and it obviously wasn't easy; her expression more or less steady, it was mainly her eyes that betrayed the complex reprocessing of ideas that was taking place within. She looked at him with doubt, with bewilderment . . . but not, he noticed, with disbelief.

It wasn't his problem. He wouldn't let her make it his problem. Once had been enough, a warning forever, and now she was on her own. He left her standing by the bank of lockers, and headed back toward the door.

And before he could reach it, he heard her say, 'If what you're telling me's true, then that's all the more reason why you have to help me.'

He looked back. She was watching him steadily.

'Because I can arrange for you to see him again.'

He stared at her.

'I even know where you live, Gary,' she said. And then she added, with an apologetic shrug, 'Sorry.'

Nothing happened for a moment.

And then . . .

'He was right,' Gary said stonily. 'You *do* use people. You're not even pretending any more.'

'Maybe I have done,' she said. 'But it was never anything deliberate. And I wouldn't do it now, if I wasn't so close to the end of the line.'

She waited a few moments longer, and then she said, 'Well?'

'What have I got to do?' Gary said woodenly.

'Just point me where I have to go. I'll do the rest.'

FIFTY-FOUR

The ward was dark, just a couple of low emergency lights picking out random areas of the floor, and all of the children's beds stood empty. Gary had told her that those junior patients who were judged fit enough had been sent home for Christmas, while those in need of continuous care had all been moved in together. She could hear many of them somewhere on another part of the fourth floor, shouting their way through a magic show. They sounded like a tough crowd to fool. Lucy had wanted a place that had some privacy, but where a call for help wouldn't go unheard; she'd done some stupid things in her life, but backing into a trap of her own devising – on this, of all nights – wasn't going to be one of them.

She picked on a chair by a high-sided cot, and sat down in the shadows to wait. She felt a little selfconscious, as if she was persisting in a vigil for a long-dead child. Which, considering the circumstances, maybe wasn't so far from the truth after all.

She wished that she could feel more grown-up, and wondered if she ever would. Perhaps being grown-up was more a matter of how you behaved, and had nothing to do with what you felt. You got older, and if you got rich then perhaps you traded in your teddy bear for a big expensive car, but somehow you never loved the car as much as you'd loved the toy. She looked down into the empty cot, the safety bars of its side throwing jailbird shadows across the mattress. The mattress had been stripped to expose the well-worn vinyl underneath. The purpose of the vinyl was obvious. She supposed that small kids would wet the bed a lot while in a hospital; sick, scared, far from home, nothing around them familiar . . . she could remember those times when her asthma had been at its worst, and how the misery that she'd felt had been almost nothing to do with her illness and everything to do with her isolation. Christine had come to see her one time, and had brought her a secret present. It was so damned secret that Lucy couldn't even remember what it had been. But she could remember keeping it under her pillow and then, when she woke at some godforsaken hour of the night, reaching up and touching it for reassurance.

Whatever it had been, she wished that she still had it now.

She'd dreamed of Christine after she'd died, mostly in the time that she'd spent on the road. There had been many such dreams, but the only one that she remembered in any detail was the first. Christine was leading her somewhere. Just a little further, she kept on saying, and Lucy would follow. They passed cars that had sunk down into the tarmac of the road as if into deep, melting snow. There had been an endless woodland of birch trees, tall and straight and with their silver bark flaking away in bands. A green wooden house with its windows shuttered at the heart of a maze. A block of dusty offices that appeared to have been deserted in an instant about fifty years before, and where not a single thing had changed since. And Christine kept saying, just a little further.

Lucy had the feeling that she could have slept on forever, and there would always have been just a little further to go. She hadn't told anyone about it. People never really wanted to hear your dreams, they only ever wanted to tell you their own.

She held her watch out into the light, and tilted it so that she could check the face.

She wondered how much longer she was going to have to wait.

The problem was that she might not get a response at all. If so, what then? But she didn't think that it was going to happen – not because of anything that had been said, but because of the long silence that followed on the internal phone when she'd simply spoken aloud the date that had marked the last night in her sister's life. No further discussion had taken place. Obviously, none had been necessary.

She lowered her watch and looked around. No matter what you tried to do to brighten a child's environment, it always looked sinister when the lights went down. The ward had been broken up into smaller, more intimate areas with windowed partitioning, and could be divided down even further with draw-across curtains. On the glass hung birthday cards and get-well cards, taped by their corners and half-opened like butterfly wings. The curtains carried a jungle-scene pattern in a brightly-coloured, almost primitive style. There were fingerpaintings on the wall by the entranceway, and a big Mickey Mouse poster above the Fire Exit sign.

From over in its direction, she heard the faint metallic sound of a latch being drawn somewhere outside.

She tensed a little, and listened.

She knew what it was. To get in here she'd had to pass through a gate at the end of the approach corridor, almost low enough to step over but high enough to contain pint-sized wanderers. On the outside of the gate was a sign that read *To be kept locked* and at floor level there had been a see-through panel. She'd had to open it to get through, and the sound that it had made was the sound that she'd just heard again.

Another sound, sharper. The gate had swung shut.

She didn't rise from her chair. Here, she had the advantage; anyone looking would have to scan the shadows for her, and until she moved she'd be just another shape among many. Whoever it was, he'd be coming down the corridor now. Past the little side-wards with their fishtank incubators and banks of life-support systems, past the nurses' thank-you board with its scores of Polaroids of the ones who'd made it back to home and happiness, past the cutout cartoon figures on the darkened office windows.

First a shadow, then the body that had cast it. Then another.

The two of them had come together.

They hesitated under the Mickey Mouse poster, blacklit and faceless for the moment. They'd thrown on their white coats, but under the coats they seemed to be shirtless and oddly dressed. They peered into the darkness of the ward, searching for her.

Slowly, she stood.

One of them sensed the movement, and stepped forward. This brought him into the limited circle of one of the emergency lights so that he suddenly became a figure of intense brightness and shadow, hair and shoulders a burned-in image while his eyes became twin pits of darkness. He'd still to place her exactly, and he was craning like a blind thing for more information. She could see both of them better, now, although she still couldn't make much sense of the way they were dressed. Their bared chests were painted in lines and streaks of colour as if for some primitive ritual, and the rest of their clothing was a weird mixture of gaudy reds and golds.

And then, like one of those *gestalt* line-pictures where you suddenly comprehend an image and then can never fail to see it again, the painted lines came together and she understood their purpose. The lines made the two men's torsos into faces, whistling faces centred on the pursed lips that had been painted around their navels. They must have come straight over from backstage at the end-of-year revue in the nurses' home, in too much of a hurry to do anything more than grab their whites to put on over their costumes. She wondered if the show had gone well.

And then she stepped out by the end of the cot, and the two of them zeroed in on her.

'What do you want?' the one under the light said.

She wasn't sure that she recognised his voice, and so she said, 'Which one of you is Doctor Wilson?'

'I am,' the man in the light said. 'So who are you?'

'Take a closer look,' Lucy suggested, 'and see if you can guess.'

Wilson looked, but it was hard to say how much he'd be able to discern. 'If it's money,' he said, 'you're making a mistake. We couldn't pay, and there's nothing you can prove.'

'Why would I want money?'

'The inquest said that he died in his own bed of a heart attack. As far as we're concerned, we'll stick by that.'

He wasn't talking about Christine. He was talking about the boy that they'd carried out of the hotel suite after desperately working to keep him alive.

Lucy said, 'What did you spike the champagne with? Butane gas?'

Wilson frowned. The hard light exaggerated the expression. 'How would you know about that kind of thing?'

So she'd been right. There had been a craze for the stuff, once – it had been cheap, simple, stupid, and deadly. A couple of medical students should have known it better than anybody but then, wasn't that always the way?

She said, 'I've seen glue-sniffers with brain damage and I've known one of them die. Butane goes straight into the heart muscle and revs it like a Ferrari. But I really don't care about some pisshead stunt that went wrong on you. I'm more interested in what happened on the motorway.'

'The motorway?'

Something in his tone seemed to cause the ground to shift beneath her.

She said, 'On the motorway, later that same night.'

'We didn't go near any motorway. We came straight back to the residence and . . .'

'Don't say any more,' the second man cut in suddenly, breaking the silence that he'd maintained so far. 'It isn't her.'

Wilson glanced at him, uncomprehending. 'What?'

'She looks the same, but it isn't her. It's the kid we saw on the ward.'

So then Wilson stared hard at Lucy, doing his best to make out whatever he could of her in the gloom, and he saw that the other man was right.

'Well, bugger me,' he said wonderingly.

FIFTY-FIVE

Everything changed after that. It was as if the worst of the tension had been defused, the main cards were on the table, and it was time to wind down and spare a little honesty. They'd never followed Christine and the proof of it was, as with all the others, they hadn't even known she was dead. They'd seen Lucy, and they'd accepted her in her sister's place without any surprise at all. The three of them sat around on a three-quarter bed in one of the better-lit parts of the ward. The guilt that they had, and which had driven them here in response to the bleeper call that she'd managed to persuade the switchboard to issue, centred entirely around the death of their colleague and the way in which they'd managed to cover themselves after.

She told them Christine's side of it. They expressed dismay, but Lucy couldn't help seeing the relief that was in there as well. It wasn't quite as they'd feared. She wasn't Christine, back in town with a long bill of demands and the leverage to make them pay. She was just the kid from on the ward. She knew where she'd seen the two of them, now; in a half-waking daze on the night of the attack that had first brought her into the hospital, she'd seen them standing at the foot of her bed.

God, if only she'd known. The distance she could have been spared.

The second man, whose name was Cornwell, said, 'It was stupid, I know. If anyone should have known better, we should. But once it was done, it was done. All we did then was bring him back to the residence and put him to bed.'

'And nobody went to silence Christine when she set off for home?'

'We never even saw her go,' Cornwell said. 'We had enough to worry about.'

'So, who ran her down?'

Both men shrugged.

'Not guilty,' Wilson said.

Lucy felt bleak.

She looked down at the coverlet on the bed, hardly seeing its pattern. She could hardly believe it. She felt as if she'd danced down the Yellow Brick Road, and straight into a yellow brick wall. She'd been so damned sure that she was heading for the story's end, where everything would come together and it would all make some kind of final sense, but where had it actually led her? She'd screwed up, it was as simple as that. She'd fired an arrow into nowhere.

Cornwell said, a little hesitantly, 'What are you going to do now?'

Lucy looked up at him. 'About you? Nothing. I've got all the baggage I need, I don't have to pick up more.'

She saw the two of them exchange a glance, but she could hardly have cared less. Then there was a sound that cut through the air of the empty ward like an alarm, and Cornwell clapped his hand to the bleeper that was hooked into the breast pocket of his hospital whites.

The sound stopped, but neither of them moved. They both seemed edgy and embarrassed, and after a moment she realised why; they were waiting for her permission to leave.

'Go on,' she said. 'If you think you can live with it, then go ahead and try. It's not my problem.'

They got to their feet. She could tell that they were trying not to seem too eager. She wondered how old they were. Older than her in years, perhaps, but otherwise . . . right now, she felt as if she'd outlived just about everybody.

Shit.

It was Wilson who stopped in the doorway and looked back.

He said, 'I'm sorry about your sister. It doesn't matter how she made a living. She didn't deserve what she got.'

'But somebody thought she did,' Lucy said, and she said it so softly that Wilson probably didn't hear.

When they'd gone, she sat alone in the silence and the twilight of the ward. She raised a finger to her forehead, and pressed gently on the spot where her eyebrows met. She'd once described what she was doing as some kind of a mission. Well, if it was, it was a mission that had ended in abject failure. All that she'd managed to do was to create a wide wake of unhappiness behind her; and now here she sat at the heart of a great impersonal city that moved around her like a dark and mysterious engine, herself unseen, unnoticed, uncared for. She wondered what her father would say, when he knew how it had gone. Or Joe Lucas, even.

Joe Lucas. Now, *there* was something that she hadn't even given herself time to consider. How was she to interpret what Gary had told her?

The shadows moved.

'I got your message,' Joe said from behind her.

FIFTY-SIX

He saw her tense. He'd approached her in silence because he knew that if he didn't, she'd probably leap up and run like a rabbit. He wondered if she'd squeal like a rabbit. They could make a hell of a noise, for their size, when you really hurt them. Joe didn't want to hurt her more than he had to. Apart from the sound and the attention that it would draw, he didn't want her to suffer. That was why he'd brought the hammer.

He'd found it in a cupboard in the dykes' place with a bunch of other tools, all of which looked as if they'd been bought for one-off jobs and then abandoned more or less unused. Probably got this one for hanging pictures. He'd have liked something that was easier to use but, what the hell, you couldn't come up with anything more certain. Lucy had risen now, and was looking at him. She seemed serious, childlike. He could remember how she'd seemed on that very first night. They'd come so far, and yet in a way they'd come no distance at all; nothing much had really changed between them, apart from that one piece of knowledge that he'd worked so hard to prevent her from reaching.

He said, 'Jack says you finally found out what you needed to know. Is that right?'

She stayed silent.

'Say yes, Joe,' he suggested.

'Yes, Joe,' she said.

He said, 'I wish you'd listened to me at the beginning. You don't know what it's been like for me, watching you follow her down. I'd have stopped you if I could. At least give me credit for trying. I was too late when I got to Chrissie, but with you I should have had a chance. If you hadn't been so damned slippery and determined I'd have done it, too.'

'You could have stopped me easily,' she said, and her voice was a still point of calm in the turmoil within him. He'd stalked the lower floors of the hospital for more than half an hour until, waiting around and wondering how he could ever hope to locate her in this warren of an institution that linked at least half a dozen buildings with its devious groundplan and basement-level tunnels, he'd seen her in

237

the company of that spook porter again. The main core of stairwell and elevator banks was the key to everything, and he should have realised it. They were just entering one of the lifts, and didn't see him; by the time he'd reached them, the doors had closed and the car was gone. He'd watched the indicator board. The car went up to the fourth floor, stopped for a minute, and then began to return. So then he waited off to one side, and when the lift doors opened he saw the porter come out alone. Joe couldn't remember his name. He was pretty sure that the porter didn't see him. After nosing around the fourth for a while he'd seen these two geeks in fancy dress and doctors' coats coming out of an empty ward, and once they'd gone he'd slipped down the darkened corridor to take a look, and there she was . . . he'd felt something in his heart move at the sight of her, and he'd wished then that none of this had ever come to be necessary. He'd told himself that the fault wasn't his, that it was something inevitable that had been set in motion by her determination to quiz just about every damned haulage driver in the country until she flushed out a witness; but now here she stood before him, saying that it never needed to have reached a point like this at all.

He said, 'How?'

'You could have told me the truth. When did you see her?'

He started to move. Not directly toward her, because that might scare her back. He needed to lull her, almost seduce her into his reach. He would pace, prowling like a big, dangerous fish in a pool. And as he paced, each time he passed would bring him in a little closer to her.

And he so wanted to talk.

He said, 'I saw Christine for the first time on the street. The first time in almost fifteen years, I mean. There were ten of us down here on a course, three days in some stuffy meeting room and two nights on the town. It was in the evening, and it had been dark for a while. We were in a big group, going from one club to another. All that happened was that I looked out and there she was, crossing the road. It was only for a second and she didn't see me, but I knew her straight away. I felt my heart go bang, as if it had stopped. You read about it and you don't believe it, but that's how it happened.'

'Did you follow her?'

He turned, ran his hand through his hair. He didn't look directly at her, but his radar told him exactly where she was.

'I couldn't,' he said. 'By the time I'd got myself together, she was gone. But then I went back again the next night, and I waited around. There was plenty going on in the area, so it didn't look so strange. I'd intended to give it a half-hour at the most; I must have

238

been there at least two. I'm standing in the middle of the pavement thinking how it's time to jack it in, and then I turn around and there she is. I act surprised. She doesn't have to act at all, it *is* a surprise. We did all that how-are-you-how've-you-been stuff, and then she checked her watch and we went for a drink. She said she had to work later, but she didn't tell me what she did. I should have started to wonder right away, but I didn't. I don't know what I thought, maybe a bar job or something like that. I was sixteen again, I wasn't thinking straight. When she left, I don't know what I felt. Desperate, somehow. But really good at the same time. As if I'd suddenly found that there was a definite pattern to it all, that the things that you'd missed and still wanted would come around again, and this time you'd be ready. I stayed in town and I managed to see her again, two nights later. This time it wasn't so good. One chance meeting was fine, but a second one worried her. I could tell that something was wrong. I couldn't stay around any longer, so afterwards I followed her home so that I'd know where to find her whenever I needed to.'

He glanced at Lucy, to see how she was taking all this. Her expression hardly seemed to have changed. But something had come into it now that he didn't immediately recognise, and when he *did* recognise it he felt a certain dismay; because instead of the apprehension or the hatred that he was expecting, what he saw carried all of the signs of compassion.

Compassion, or pity. It was difficult to tell.

He looked away from her again.

He said, 'After that I drove down a couple of times, just to sit in the car and be near to her. I'd wait for her, watch her go in, see the lights in the windows. She always came home alone. Sometimes I think she got the feeling that someone was out there. Then I'd turn the car around and head back in time for the morning shift.'

Lucy said, 'What happened December seventeenth?'

He stopped. Turned. Slipped his hand into the long, deep pocket of his overcoat, where the hammer was. a head-down weight and its handle seemed to reach up to meet his grasp. It might have been shaped for his grip, and his alone.

He said, 'It was late. I'd been there a couple of hours, listening to the radio in the car. I saw a minicab drop her at home, and I couldn't believe the way she looked. She was knockout. But when she came out again just a few minutes later, she was in ordinary stuff and she was carrying that cheap-looking bag. It didn't take a genius to put it all together. I tracked her out to the North Circular road. She started looking for a ride and I was going to stop and pick her up, but someone else beat me to it. So I followed them.'

'You caught up with her on the motorway.'

'She saw me in the service area and came over. We were both past pretending. She said that she'd finally drawn the line, she was going home.'

'Why was she hitching? She must have had money.'

There was about a bed's length between them now but Joe had stopped, his hand out of sight, his grip in readiness on the hammer . . . and all of his designs momentarily edged aside by the sheer vividness of his memories.

He frowned. She'd asked him a question.

Then he said, 'You mean, money she'd made? She left it. All that she was bringing out was the stuff she'd arrived with. You should have seen her. She wasn't downcast. It was as if she'd been let out of a cellar and into the sunlight.'

'And you killed her.'

There it was. Not an accusation, but a statement of fact; if she'd tried to put it in any other way, he'd probably have tried to deny it.

But it was almost as if she was inviting him to explain, and so he said, 'Not because of what she'd been doing. She had hope again. After what she'd been through, she thought she was looking at a golden country just ahead. What I did was to give her a little push, and launch her into it before her dreams had the chance to die. Dreams always do, that's the problem with them. Mine did. But hers never will.'

Lucy said, 'You really loved her, didn't you?'

Joe looked down. 'I adored her. But I don't expect anyone to understand.'

'I do,' Lucy said.

He looked at her, with some wariness. In this light, and even at this distance, it might have been Christine Ashdown herself offering him personal forgiveness.

And, feeling almost like some would-be seducer who himself had become seduced, he said, 'Really?'

'Of course I do, Joe. Come here.'

She held out her hands to him, and what could he do? He was lost. He held back for a moment and then, almost without conscious control, he found himself stumbling blindly into her embrace like a man falling into a mirror. Although he was easily a head taller, she seemed to enfold him completely; he screwed up his eyes and, with his face pressed into the warmth of her shoulder, he whispered Christine's name. He felt a gentle hand behind his shoulders, pulling him close.

She rocked him. She spoke his name. She told him that everything was all right.

But of course, it wasn't.

He was able to hold it all back for a moment, but then reality returned like a swing. This wasn't Christine, and he'd done what he'd done, and there was no going back or rewriting the past or even pretending that things were any way other than how they were. He opened his eyes, and through the veil of her hair he saw the empty child's bed and the cartoon figures on the wall above it. His hand reached again into where the hammer lay waiting in its hung folds of cloth, and as he took one sharp and painful breath he started to draw it free.

This wouldn't take more than a minute. The first blow would drop her, and from then onward she'd feel nothing. He'd have to beat and beat until the essence of her was finally extinguished, scattered and dispersed like so much spit and spray, but in a sense that would only be so much hard labour. The real work, the true creative act, lay in that initial decision to move.

He slid his free hand up to the back of her head, cradling it gently with his fingertips. It had a delicate feel, like a shell; and, like a shell, it seemed an absurd and fragile defence for something so vulnerable. He held it like an orb, like one of those junk table lamps of his sister's where a porcelain hand lifted a round opal globe, while his other hand made to put out its light for good.

But the hammer snagged on the material of his coat, and she seemed to sense something of his intentions, and as he fumbled to pull it free she pushed his other hand aside, and as the hammer still refused to become untangled he saw her take one swift step backward.

Now she was out of his reach, and watching him.

This was all wrong.

She'd got herself away from him far too easily. He seemed to lack the strength that he needed. He didn't need much, but it simply wasn't there. Even his balance was starting to go. He tried to tear the hammer free, and managed only the feeblest of tugs. It seemed that after taking that one, painful breath, he was now unable to take another.

So then he looked down.

The hilt of the knife stood almost at right angles to his chest, just below the sternum. Nothing of the blade was visible at all, and he could see no blood. She'd pushed it all of the way in, couldn't even have hesitated. He stared at it stupidly, unable even to begin to accept the implications of what he saw.

He tried to yell, but managed only a rattling sigh.

His legs gave way.

He didn't see her move but suddenly she was with him again, her arms around his shoulders and holding him tightly. She seemed to be guiding him down, helping him not to fall. He could feel the hard floor beneath him, the warmth of her hugging him so close. She brushed the stray hair from his forehead and she was talking to him, softly. *It's all right, Joe*, she was saying, *It's all right*. And he was grateful for that, because he knew that he'd have wanted to do the same for her, and he tried to tell her so only he knew that it was probably already too late. He coughed, and something came up from his lungs in a bubbling flood, and even though she tilted him forward to help him get it out the act left him feeling no better.

He'd started to sweat, but he was cold. Maybe he was shivering now, it wasn't easy to tell. It didn't hurt. Nothing hurt. Looking up at her face, he saw tears; not his own, but hers. She tried to wipe them on her sleeve, but it was difficult to manage without letting go and that was something he didn't want her to do. He couldn't tell her, but she seemed to know. He could look up into her face and, yes, he really *could* see Christine there, and this pierced him more deeply than any blade ever could. It was more than he could ever have dared to hope for in his life; Christine Ashdown holding him close, Christine Ashdown shedding tears for him alone and nobody else.

Christine Ashdown, cradling him with love and forgiveness.

In the life that had seemed to contain far more darkness than any man's should, it was a moment of pure light and peace.

At which point Joe Lucas turned his face to the golden country, and launched himself off.

FIFTY-SEVEN

It wasn't the first time that she'd seen the sun rise over a service area.

The light was grey and the morning was cold and she was somewhere in the Midlands, she couldn't exactly say where. That was one of the problems, they gave these places names but in truth they existed in some void that was without identity, community, or geographic purpose. In some cases you could often find a service road around the back somewhere, which looked like a farm track but which actually linked into a road that wasn't motorway but which had houses, postboxes, farm gates, whatever; it would be marked by some notice forbidding its use and when she looked at it, she'd feel as if she was looking at the escape route to some other reality that was less bleak, more human, and about as reachable as the territory on the far side of a minefield.

This place wasn't much. The usual fuel court, the usual freezer-and-fryer restaurant behind it in a long, low block where everything was bright and nothing looked quite real. She'd gone in there looking for a phone, and it had been like walking into some lifesized Fisher-Price toy. There had been exactly three people in there, two of them staff and the other a biker half-asleep at his table.

Ah, the good old days.

They'd no phone inside but there were supposed to be three over by the fuel court; she must already have walked by them and when she saw them, she understood why. She'd been looking out for boxes but these were the modern, sod-the-public kind, where you stood out in the weather and shouted at the receiver with one finger stuck in your ear like some manic folk singer. And then when she checked she found that she'd no change, and the woman at the fuel court's cash window wouldn't give her any unless she bought something, which made Lucy decide that she was damned if she'd spend anything here simply as a matter of principle, and so she went back to the phones and dialled up the operator for one more collect call.

The spot wasn't exactly sheltered, either. The wind cut at her, its edge sharpened by her fatigue. She doubted if there would be snow in time for Christmas, but there would almost certainly be rain.

She was dressed in the clothes in which she'd originally travelled down. Christine's clothes, and Christine's valise. Everything else had been gathered together and stuffed into a couple of black plastic trash bags which she'd dumped on the pavement with a lot of other rubbish that was awaiting dawn collection, just a short way down from the entrance to the mews. The house had been quiet, and someone had been through all of her stuff, but nobody had come downstairs and she'd been inexplicably glad to get out of the place. She'd wanted to leave a note, but didn't dare. She was supposed to be covering tracks, not making them.

Whoever came to rake out the hospital incinerator sometime later on in the day would find an ash content rather higher than was usual. Nobody would quiz the content of the ash. No-one ever did. Gary, having become aware of Joe's presence when he'd emerged from the lift, had taken to the stairs and followed him back up. He'd seen everything from behind glass and, when he'd realised what had happened, had come through and calmed her down and then gone for one of the shuttered wagons. It might have been the one that she'd once ridden in, it was impossible to tell. She'd taken out the knife herself. It was now in the river.

That covered just about everything, except for her money. She'd kept the money. Sentimental gestures were fine but, hey, the money itself didn't give a damn, so why should she?

As her call was ringing out, she looked down on what she could see of the road. Early as it was, freight was already on the move. Damn it, she hadn't seen an open road or a lorry in weeks. She'd a feeling almost of poignancy, as if connecting with some primitive urge to be rootless, to be up and going – it didn't matter where and it didn't matter why, the urge to move was all. As soon as she'd finished her call, she would head down for the shoulder by the sliproad. There was even a good chance of connecting with someone she knew, which would be great – she felt as if she'd taken enough risks in the past year to last her several lifetimes over.

The call went through, and again she heard her father's voice.

'Got a Christmas present for you, Dad,' she said. 'We're coming home.'

It wasn't the first time that she'd seen the sun rise over a motorway service area.

But it would probably, she reckoned, be the last.